DAWN OF HOPE

Spitfire Mavericks Thrillers
Book One

D. R. Bailey

Also in the Spitfire Mavericks Series

A Fool's Errand

DAWN OF HOPE

Published by Sapere Books.

24 Trafalgar Road, Ilkley, LS29 8HH

saperebooks.com

ISBN: 978-1-80055-949-3

I would like to dedicate this book to my very best lifelong friend, Angus. We met on our first day at secondary school in 1970 and have remained friends ever since. We spent our school days around each other's houses and getting into scrapes. We've shared good times and bad. I well remember dragging him, long-suffering, to a nightclub after one particular break-up with my then girlfriend. To his credit, he came and kept me out of trouble. I'd say we caused a few ruckuses in our time, and we even played in bands together, a pastime he still pursues to this day. He was a bit of a ladies' man if truth be told, so I was more than happy to see him finally get married to a lovely girl and have three great kids.

As life has gone on, inevitably, we went our separate ways and have seen much less of each other as the years have gone by. In my mind, our friendship remains undiminished for all of that. One thing I recall is his great love of Spitfires, and he even managed to achieve his great ambition of flying in one. I hope that by dedicating this book to him, in some small way it validates the great value I place upon our friendship over all these years, and all the great times we spent in each other's company.

CHAPTER ONE

August, 1940
South-East England

I was flying as part of Squadron 696 above the cloud cover at twenty thousand feet when the bandits came out of the sun.

"Break, break! Red section, break," I shouted over the radio as my section split left and right. Three ME109s buzzed down like angry wasps. I banked hard left.

My Spitfire responded nicely, as it always did, and I climbed straight up, hoping to come over the top and behind the raiders. Our target of a dozen or so Heinkel bombers was now forgotten as yet another dogfight ensued.

As I pulled out of the loop, I saw one of the Messerschmitts was a sitting duck. With safety flicked off, I fired and felt the Browning guns kick into life. The burst went wide and the 109 banked right to avoid me. I gave chase, with one eye on the two pilots in my section, one of whom was being pursued.

"Jonty, there's one on your tail," I said frantically, still trying to run down my own quarry.

"I know, Scottish, but it's OK, I've got this," Pilot Officer Jonty Butterworth said with his usual insouciance, as if he was merely taking a stroll in the park.

A fleeting thought that one day this attitude would get him killed crossed my mind, and I spun my craft while the 109 tried to outfly me. He passed across my sights once more. I fired and missed again, swearing under my breath.

"I told you, he couldn't hit a barn door, Jonty." It was Pilot Officer Willie Cooper, the other third of my section and a New Zealander on secondment.

"Shut it, Kiwi, and watch your back," I laughed.

The 109 suddenly seemed to accelerate away and disappeared from my line of vision.

"Damn!" I swore.

In the meantime, Jonty was still weaving to avoid the Messerschmitt, which was taking potshots at him. Jonty was a skilful pilot and the 109 was unable to draw a bead enough to actually hit him.

"Where's the third one?" I said as I turned to try and go to Jonty's assistance.

"He's here." Willie screamed past in front of me with another ME109 in hot pursuit.

"I told you to watch your bloody back!" I shouted, still heading for Jonty's bandit.

"Yeah, I know, but where's the fun in that?"

From the corner of my eye, I could see Willie climbing ever higher. I left him to it and zeroed in on Jonty's 109, who seemed oblivious to my approach. He was about to cross my line of vision and I fired again, hoping he'd fly into a hail of bullets.

To my immense satisfaction, he did, and smoke began to pour from his engine.

"Thanks, Skipper," said Jonty, pulling out of a steep evasive dive.

Willie appeared again out of nowhere, seemingly unscathed.

"Where's your bandit, Kiwi?" I asked him as he settled in on my wing.

"Lost him."

"Fine, let's rejoin the squadron and get after the Heinkels."

Jonty arrived on my other wing, and I altered course to our original heading.

"'Twas in my trusty Spitfire, victoriously I flew, as yet another bandit, was shot down from the blue."

"Shut up, Jonty," Willie and I said together.

Jonty was well known for his verses, which he made up and liked to recite when drunk in the mess or at the local pub. Naturally, we would rib him about it.

"Philistines," he laughed. "Don't worry, I'll give you the full version later."

"I can hardly wait," said Willie, somewhat acidly.

"You Kiwis just don't appreciate fine literature."

"Oh, I do, I read *Lady Chatterley's Lover* from cover to cover…"

"That's hardly in the same class as…"

Another voice broke into this banter. "Red Leader, where the hell have you been?"

Flight Lieutenant Brent Judd's clipped tones came over the radio. He was in charge of Blue Section and, while we were in the air, the squadron as a whole. Today flights A and B were up with two sections in each: Blue, Red, Yellow and Green making twelve Spitfires in total. Lieutenant Judd was a bit of a tartar in the air, a stickler for the rules. Rules were there to be broken as far as I was concerned.

"Sorry, Blue Leader, we got waylaid. One kill and two got away."

"Right, well, we'll be on the main force in a few moments, so get back in formation."

"Aye, aye, Skipper."

My section joined the rest of the airborne Mavericks and I resumed scanning the sky for enemy planes. I wondered why the ME109s had given up so easily and thought they still might come back on a sneak attack.

Within a few minutes, we spotted the Heinkel bombers flying in from Dover. The air was thick with flak from the ack-ack batteries on the coastal defences.

"Right, let's give Jerry something to think about. Watch out for fighters and try not to get shot by our own guns," Judd admonished us.

Over the radio came cries of "break right" and "break left" as the sections peeled off and went on the attack.

Shooting bombers was a very different kettle of fish from shooting fighters. The bombers can't manoeuvre and rely on their gunners for defence. They were going to be sitting targets, wallowing along on their course and hoping to get through to release their deadly payload. Still, it was easier said than done, I brooded, leading my section into the thick of it. We had to stop them at all costs and try not to get killed while doing so.

I scanned the bombers, ready to pick a mark, fire and avoid getting hit in the process. At the same time, I was watching out for their fighter escort, who would no doubt swoop down on us like avenging angels as soon as we opened up. I knew there were at least two ME109s out there, and no doubt more.

"OK, Red Section, take as many of these bandits as you can, and watch your backs," I told Willie and Jonty.

We split and I saw an easy run to a Heinkel dead ahead. Figuring I might as well take it, I closed in.

The Heinkel has a forward gun in front of the pilots, a top gun facing the rear and a gun under the aircraft. Because of this limited movement, I tried to come in on the right trajectory and avoid getting shot.

I was flying in from their left and fired a burst which raked the side of the bomber. The port engine started to smoke, and it went into a dive. It was a goner, so I didn't stick around but circled for another attack. Other bombers were already going down and it looked, so far, like we were unscathed.

I was scanning the skies, zeroing in for another kill when Jonty shouted, "Bandits, bandits, six o'clock."

I fired a burst at the next bomber in my sights and broke off. A 109 was flying up towards me and I wasn't about to get lacerated with gunfire. Bullets zinged past my canopy as I pulled a roll left and then right. The Messerschmitt wasn't shaken off. It resembled nothing so much as a shark with a big yellow nose. It was easily recognisable by its shape and high manoeuvrability.

"Need some help, Scottish?" came Willie's voice in my ear.

I bit back a sarcastic rejoinder and said, "Yes."

"Roger."

Without warning, Willie's plane appeared, flew past me and raked gunfire across the 109 that was doggedly on my tail. It burst into flames and exploded.

"Nice shooting for a Kiwi," I said, breathing a sigh of relief.

"You owe me a beer," Willie shot back. He had an ever-ready wit and a comeback for everything. Nevertheless, or even because of it, we had become firm friends.

I banked away to the left, as more 109s were attempting to wreak havoc on our squadron. Meanwhile, the remaining Heinkel bombers were getting away, since the 109s kept us fully occupied.

"Bloody hell, get off my tail!" shouted Jean Tarbon, a Canadian pilot, who dropped into a spinning dive closely followed by a Messerschmitt. I gunned the throttle and got behind the 109, firing burst after burst until it started to smoke.

"Pull up, Bear, before you crash your bloody plane," I told Jean as the stricken 109 spiralled away.

I had used a lot of ammo on that one, and I turned again to see Jonty with yet another enemy behind him. There was no support, as everyone seemed occupied either in a fight of their own or going after the Heinkels.

I looped over and came screaming down on the 109 behind Jonty. "I've got him, Jonty, I'm on him," I cried, pressing the trigger. It clicked and nothing happened. I pressed it again and again. The bloody guns were empty. "Damn, my ammo's gone."

"Not to worry, Skipper, he won't catch me," said Jonty cheerfully, going into a steep banking turn.

However, I could see he was going to get caught and his luck wasn't going to hold. Then I saw with relief Lawrence "Ace" Calver's craft on an intercept with the 109.

"Thank God, Ace! Jonty's in trouble, can you take that one?"

There was no answer, although Lawrence kept coming.

"Ace, shoot, for God's sake, shoot!" I shouted.

He didn't respond and the 109 opened fire, narrowly missing Jonty. The next time he might be on target.

"Ace, shoot the bloody Jerry!" I screamed down the radio.

Lawrence did nothing and the 109 fired again. This time, Jonty's Spitfire began spewing black smoke and started to head earthwards. The 109 broke off his attack, evidently seeing Lawrence's plane, and banked away quickly.

"Jesus!" I swore. "Jonty, Jonty, bail out!"

"Tally-ho, Skipper! Got a spot of trouble here," came Jonty's calm tones. His canopy was shoved back and then I saw him leaving the cockpit. Shortly afterwards his chute opened, and I turned away knowing he was safe.

"Sorry, Scottish," said Lawrence finally. "Problem with the guns."

I was seething and did not answer. I turned back towards the Heinkels, but they were gone. The other members of the squadron must have shot them down. The remaining 109s were hightailing it back to France.

"Form up, Mavericks, let's head for home," said Judd, now our mission was over. My kite was useless anyway due to the lack of ammunition.

I joined up with the rest, and Willie took up his position on my wing. I felt a pang not seeing Jonty on the other one, but I knew at least he would be OK.

"Is Jonty all right?" asked Willie.

"Yes, he managed to bail."

"Phew! He's got more lives than a cat."

"At least a cat doesn't keep reciting his frightful verses."

We both laughed at this as the tension from the battle eased. It was stomach-churning stuff while out there in the air in combat. I put Lawrence Calver to the back of my mind, although I had not forgotten his failure to save Jonty.

We flew in formation back to Banley Airfield, in what was loosely part of East Anglia, just north of Chelmsford. Our squadron, the Mavericks, had been shoved somewhat out of the way in this outlying airfield. I pondered whether it was our reputation for being a motley band of fliers who had been kicked out of every other squadron in the RAF. However, we still came under the Air Force group protecting south-east England and London. Our Spitfires could reach Seven Sisters in around twenty minutes from scramble.

As the control tower hove into view, I glanced left where there was a large red-brick mansion situated not far from the airfield. It belonged to one General Grimthorne, who was serving on the army staff of the Eastern command. It also happened he was on extended leave, and I spotted the venerable officer sitting in his garden, taking tea on his well-kept lawn.

"Are you thinking what I'm thinking?" Willie chimed into my thoughts.

"Why not? It would be rude not to."

We broke formation and dropped down low until we were just skimming the tops of the trees, heading for the general's house. Without warning, we burst over the top of the general's garden, no doubt destroying his peace and quiet. I had the fleeting image of a teacup going flying and the general shaking his fist at us in my rear-view mirror.

"Oh, we got him good this time," Willie guffawed.

I chuckled too.

Buzzing the general's house had become something of a pastime for some of us in the squadron, and his irate responses simply acted as a goad. The Spitfires certainly made a distinctive noise and having one appearing out of nowhere while you were having a quiet cup of tea was guaranteed to spoil your afternoon.

Having wreaked minor havoc on the general's peace of mind, we turned back to the airfield, landed and taxied to our standings. I jumped down from the wing whilst my aircrew went to perform their ministrations and get her ready for the next outing.

"She ran out of ammo!" I called out to the leading aircraftman who was my chief technician.

"Sorry, sir."

It wasn't his fault, of course, just one of those things. I had been a little too trigger-happy, I suppose. Just then I spied Lawrence Calver and my anger about Jonty came flooding back. I ran up to confront him.

"Why the hell didn't you fire?" I demanded, putting a hand on his shoulder.

He spun around. "I say, old bean, steady on."

"Why didn't you bloody well fire? You could see Jonty was in trouble!"

"I told you," he replied coolly. "My guns jammed."

I regarded him with impotent fury. "That's a load of flannel and you know it."

"Are you accusing me of lying?" he said, raising a sardonic eyebrow.

"I am accusing you of being economical with the truth," I retorted through gritted teeth.

"My gun jammed. Jonty got away. Let it go, old man."

"We'll see about that!" I turned on my heel and headed straight for the CO's office, determined to have it out now that my blood was up.

I stalked over to the building housing the main control tower. This was a large brick-built affair with a gallery below the tower itself where people could stand and watch the planes come and go. Inside, on the ground floor, were offices and so forth.

Once inside, I knocked on the door of Squadron Leader Richard Bentley's office.

"Come!" His stentorian tones sounded from inside.

I looked over the familiar spartan interior, with a wooden floor, plain light blue walls, a large desk, charts on the wall, and filing cabinets. In one corner his adjutant, Section Officer Audrey Wilmington, had a desk and was, as usual, typing away furiously.

I snapped a crisp salute at Bentley. Audrey flicked a glance at me but no more.

"As you were," he said and gestured to a chair in front of his desk.

I'd always felt he was the picture of a squadron leader, complete with a handlebar moustache, bushy eyebrows and the pipe he smoked. Thankfully, this was sitting on his desk in its rack. I wasn't a fan, since it stank the place out every time he used it. I couldn't imagine how Audrey tolerated it.

"Flying Officer Angus Mackennelly," he said affably. "What's got your goat?"

I must have been wearing a furious expression and along with my Scottish red hair, I probably looked a sight. Besides, I was still in my flight gear.

"That bloody moron, Lawrence Calver," I said heatedly without preamble.

"Lawrence?" Bentley sighed. "What's he done now?"

I related the details of the incident, as well as the exchange with Lawrence on the ground and became annoyed all over again. Bentley heard me out without interruption. He was known for his infinite patience, and he needed it as far as the Mavericks were concerned.

"I see, but what makes you think his guns *didn't* jam?" he asked reasonably.

"Of course they didn't bloody jam — he fired them afterwards."

Actually, I had not seen him do that, but I was a little carried away at this point.

"I see, I see." He nodded sagely. "But in any case, what possible reason could he have for not trying to help Jonty?"

"You know why, sir, as well as I do."

Bentley frowned, puzzled. I couldn't believe he didn't know about Jonty's sexuality. Everyone in the Mavericks was aware of it.

"No … I don't believe I…"

I stood up and paced the room, frustrated by what I felt was his obtuseness, but I was aware I needed to be careful how I phrased things.

"Sir, Lawrence doesn't like Jonty. He has made comments about his … sexuality."

Bentley regarded me for a moment. "Sit down, Angus, you're making me giddy."

I obeyed and sat glowering at him. He was quite impassive and picked up his pipe. He started to absently scrape out the bowl. "You're telling me that Lawrence would jeopardise the life of a fellow pilot and officer because he thinks he's queer?"

"That is exactly what I'm saying," I replied hotly.

"On what basis are you making this accusation?" It wasn't combative; he was simply asking me objectively.

He had a point. How did I know? I told Bentley of my suspicions. I explained how I'd heard some very violently anti-homosexual views from Lawrence Calver expressed to others, and with veiled references to Jonty. He had so much as intimated that he'd like to plant a few well-placed hits on anyone who was queer if he had the chance.

"Right, but you've no proof, have you? No *actual* proof." Bentley leaned back, opened a tin of foul-smelling tobacco and began to stuff his pipe. "Even if you are right and even if I could prove it, we're in a war, dammit, and Lawrence Calver is one of the best damn pilots I've got. More kills than anyone else in the squadron."

I still wasn't quite ready to give it up. "But surely…"

Bentley held up his hand. "We need him. This squadron needs him. Make no mistake: if, and mark you *if*, he did what you are saying, I'm not defending that. In fact, I find it quite abhorrent — yes, indeed, abhorrent." He leaned forward. "But this is a war. Things are different in a war; sometimes we have to tolerate things we don't want to."

"Yes, sir," I said, deflated.

"You see that, don't you?" He picked up a match, struck it and put it to the pipe while puffing vigorously.

I glanced at Audrey, who was wrinkling her nose.

"Yes, sir." There was nothing else to say.

"Right, well, then let's hear no more about it," he said with finality. "Anyway, while you are here, there's something I need to discuss with you." He coughed discreetly. "Ahem, Audrey, if you could."

She stopped typing at once and said, "Yes, sir, of course, sir. I'll go and get myself a cup of tea."

"Indeed, yes, good. Take a half hour, if you will."

"Sir."

She put on her cap and left the room. She locked eyes with me briefly, speculatively, before shutting the door. She was attractive — blonde, with a very pretty face, blue eyes and rosebud lips — and the thought *had* crossed my mind. However, I wasn't going there, not with her being the CO's adjutant.

"Now," said Bentley, puffing on his pipe and filling the room with fumes. I tried to pretend I didn't notice. "This is something most important, for your ears only." He lowered his voice confidentially. "There is a suspicion that we've got a German spy in our midst."

"What?" I exclaimed loudly.

"Hush!" He put a finger to his lips. "Walls have ears."

"Are you serious?" I said more quietly.

"Absolutely."

"But how can you be sure?" I was incredulous. How could we possibly have a spy in our squadron? And why would there be?

"We are beginning to suspect Jerry is being fed information about our movements and the movements of other squadrons. Just a few incidents where it was almost as if they knew we were coming. We are also privy to classified information which they could be feeding to Jerry."

"Oh?"

"Yes."

I mused on this for a moment. It could perhaps be true. After all, on the last sortie the ME109s had suddenly appeared without warning.

"So, if there is a spy?" I asked him.

"I want you to find out who it is." He pointed the stem of the pipe at me for emphasis.

"Me?"

"Yes, you."

"Why me?"

"Because I think you're the man for the job."

"So, you don't think I'm the spy then, obviously."

Bentley guffawed at that. "I can't think of anyone less like a spy, frankly. No spy would have managed to get chucked out of every outfit from Kent upwards."

"True." I shrugged. He wasn't wrong. For one reason or another, my attitude was not tolerated in other squadrons. They said I was a bad 'un who wouldn't obey orders — a maverick, and that made me eminently suitable for a squadron of that name. There were other reasons, indiscretions. I had foolishly gained a reputation as a bit of a ladies' man, and not only for single ladies. If I was a spy, I would have been very careful not to rock the boat. Instead, I'd practically blown holes in every metaphorical boat I'd been placed in.

"Right, anyway, you're to find the spy. Any questions?"

I regarded him, flabbergasted. "Yes! How?"

"I'm sure you'll work it out. In any case, those Johnnies from … what is it? Oh yes, MI6. They'll be up to see you and will give you some tips. Just keep this to yourself, mind. As soon as you think you know who it is, let me know."

I hesitated. "What if *you're* the spy?"

"What?"

"Well, if you were the spy, that's exactly what you *would* say."

He shot me a triumphant glance. "There, you see, you're the man for the job, all right."

Having given me my orders, he started to shuffle the paperwork on his desk, his pipe clenched between his teeth. This was usually a signal to go.

"Will that be all, sir?" I asked him.

"Yes, yes," he said absently and then, "Wait, no. I want you to watch Lawrence's back."

"What?" It was my turn to show surprise.

"Yes, yes, just keep an eye on him in the air, best pilot and all that."

"Sir, is this some kind of joke?" I could hardly believe he would ask me to do so, after what had just transpired.

He looked up. "No, perfectly serious. Just keep tabs on him in the air, make sure he doesn't get shot down, that sort of thing." It was almost as if he'd forgotten my initial reason for coming into his office.

"Yes, sir." I stood up and saluted.

Bentley was already absorbed in some paperwork on his desk by the time I walked out of his office. I could not believe that he'd asked me to watch Lawrence's back after all I had said.

However, I pushed it to the back of my mind, intrigued by the spy business. A traitor in our midst was very worrying.

As I left the tower building, Leading Aircraftman Dominic Redwood walked up to intercept me. Redwood was in charge of the ground crew maintaining the Spits. Each plane had a specific technician assigned to it, but he always took a keen interest in all the aircraft.

"Sir," he said, saluting as he came up to me.

I returned the salute. "Techie?"

"Sir, I examined your guns. You said you ran out of ammo?"

"Yes, I was a bit too heavy on the trigger."

He looked quite abashed. "No, no, it's not that, sir. I don't think you were carrying a full load."

"What?"

"The ammo, sir, I think you were short of ammo."

"How do you know?"

I couldn't imagine how he could tell if all the bullets were gone. All the pilots knew we had only around sixteen seconds of ammo in any case. We fired in two-second bursts to conserve it. I thought back, but I couldn't remember how many times I'd fired or for how long.

"I don't, sir, it's a hunch."

"Don't you check, before we go up?"

"Yes, of course. We double check, and from now on I'll be triple checking."

"Right." He waited to be dismissed now he'd floated his suspicion. "Thanks for letting me know."

"Yes, sir."

Redwood saluted and left. I watched him go while musing over what he'd said. What if he was right? What if someone had tampered with the ammo? But when, and how? I made my way to the pilots' hut, deep in thought.

CHAPTER TWO

I spent an hour or so brooding and listening to some sort of concert by Vera Lynn on the wireless. I wasn't a massive fan of her nostalgic, rousing anthems, but the others were enjoying the music, so I said nothing. I would have preferred something a little jazzier myself. As I was being particularly morose, nobody spoke to me. The Lawrence Calver incident still rankled and at the same time I was mulling over the spying issue. I wondered if Jonty had landed OK, and when he'd be back. It might take him a while to find his way to the squadron.

There were no more sorties on my shift, and when it ended, I took a ride to my quarters at Amberly Manor in a jeep driven by our batman, Bruce Gordon, a sergeant assigned to see to all our needs. Very good at it he was too. He was old school, around forty-five with greying hair, a salt and pepper moustache, a kindly eye and an acidic tongue. For some reason we all called him 'Fred', although nobody knew why or when that had started. He took it in good part and enjoyed the nickname.

We approached Amberly Manor in short order — a sprawling red-brick Edwardian pile set in its own ample grounds and owned by Lord and Lady Amberly. John, Colonel Lord Amberly, was currently serving in the army and was not often home. Barbara, Lady Amberly, however, was another matter. The temptation was strong, and there was a mutual attraction for sure. I didn't know how weak I might be in the face of a continued onslaught.

"Good day, sir? I heard you shot down a 109 and a Heinkel," Gordon was saying, jerking me back to the present.

"Yes, a lucky day. Poor Jonty got hit but he bailed out."

"Oh dear, poor lad, I hope he's all right," Gordon said sincerely. He liked Jonty and looked out for him like an old mother hen clucking over his brood. He had no issues over Jonty's sexuality and was fiercely defensive of him.

"Yes, I'm sure he'll be back right as rain very soon."

"Ah good, good."

We drew up in front of the vast building, and I was about to jump down from the jeep when Gordon said suddenly, "Erm, Lady Amberly has requested you dine with her."

There was something in his voice that held a hint of more than just dinner. I had dined with her before, naturally, in the company of the other officers and with her husband John. This was different.

"Did she indeed?"

"Yes, sir. I took the liberty of accepting for you." There was a twinkle in the batman's eye as he looked over his shoulder at me. Not much escaped his sharp perception.

"Right."

"Then, shall I draw you a bath, set out your dinner jacket?"

"If I'm dining with the upper crust, then I suppose I must make an effort," I sighed.

Formal dinner with the host wasn't what I had in mind. A few whisky chasers and a mug of cocoa before bed, perhaps with a good book, was more my style. "Right then, Fred, I suppose I'd better get to it and not keep the lady waiting."

"Never a good idea to keep a lady waiting, sir, no."

I laughed. He was a card, all right, and from his sardonic tone, I knew he was speaking from experience.

Only a little while later, I found myself at the door of Lady Amberly's private parlour. The mansion in which Lord and Lady Amberly lived consisted of more rooms than I could count, a skeleton crew of servants, and overall, it seemed the very epitome of faded opulence.

I knocked on the door and opened it. It reminded me of the nursery rhyme about the spider and the fly. I immediately noticed the small rosewood table and chairs set for two. There was a fire burning in the grate, which lit the room quite comfortably, along with the candles in a candelabra on the table. Her Ladyship evidently wanted to create a mood. The room itself was actually quite a reasonable size, containing a lounge suite and a daybed. The daybed caught my eye, but before I could speculate about its function in here, Barbara claimed my attention.

"Welcome, Flying Officer Mackennelly." She got up from one of the armchairs and held out her hand.

I took it and kissed it lightly, as she would expect. Her fingers trembled slightly in mine, as if in anticipation. Of what this might be, I pushed firmly to the back of my mind. "No need for that, Barbara," I replied, smiling. We were on first-name terms by now.

"I was simply responding to your attire. There was equally no need for you to have been so formal." Her tone was a little arch, chiding me gently and filled with artifice.

"Well, I am dining with the Lady of the Manor. So, I thought..."

"You thought. Perhaps you shouldn't think quite so much, Angus. And I'm not always a lady, depending on the circumstances. I don't necessarily expect you to be a gentleman either." This was so loaded with innuendo as to raise the blood pressure a mite, and it did.

I looked her over. She was devastatingly attractive. Her auburn hair hung loosely about her shoulders, rather than being done up in her usual style. She was slim, around thirty years of age, with a fair and flawless complexion. Her green eyes were holding mine with so much promise in them, I could hardly articulate my thoughts. She was wearing a simple wrap-over dress and mules with feathers. I tried not to think about what was under that dress.

Damn, I thought. *Here we go again.*

It would not be the first time I had yielded to the lure of a beautiful woman, and she was stunning. I had told myself not to get involved in any more affairs, but it was to no avail. She had only to reel me in with the lightest touch.

"Shall we?" She indicated the table.

"What? Oh, yes." Dinner had somehow escaped my mind.

I sat down while she laughed at my discomfort. She rang a silver bell and a maid appeared at once. Shortly afterwards, a potato and leek soup was served with rolls and pats of butter.

"Butter, eh?" I said with satisfaction, spreading some on a roll.

"We make it here, from our cows."

"Of course."

"We grow the leeks and potatoes," she added unnecessarily.

I nodded and the conversation turned to safer topics for the moment. Lots of produce was grown at Amberly, particularly now we were on a war footing. The soup was delicious and was followed by ham, potatoes and cabbage. I didn't ask where the ham was from and appreciated the generous portion I was served. She had rations like everyone else, but the RAF probably also provided a generous allowance to feed us, and then there was the black market. Barbara was shrewd if nothing else. Sticky toffee pudding finished off the ensemble.

We enjoyed a glass or two of wine from the cellar, and the maid left us some port before being dismissed.

Barbara poured two glasses. I sipped delicately and found it well matured. Delicious, in fact.

"You know, it's normal for the ladies to withdraw after the port is served," I quipped.

"Oh, but not this lady." Barbara took another sip and then stood up. She walked over to each of the doors slowly and deliberately, swaying her hips. It was a show put on for my benefit. I said nothing but I felt the room grow a little warmer. She locked each of them in turn.

"What are you doing?" I asked her, though it was obvious.

"Making sure we are not disturbed."

She returned to the table and sat down, but with her chair pulled out. As she crossed one leg over the other, the skirt fell away to expose her smooth, bare leg. She let the mule dangle from her foot.

"John's away, you know, for some considerable time," she informed me.

"I … I see…"

"And I have … let's say … needs, Angus, not to put a too fine point on it."

"Oh, and I'm to…"

"Yes, you are." She was suddenly on her feet and reaching for my hand. She pulled me up and towards her. I didn't resist.

"Why me?" I asked her.

"You're the most attractive man in the squadron for one thing, and for another, I've wanted you ever since you got here." Her voice was pitched low and husky. It was now unbearably tense in the room.

"Oh."

With one swift move, she undid the tie on the dress and it fell open, leaving me to speculate no longer what was underneath it. There was nothing and she was everything I had imagined and more.

"What are you waiting for, Angus?"

"I…"

"Kiss me."

I obliged, being unable to resist. Her lips were soft and yielding, with the taste of port still lingering on them. Her arms pulled me in closer, and I was lost in her embrace.

Just as I always did, I threw scruples to the winds and let the future go hang. Her need was overriding and now, so was mine. I discarded what little caution I possessed and lived in the moment.

Tomorrow would take care of itself.

CHAPTER THREE

I awoke to the sun streaming in through the blinds in a strange room. It wasn't mine. Then it came flooding back. A night of unbridled passion where Barbara had truly unleashed herself on me, and I had reciprocated willingly and with great fervour.

She was lying beside me, asleep, her tousled auburn hair glinting in the shafts of light. She opened one eye and then the other as I stirred.

"Morning, lover boy." Her smile was quite devastating and easily unmanned me.

"Hello."

Her lips swooped in for a kiss and then she wanted more. Reluctantly, I had to call a halt to the proceedings.

"Sorry … I've got to get dressed and have breakfast. I'm due on shift."

"Oh!" she pouted. "Damn this bloody war."

"If not for the war, I wouldn't be here," I pointed out.

"True, true." She left the bed and walked naked to her wardrobe. It was a delicious sight from my perspective. "Enjoying the view?" she said, throwing on a robe.

"Very much so."

"Well, you can enjoy it again later."

"Really?" I got out of bed myself and began to pull on my trousers.

"Yes, I'll let you. In fact, I want you to. Actually, I insist on it. Here." She tossed me a dressing gown.

"I can't wear *that*. It's your husband's."

"Yes, don't worry, he's got about six. Just get Fred to bring it back later."

"Was Fred in on this?" I demanded, putting on the gown and picking up my clothes.

"My lips are sealed."

I laughed. "And how long is your husband away for?"

"Oh, long enough for me to get the maximum enjoyment out of you." She strolled up to me and put her arms around my neck.

"Oh, so I'm the entertainment?"

"Yes, very much so. Did you want to be more?" Her eyes were teasing me.

"I'm fine with that, but look, we have to be discreet. I can't have everyone knowing."

"Of course, and neither can I, for obvious reasons. I promise I'll be the soul of discretion. Now go, but you better come back later." There was a hint of vulnerability. In a way, I was gratified. It made me feel wanted, at least.

"What about the staff?"

"Don't worry, they are very discreet too. Now, go on, before you distract me further."

"Oh, I'm distracting *you* now?"

We both laughed and I slipped quietly out of her room and headed back to my own. It was a heady moment, she made me quite giddy. She had been loving and ever so passionate, more than many women I had known, and I had known a few. It was a little disturbing how easily I'd slipped into the affair. I hoped I would still be able to look her husband in the eye when he returned home.

I was pensive as Gordon drove me to the airfield.

"Penny for your thoughts, sir?" he ventured at length, since I was usually a lot more voluble.

"You know exactly what my thoughts are, Fred. Come on, don't act all innocent with me!"

"Sorry, sir, the lady was most, let's say, insistent. Besides, I thought you might be lonely."

I laid my head back and laughed. That was rich. "So happy you are concerned about my welfare, Fred."

"All in a day's work, sir, all in a day's work. Oh, and don't worry about the dressing gown. His Lordship will never know."

"I bloody well hope not, or there will be hell to pay. I haven't another squadron to go to, so I can't mess this up."

"I'm afraid they'd ship you off to Africa or somewhere, sir, if it comes to that."

"Great, just bloody great. We have to avoid it at all costs, then!" I said with feeling. Gordon was no stranger to my past. We had discussed it over a beer. Among other things, he was a sympathetic ear.

"Don't you worry, sir, I'm watching your back. You can have your fun, and nobody will be any the wiser."

"Thanks, Fred, you're a stalwart chap."

"It's…"

"All in a day's work, yes I know." I finished his favourite saying for him. He smiled appreciatively.

We bowled up to the pilots' hut and before I could jump out, Audrey Wilmington, the squadron leader's adjutant, approached. It was unusual for me to see her at all, let alone twice in two days. She was looking smart as usual and rather beautiful, or perhaps it was simply me riding on the cloud of last night's passion.

"Sir," she said, "there are some gentlemen to see you."

I climbed from my seat, so I wasn't talking down to her. "I've got to get on shift," I protested.

"Bentley's orders, sir. I'm to escort you." She was implacable, and besides, if Bentley had said so, then there was no more to be discussed.

"OK, fine." I saluted Gordon and waved him away. Then I walked beside Audrey back to the main building. "Who are these people?"

"They are from the ministry, that's all I know, sir."

Then it all came back to me. MI6 was due to visit me, and I guessed this must be them. I said nothing further on the subject, since Audrey wouldn't be aware of who they were or why they were here, considering the object of their visit.

"By the way, sir, Bentley's on the warpath," she said in confiding tones. She shot me a smile. I wondered why I hadn't simply asked her out instead of getting myself embroiled in forbidden territory once again.

"Oh?" I returned to the matter at hand.

"Yes, General Grimthorne has been on the phone."

"Oh!" I could certainly guess what this was about.

"Apparently the general isn't happy about pilots barnstorming his house," she continued with a smile playing around her lips. I wondered if she knew it was me and Willie who'd done the last low-flying run over the general's garden.

"Right."

"Just warning you, sir, that's all." She stifled a giggle and I tried not to laugh.

"Warning noted."

We had arrived outside an office in the main building. Audrey knocked on the door, opened it and ushered me in. Before I could say anything, she closed the door behind me.

In what was otherwise a bare room, with a table and chairs, were two men who appeared almost identical in appearance. They were wearing buff raincoats and hats. Each of them had black hair and a moustache.

"Flying Officer Mackennelly?" said one of them.

"That's me," I agreed.

"Take a seat."

I did so, sitting opposite them across the table. If they were trying not to look like secret agents, they were doing a bad job of it.

"Now," said the second man. I noticed on closer inspection that his eyes were blue and the other man's eyes were grey. Also, there were differences in facial features, and one had a red tie and the other blue. Apart from that, they seemed cast from the same mould. "Do you know who we are?"

"Well … no," I admitted.

"Good, and you don't need to. We're from MI6 — that's all you *do* need to know."

This was beginning to sound like a cheap novel, but I held my peace. They were, I was sure, deadly serious. "Right. The boss said you'd be coming." I nodded, trying to be affable.

"Squadron Leader Bentley? Yes indeed."

I waited for them to say something further, but they appeared to be scrutinising me thoroughly before continuing, which was slightly unnerving. Eventually, red tie spoke. "Nothing we say to you can leave this room."

"No, nothing," said blue tie.

"We are here because you've been tasked with finding a spy in your squadron."

"Yes, Bentley told me, but I don't understand how there could be."

"There are things you don't know, and we can't tell you."

This wasn't entirely helpful and, if I was honest, extraordinarily irritating.

"What we can say is there is very strong evidence pointing to it."

"Very strong evidence indeed," intoned blue tie.

I was tempted to enquire if the room had an echo but realised this wouldn't endear me to them. It was probably not a good idea, on balance. They didn't seem like men with any kind of sense of humour.

"What should I be expecting to find?" I asked, trying to be more practical about it.

"We imagine they have some kind of radio equipment, an accomplice on the outside for passing information, regular places they go to, that kind of thing. They will have habits to disguise their activities, and that is what you must discover. Look for patterns of behaviour, things done over and over again."

"OK." I nodded slowly.

"You have some foreign pilots, am I right?" Blue tie deviated from his role as the parrot of the duo.

We were quite a diverse squadron. We had a Czech, a Kiwi, a Canadian and an Indian, among others. They were all excellent men in my opinion, and courageous to boot. I could not imagine any of them being a spy.

"Well, yes, but…"

"Look at those first. Believe us when we tell you, it will be the person you least imagine. It always is."

"Right."

"Any other questions?"

I actually had many, but it didn't seem as if this pair would be disposed to answer them. I had not the first idea how to go about finding the spy, but I was disabused of any notion they would be willing to deliver a rapid training programme in order to clue me up.

"How do I get hold of you if I need to?"

"Get a message to Thompson at London HQ, codename Ratcatcher. We'll be in touch with *you*."

"OK, but..."

"Just find the spy, there's a good chap." Red tie smiled as they both stood up.

"Toodle pip," said blue tie and before I could say anything else, they were gone.

"Well..." I said to myself.

I could hardly believe they had come all the way for *that*. I had expected a proper briefing, certainly more than what had amounted to little more than a pep talk. It left me none the wiser. I could have figured out the spy had a radio for myself. However, two things got me thinking. One, the idea that the fellow had certain habits, and the second, that it might be a foreign pilot. It irked me no end to consider the possibility, but perhaps they were right and I *should* look there first.

I strolled back to the pilots' hut deep in thought, only to walk in on Bentley giving a rare briefing.

"Ah, Scottish, so nice of you to drop in," he said in a voice laced with sarcasm, which drew some laughs from the others.

"Sorry, sir, I had a meeting," I replied, feeling rather aggrieved since he knew exactly where I had been, and it was on his orders. I took a seat, deciding discretion was the order of the day.

"I won't go over everything again, you can ask one of the others, but the long and the short of it is, we've been fighting Fritz and his bombers on our own shores for more than a month and a half, as you know. Intelligence tells us he's upping the ante. We're in for it, and no mistake. We are expecting enemy bombers loaded with ordinance in the next few days, and a lot of them. The Germans are preparing for a big push, but we're not about to let them knock on our doors without an appropriate response. We are certainly not going to be holding the door open for them to walk in."

This wasn't good news, although some action was always welcome in a weird kind of way. It was what we had trained for, after all.

"On another matter," Bentley began, "I've had General Grimthorne on the blower to me yet again. I say *yet again* because in spite of my strict instructions to the contrary, some of you blighters have been buzzing his bloody house!" He gave us all an irascible stare.

This intelligence was met with raucous laughter. Bentley was unimpressed.

"It's no laughing matter. Believe me, the general was threatening to talk to the high-ups in Fighter Command if you people don't cease and bloody well desist! I do not need the brass crawling all over my airfield. For Christ's sake, can you find something else to waste your bloody time on?"

"The general is a starched shirt. It's just a bit of fun, letting off steam," said Lawrence defiantly. There were murmurs of agreement.

Bentley regarded him with a fulminating eye, but since Lawrence was now his favoured pilot, he refrained from the pithy retort which was obviously forming in his mind. Instead, he just said, "Yes, well, don't let it happen again! Dismissed!"

With that, the squadron leader stalked out of the hut while more laughter followed him.

"Good on you, Ace," one of the other recruits, Charles Forster, piped up.

Even though I agreed with Lawrence, this made me unaccountably annoyed. I had taken yesterday in bad part, and now anything he did was bound to irritate me.

"Personally, I think the whole squadron should go over the general's house next time. Who's with me?" shouted Lawrence, buoyed up by this support.

"I think we should listen to Bentley," I pitched in, just to be obstinate.

"That's rich! Wasn't it you and Kiwi over his house yesterday?" Lawrence retorted.

We locked eyes for a moment, but before either of us spoke the phone rang. Jean Tarbon answered it and put it down, looking grave before shouting, "Scramble, scramble, you reprobates! The bandit hoards are upon us!"

The next minute the alarm sounded, and we were running for our planes, everything else forgotten in the adrenaline rush.

Dominic Redwood was waiting, as usual, to help me into my kite.

"It's fully loaded, sir, I checked it myself. In fact, we put in as much ammo as we could get away with."

"Good work, Techie," I said, climbing onto the wing and into the cockpit.

After some rapid checks, we spun up the prop and, in a few moments, I was up and away into the blue yonder.

CHAPTER FOUR

"Red Section, stay on me," I said over the radio as we headed for the south coast. We were all flying in formation, with Blue Section in charge as usual.

"Wilco, Scottish," came Willie's drawl.

"Roger it, Chief!" It was the Czech pilot, Tomas Jezek. He was standing in for Jonty, who had not yet returned, and I needed a third on my section.

"Everyone on me," Lieutenant Judd's voice cut in. "We've got some other squadrons joining us, including some Hurricanes, so keep your eyes peeled. I've just had word the bandits crossed the Seven Sisters, so let's be alert!"

Jerry was on our home turf now, and over the Sussex Downs. I eased off the safety on my guns, and carried on looking left, right, up and down for any sign of ME109s. This was the plane we had to worry about the most. We'd be on the main bandit pack in less than ten minutes.

"Red Section, ready for action?"

"Oh yeah, just let me at them!" Willie replied at once.

"I want to shoot some Germans for sure," said Tomas.

Just then I looked above and saw the familiar sight of six 109s dropping out of the sky.

"Well, now's your chance. Bandits at twelve o'clock. Break, break!" I shouted, pulling a hard left.

The rest of the squadron split up as the Messerschmitts bore down on us and then they also broke formation, swooping into the attack.

My whole attention was taken up by one of the 109s who had decided I was an easy mark and was heading straight towards me. I couldn't break left or right again, as I would offer up a big target. It was a game of chicken and one I was by no means comfortable with. I wondered what to do, and as I closed with the enemy plane, I decided to try a risky manoeuvre.

I rolled my craft, trying to keep on course, and as I did so I fired off a couple of bursts, hoping that some of the bullets would hit home. As I levelled off, the other plane appeared to be completely unscathed, and then suddenly it pitched up violently. Reflex action kicked in and I fired again at the belly of the 109. It burst into flames and exploded in mid-air.

"Good God!" I said. I must have hit it the first time and then the second volley ignited the fuel. I banked sharply to avoid flying into the debris.

"Nice shooting, Red Leader." It was Lieutenant Judd.

"Yeah, that was a close one, Scottish!" Willie's laugh cut in over the top.

"They've retreated; let's head on to the main force," said Judd. "On me, squadron."

We formed up again and wheeled right, as the bombers would by now have gone past us due to that little diversion. On the other hand, we would be approaching from the rear, which could be advantageous. Other squadrons were engaged already.

"I hope they leave some for us!" said Tomas.

"I'm sure they will. Anyone down?" I asked.

"Nope, we were lucky," Willie replied.

Tomas's wishes came true as we saw the main flight of bombers below us consisting of Heinkels and some Stukas. There were certainly enough to go around. A couple of other squadrons, Spitfires and Hurricanes, were already cutting into them.

"All right, let's get them! Watch out for the escort," said Judd.

"Break, break!" The calls went over the radio, and we headed in to do the maximum damage we could.

The Heinkels were easy targets and although the air was thick with tracers from their guns, we easily outmanoeuvred them. I took down one and then a second in two short bursts. They were lucky shots, as quite often it took more. Then, banking left, I saw Lawrence Calver diving with a 109 on his tail.

"Damn!" I said under my breath. It was really the last thing I needed, but Bentley's words came back to me. I had to protect him, so I dived too.

The 109 didn't see me coming, and I fired a burst which raked his tail. The rudder and tail parted company, and the plane spiralled downwards out of control.

"You're clear, Ace, I got him," I said, pulling away.

"Thanks, Scottish."

"You're welcome."

The whole thing stuck in my throat, but I didn't have time to think about it. I turned back into the main pack, knowing I'd only a few more bursts left, and we'd be running low on fuel. More squadrons would be in to relieve us.

There were two Stukas on my right, and I turned towards them. They were unable to respond, and I fired two bursts across their bows, hitting them both and downing them. Almost mesmerised, I watched them dropping out of the sky. Those few moments of inattention nearly cost me my life.

An ME109 had crept up behind me, and I was startled to see it in my rear-view mirror. My heart began to pump nineteen to the dozen. They said death in the air came quickly and when you least expected it. They said only a few seconds could make the difference. I had had those few seconds, and I had not been looking. Now I was going to pay for it.

"Damn!" I said, thinking my time had definitely come. I had no time to react, and he had all the time in the world to open fire. I started to pull right, hoping at least to perform some kind of evasion tactic before the inevitable, when the 109 burst into flames.

"Got him for you, Scottish." To my immense relief, I heard Willie's cheery voice. "You really should pay more attention."

I breathed a big sigh. "I know. Thanks, Kiwi." I wouldn't allow myself to get caught napping again.

Judd's voice came over the radio, to call it a day on our sortie. "This is Blue Leader, disengage, disengage, and return to base."

I was glad to hear it, although there were still more bombers to hit. However, two more squadrons had arrived, and I was nearly out of ammo. No doubt others would be in the same boat. We turned away from the combat and formed up. This time, I was keeping a weather eye all around me. I didn't want to be taken by surprise again.

"Well done, chaps, a good result. We got some and lost none," said Judd as we resumed formation and headed home.

There were no further incidents, and in spite of urging by Lawrence, none of us was keen to annoy the general again, at least not so soon. I purposely refused to join in, anyway, since my animosity towards him was increasing rather than diminishing.

As I landed and taxied back to my spot, I noticed an army jeep not far from us with a familiar figure standing up in it.

"All good!" I told Dominic Redwood while I jumped down from the wing. He nodded and went to inspect his beloved aircraft.

The person in the jeep was Jonty and he was singing lustily at the top of his voice.

"Jonty was a warrior, a warrior was he, he kicked the Hun right up his bum and back to Germaneee…"

Beside him was an orderly with a long-suffering look on his face. I felt for him. Jonty could have inflicted his ditties on him for Lord knew how many long hours.

"Ah yes, the bloody Hun, I kicked him up his bum, his bum bum bum, and I'll say that was fun…"

"Jonty!" I shouted, hastening towards them.

Jonty curtailed his singing. "Skipper, is that you? Skipper?"

"Yes, Jonty, where have you been, you old soak?"

I said this because I'd spied an almost empty bottle of Scotch in his hand, which he was waving about. This would be typical, as Jonty was certainly partial to a drink or two. However, he appeared to be completely half-cut.

"How have I been?" he said, bursting out into song again. "I've been all the way from the briny sea, all the way and up to thee. I'll tell you a tale and it's a hoot, since I floated down in my parachute. Oh, my name is Jonty, Jonty is my name, I'm a jolly pilot and a pilot I will be, I'll kick the bloody Hun and make him run run run, back to Germaneee…"

"For God's sake! Can't we make him stop?" said Willie, who had evidently also spied Jonty and caught me up.

"We *have* to stop him! For the sake of that poor corporal if nothing else," I said, laughing.

"Hey, Jonty, that's enough of your tuneless bloody shanties," Willie yelled out.

By this time, we had reached the jeep and Jonty ceased his singing.

"Kiwi, my boy, is that you?"

"As I live and breathe."

"Oh well, ohhhhhh..." Jonty suddenly pitched forward and fell headfirst out of the jeep. Fortunately, we managed to catch him and lower him to the ground.

"Excuse me, lads, sir, I'm a bit dizzy, you know."

"Well, stay there until we can get you home," I told him.

"Home, ah yes, now there's a thought. I wanted to go home, you know, been wanting to for a few hours."

With that, he closed his eyes and promptly fell asleep.

"There's one problem solved," said Willie sarcastically.

I nodded and decided to try and mollify the poor soldier who had brought Jonty back. "Corporal, thanks for bringing him up here," I said to the orderly, who was looking somewhat relieved.

"That's OK, sir. I was coming up this way anyway, to my barracks."

"Where *did* you pick him up?"

"He landed somewhere in Kent, and then my CO told me to bring him to you."

"And has he been like that the whole way?" I hoped not, but my instinct told me otherwise.

The orderly made a face. "I tried to stop him, sir, I really did, but he insisted on buying the whisky and said he wasn't on duty. Then he ... well ... he started singing..." He trailed off and rolled his eyes.

"Poor you. Was it *very* bad?" I asked sympathetically.

"It was all right to start with, sir, but honestly I've never wished more for a pair of earplugs."

We all laughed together. I was glad the orderly could see the funny side. No doubt he'd have a few stories to tell his mates.

"He's not that bad *all* the time," I said, trying to mitigate Jonty's behaviour.

"Don't believe him, yes he is!" Willie put in.

"Well, you can leave him with us now. I'm sure you'll be happy to do so."

"Never happier, sir, and that's the truth." The orderly smiled.

I reached into my pocket and found a couple of notes. I held them out to him. "Here, have a drink on us. I'm sure you deserve it."

"Oh, I couldn't possibly." I could tell he really wanted to, but was perhaps trying to be polite.

"Take it, please. Don't worry, we'll get our money's worth out of him when he sobers up."

"All right, don't mind if I do, and thanks."

The corporal accepted the proffered notes, put them away safely, flicked me a salute and drove away.

"I bet he's glad to see the back of Jonty," said Willie.

"Yes, and now he's our problem. Let's get him back to Amberly before Bentley sees him in that state."

We carried him none too gently to the hut and put him in a chair while I went to find Gordon.

We flew one more sortie that day to pick up some stray bandits. However, by the time we reached the rendezvous, they were nowhere to be seen. After a quick coastal patrol, we headed home and ended our shift. The promised onslaught had not quite arrived, but the last lot of bombers had been much larger in number, which was perhaps a sign of things to come.

We had managed to get rid of Jonty without too much trouble, and Gordon had proven his mettle as usual by removing him in short order. I headed home with Gordon a little later on.

"Is sir dining tête-à-tête this evening?" the batman enquired.

"I wasn't aware of it," I shot back.

It also didn't seem like a good idea to be seen too often dining alone with the lady of the house. I didn't want our affair to become conspicuous. I had no doubt I would be seeing Barbara that night, but I also didn't want to presume.

"Perhaps it would be best to eat with the other officers," he said, as if reading my thoughts.

"Yes, perhaps."

I had a bath, which Gordon kindly drew for me. Amberly had no shortage of hot water, and I was grateful for such small comforts. I put on a clean uniform and headed for the dining room.

Jonty was there, holding his head, along with Willie and a few others. I took a seat between Jonty and Willie. "What's for dinner?"

"A rather delicious stew," said Willie, indicating a plateful of what looked like beef, carrots, mash and some Brussels sprouts.

This elicited a groan from Jonty. "Don't talk about food to me."

"Serves you right for downing the best part of a bottle of Scotch," I said unsympathetically.

"Well, what else was I to do on that infernally long journey in a smelly old jeep?"

"You could have made conversation or gone to sleep, instead of singing the ears off that poor sod."

Jonty let out a big sigh. "True, true," he acknowledged. "I probably was a bit of a bore, wasn't I?"

"Probably?" Willie snorted.

A maid brought me a plate of stew loaded with mash and Brussels sprouts. Jonty ventured a look at my plate and decided perhaps he was hungry after all. A portion was duly supplied to him, and he attacked it with gusto as if his hangover had mysteriously vanished. This was Jonty all over, a little volatile but seemingly unruffled in a crisis.

"And what have you lot been doing while I was away?" he demanded, having consumed a plateful and asked for another.

"Shooting down Germans. We wanted to have a masked ball, but unfortunately Jerry had other ideas," said Willie in acid tones.

"Blast, I missed all the fun."

"Don't worry yourself. Apparently, they are coming for us in droves; you'll get plenty of chances," I told him.

"Jolly good!" Jonty rubbed his hands together in what I took to be foolhardy glee.

"Just watch yourself out there, Jonty. You had a lucky escape," I said earnestly.

"Ah well, you know, 'I bear a charmed life…'"

"Oh God, don't start with the Shakespeare!" Willie complained.

"Are you insulting the bard?"

"No, I just don't want to hear it at dinner."

"Afterwards?"

"No!"

"Philistine!"

Further insults were traded and then talk turned to other things. It seemed as if Jerry was in earnest about trying to soften us up for an invasion. However, we were all determined not to let them at all costs. The costs might be very high indeed, I mused, over a dessert of apple pie and custard.

After dinner, I opted to repair to my room and was considering getting ready for bed when Gordon knocked on my door. I opened it and he handed me a note.

"It's from Her Ladyship," he said quietly.

"Thanks, Fred." I took it from him, and he tipped me a wink, before disappearing down the corridor.

Once back inside my room, I opened the letter. It read: *I'm waiting for you, come to me, please, darling, Barbara xxx*

It couldn't but make me smile. After all, who wouldn't want to be wanted, and by such a beautiful woman? Why was it my luck to go for the married ones? I wondered, as I disrobed and put on my pyjamas. It would be best to be prepared this time, I thought, shrugging on my dressing gown. I wasn't wearing her husband's clothing again, that was for sure.

It was late and most of the others would be in the land of nod. If I ran into anyone, I would say I was taking a stroll as I couldn't sleep. The house was big enough to take a long walk in at any rate, so it was a plausible story.

As luck would have it, nobody was about, and I reached Barbara's bedroom door unchallenged. She and John had separate bedrooms, in the style of the upper classes of yore. It made me feel a little better that I wasn't necessarily making love to her in their marital bed.

I knocked lightly, opened the door and slipped in. As I closed the door behind me, Barbara came up and slid her arms around my neck.

She was gorgeously fragrant, fresh from a bath, with a lingering scent of something. Her skin was smooth and supple under a black satin negligée, and she tilted up her lips to me for a kiss. I obliged and her hands moved under my dressing gown and pyjama top.

"I've missed you," she whispered, nuzzling my lips gently. "I've missed you so much."

"Really? I've only been gone a few hours."

"Too many hours for me."

She kissed me again and I was lost in that kiss. Things seemed to be moving quite rapidly with her. A fleeting thought crossed my mind as to whether she was becoming attached to me already. It seemed an impossibly short space of time for that to happen.

"Well, I'm here now," I said, a little prosaically.

"Just like a man!" She laughed and took my hand. "Come on, come to bed."

I wasn't about to be disobliging and followed her without demur.

CHAPTER FIVE

I went back to my own bed in the early hours. Although Barbara didn't want me to go, I felt it was politic to do so. Besides, I had food for thought.

"My relationship with John isn't everything you think it is," she'd said after we had made love.

"I didn't think it was anything particularly," I replied, as it truthfully had not crossed my mind until she invited me into her bed.

"We aren't intimate, at least not often. He doesn't satisfy me. Does that shock you?"

"No." It wasn't an unfamiliar story. I'd heard it before from other married women. I didn't say so, however.

"I like you," she continued.

"I like you too."

"No, I *really* like you." Her hand stole into mine, held it tightly.

"OK."

She regarded me with an expression that seemed a little hurt. I didn't know what to say. I hadn't really formed any feelings for her, although I might.

"You're a special man. I knew it from the moment I saw you."

"Thank you. It's kind of you to say so."

"I told you: I wanted you, I was determined to have you, and now I've got you." She looked at me defiantly, challenging me to deny her.

I wasn't about to. After a moment, she let out a long sigh and leaned over to kiss me.

"Ignore me, darling, it's just the war…"

"Yes, the war," I agreed as I kissed her back, and it led on to other things. But I knew it wasn't just the war and wondered if this time I was getting myself in too deep.

Normally I wouldn't pay emotional matters any mind. I was, perhaps, a little callous in that way. I was certainly regarded as such by the husbands when they found out. Words were had, strings were pulled, and I found myself posted somewhere else in short order, sometimes with tearful goodbyes.

Barbara was different, and I wondered if I shouldn't cut it off before things went too far. I also knew I wouldn't, because I was unable to. Women were my weakness, but Barbara had stolen under my defences already. I found myself thinking about her and it was not a good sign. Attachment wasn't healthy for a fellow in the forces. At least, that was the way I'd thought up until now. Things changed, and so did feelings.

At breakfast, I relegated Barbara to the back of my mind. There were more pressing things to consider. I was going over who might be the most likely person to be a spy. My attention had settled on Tomas Jezek. He was a Czech pilot who had managed to escape before the Nazi invasion. He was one of the lucky ones. Fiercely anti-German in sentiment, it was almost a passionate hatred that he had apparently conceived. He had personally shot down several German aircraft with great relish. However, wouldn't a spy act exactly that way? They would appear to be very partisan.

I had to start somewhere, and so Tomas might as well be my first suspect. I decided to observe him more closely, his movements and habits, and hopefully come up with a plan to discover if he was a spy.

"You're very quiet these days, old man," Willie observed. I had hardly spoken a word while eating my scrambled eggs on toast and drinking my coffee. I was rather pleased they were eggs from real hens and not the powdered kind.

"Sorry."

"Penny for your thoughts?"

"Oh, you know, just things…" I wanted to talk more, but I couldn't. The spying thing was very hush-hush, and I didn't want to mention Barbara. Willie was a friend, but how much even friends could be trusted with juicy pieces of gossip, I no longer knew.

"Ah well, you know what we say back home: a beer cures all ills."

"It's a bit early for beer, old bean."

He laughed. "Never too early, but we do have to fly, so…"

"Yes, we do."

He sighed. "Bloody Fritz, spoiling all the fun."

"You'll get home one day." I patted him on the shoulder sympathetically.

"Sure, but in the meantime…"

I pushed my plate away. "Let's get to it."

"What say you to mixing it up with the general later?" he said as he followed me out.

"You know what they say…"

"Rude not to."

We laughed and collected Jonty as we headed for the jeep where Gordon would be waiting to drive us in.

There were no briefings from Bentley, thankfully, and no dire warnings about the general. In fact, it was quiet all around. Too quiet, as the cliché went. Tomas was reading a book in a corner of the hut, and I decided to engage him in conversation.

"Tomas, how's things? Recovered from yesterday?" I asked, sauntering over quite casually. I hoped he wouldn't find it unusual, as we weren't particular friends.

"Ah, you know, Scottish, I wish I was home, but I can't complain, isn't that what you British say?"

"Yes." I laughed.

"It's shame I can't join your section. I enjoy it yesterday." His accent was quite thick, and he missed a word or two every so often.

"Yeah, well, I would if I could, but I'm only allowed two. Jonty and Kiwi have been with me for a while."

We exchanged a look that meant we were both thinking the same thing. Who knew when the next sortie would be their last one, and another good man gone?

"Sure, and I hope for you it stays like that."

"Me too, Tomas, me too. Anyway, you did well and thanks for yesterday."

"You are welcome, Scottish, anytime."

There seemed nothing more to say and he went back to his reading. I went outside, as the hut was stuffy and nothing much was happening. I walked to the edge of the runway, looking at the planes. Jonty came up beside me and startled me.

"God's sake, Jonty, must you creep up on a fellow like that?"

"Sorry, Skipper."

"It's OK."

Jonty was silent for a moment and then said, "He's a strange one, that Tomas."

"How do you mean?" I was on the alert at once.

"Oh, you know, a bit of a loner by all accounts. He goes off somewhere or other every day or so."

"Really? Where?" This was becoming more interesting by the minute.

"I don't know. He just sort of disappears."

"I see."

"Odd, though, don't you think?" He shot me a speaking look, and I wondered if he somehow knew about the spy. I wasn't going to ask him, however.

"It's his business, whatever it is." I shrugged.

"I suppose you're right."

I resolved to discover where Tomas was going, but I had no time to muse on it further as the others came pelting out of the hut.

"Scramble, scramble!" shouted Willie, heading for the planes.

"I think that's our cue," I said to Jonty and we both set off at a run.

We were in the air in no time and heading for Kent and Dover. A large force of bombers was on its way, very likely heading for London. We were joining up with some other squadrons in an attempt to down as many as we could before they got there.

"Stick with me until we sight the bandits, and watch out for rogue fighters," said Judd over the radio.

"Roger," I said.

We stuck in formation, and like everyone else I was scanning ahead, above, behind and below in a constant effort not to be taken by surprise. I didn't want a repeat performance of the previous day, and I doubted my luck would hold a second time. As it happened, we encountered no fighters at all and finally we were looking down on a massive flight of German planes.

"Well, will you look at that?" said Willie.

"They are trying to overwhelm us with numbers. I don't know if we can get them all," I replied.

"We can give it a damn good try!" said Jonty, butting in.

"All right, all right, let's keep our minds on the job!" came the quiet voice of Judd. He let us get a little closer and then said, "Break, break."

This was the signal to attack. We banked our section left and then split. We flew with engines screaming down onto the bombers.

Their defensive guns opened up at once, but I was in a good position coming in above and from the side. I raked a few bursts as I dived, and then pulled up and out again. I thought perhaps I had hit at least one or two of them as I banked away.

"Nice shooting, Scottish."

It was Willie, who always seemed to be my shadow and had saved me more than once. I saw his plane pass under me and dived back into the fray. All around, Spitfires and Hurricanes were whirling and diving too, cutting a swathe through the bombers who continued inexorably on their allotted course.

I reckoned their fighter escort would not be far away, and just as I'd made my second run, I spotted them up in the clouds.

"Bandits! Bandits at two o'clock, 109s. Watch your backs."

I broke off my attack, deciding to meet the raiders and try to divert them from our fighters. I steered a course towards them and found Willie and Jonty on my wings.

"Tally-ho, old sport, are we going hunting?" said Jonty in jovial tones.

"Just concentrate on the job and try not to bloody well get shot down!" I told him.

"Yes, sir, Flying Officer Scottish, sir," said Jonty.

He was incorrigible and he knew it. The 109s clocked us and broke right and left.

"All right, break, break," I said tightly as the adrenaline started to kick in. I pulled a steep climb and hoped to get above the fighters. Jonty was off doing his own thing, and Willie was out of my line of vision. I levelled off and to my relief, there were no 109s on my tail. However, down below me I saw one at least, and dived down in the hope he wouldn't see me.

The clouds were obscuring my view, but all of a sudden I was up close. I squeezed the trigger on reflex, and clearly saw the bullets shatter his cockpit. His nose dipped down and he headed straight for the ground. Without waiting I banked away to the right, and as luck would have it another 109 was right in my sights. I squeezed the trigger again and noted with satisfaction smoke pouring from his engine. It was obviously my lucky day. Perhaps I could make it three.

Then I saw Willie and this time he was in trouble. He was weaving and rolling just below me, trying to avoid the 109 on his tail. I turned and pointed the nose down on an intercept with the enemy plane. He was crossing my path and before he realised it, I fired a burst and then another. The aircraft barrel-rolled and then went into a stall, dropping out of the sky.

"Thanks, Scottish, I was having a spot of bother there."

"Just returning the favour, you reprobate!" I replied, relieved I had managed to get his pursuer.

"Shall we head back to the main fight?" he said.

"Yes, but where's Jonty? Damn..."

Over to our left, I could see Jonty closing fast with another 109.

"Jonty, what the hell are you playing at?" I shouted into the radio.

He was coming alongside the German plane, which seemed to be having engine trouble as it was flying rather slowly.

"Just having a bit of sport, Skipper, not to worry," he said airily.

We watched in disbelief as he put his wingtip under the wing of the other craft, did a thumbs-up to the German pilot and then rolled his plane, tipping the 109 over. It went into a sharp spin and dived, spiralling over and over until it crashed to earth.

"For God's sake, Jonty, you bloody lunatic!" I shouted. "Why couldn't you shoot him down, like normal pilots?"

"Oh, but where's the skill in that?" Jonty replied, unmoved by my anger. "Besides, I'm out of ammo."

"You're a blighter and no mistake! I hope Judd didn't see you."

Judd took a dim view of such antics in combat. Bentley would have even less of a benign opinion about it and would most likely tear Jonty off a very large strip. After all, Jonty could have damaged his own plane in such a foolish manoeuvre and got himself killed.

"Anyway," I continued, "if you're out, we'd better skedaddle. Blue Leader, permission to disengage? Jonty's out of ammo and my fuel looks a bit low."

"Granted, Red Leader. We're about to leave off anyway."

"Red Section, let's make tracks," I said as we formed up and retreated from the fray. The battle receded behind us, and although we kept a lookout for 109s their attention was obviously on protecting their bombers and not on the likes of us.

We swept back over the Thames and headed towards East Anglia. With some distance still to go, I saw that my fuel gauge was now showing empty.

"Chaps, it looks like I'm going to have to ditch. My fuel is out, and the Merlin is running on fumes," I said over the radio.

"Oh no you're not, Scottish, there'll still be a bit left. Those fuel gauges are dodgy," came Willie's rejoinder.

"It won't be enough."

"It will if you listen to me. Get some height with what you've got left, as high as you can."

"What?"

"Just do it, Scottish, trust me," said Willie urgently.

I shrugged and pulled up, taking the Spitfire to the ceiling or as close as I could get her. The engine began to stutter as I levelled off. Willie was a more experienced pilot than I was and had been flying crop dusters and other planes at home from a young age.

"It's about to cut out — then what?" I asked him.

"You'll glide it in," he told me calmly.

"I'll what?"

"Glide it in, Scottish, piece of cake."

"Maybe for you, but I didn't get much gliding time before I got onto powered engines."

"We'll be with you all the way, don't you worry. Just do what I say, and you'll be fine," said Willie, sounding far more confident than I felt.

"All right, well, it's still going anyway … damn…" The engine died as I said it and suddenly there was silence and the rushing wind. I could hear the two Spitfires, one on either side.

"Just keep the nose up. I'll help you with the course. You'll start to lose height as we go, but it should be OK."

"Should be? Just now you said it will be!"

"Margin for error and all that." Willie laughed.

"OK, well, I'm not a glider pilot so … help!"

With instructions from Willie and rising apprehension in my breast, I managed to stay in the air although, as he had predicted, I was slowly losing height. I put this slow rate down to the ample wing coverage of the Spitfire. Willie and Jonty kept talking to me and we were also soon in contact with the communications control room at the airfield tower. My heart was pounding nineteen to the dozen all the way and the adrenaline was coursing through my veins.

It was with mighty relief when the airfield hove into view.

"Right, we're nearly there," said Willie. "All we have to do is land it."

"Yes, great. Land it, yes indeed," I said with more confidence than I felt.

"OK, so do you remember from your training? There's an emergency lever for the undercarriage, you need to pull it," said Willie.

I did remember now he mentioned it. I pulled the lever and was glad to hear the undercarriage go down. At least I wouldn't be landing it on the wings. I started losing height more rapidly and the sensation of the ground rushing towards me without any power was unnerving, to say the least. However, with gentle coaxing, I finally touched her down on solid ground without incident, although I could see a fire tender making its way towards me just in case.

A cheer went up from Jonty and Willie as I did so, and I coasted the plane as far as I could before finally coming to a stop. In a few moments, Redwood was up beside me, helping me down.

"Well, that was a bit of a blinder, sir," he said.

"I don't know about blinder. I'm a nervous wreck, and I need a stiff whisky," I retorted.

"All in good time, sport," said Jonty, coming up beside me and clapping me on the shoulder.

"Pretty good, for an amateur glider pilot," said Willie with his usual sardonic laugh.

"Thanks, Kiwi." I shot him a wry smile, for once not in the mood to engage in banter and grateful for his help in getting me back in one piece.

"You're welcome."

We made our way towards the buildings, as we'd stopped about halfway down the landing strip. The technicians would move the planes to their parking spots. Behind us, we could hear the roar of the rest of the squadron. Lieutenant Judd would have held them back until I had made it home safely.

As we neared the pilots' hut, there was a lone figure watching us. It was a woman in WRAF uniform with corporal stripes on her arm. She had black hair tied back and covered with a forage cap. Her brown eyes surveyed me coolly. She was a seriously good-looking lass, I decided, the closer I got. An English rose, perhaps? With a small nose, perfect lips. I quelled the thoughts at once.

"Hello, and who's this?" said Jonty as we drew level with her.

"Corporal Angelica Kensley, sir," she said, snapping a crisp salute.

"Well, Corporal Kensley, what can we do for you?"

"I just wanted to say well done, sir, to Flying Officer Mackennelly and, well, all of you. I was on the comms listening to the way you talked Officer Mackennelly down. It was jolly … brave." She shot me a tremulous smile.

"Thank you," I said, nodding at her graciously. "I can't say I felt very brave, and the honours go to Kiwi here. I wouldn't have made it without him or Jonty."

"Anyway, we were all listening with bated breath, and we're glad you made it back safely."

"And you came all the way out here to say *that*?" Jonty enquired with interest.

"Yes, and why not?" She stuck out her chin defiantly.

"No particular reason, just, well … it shows a jolly good devotion to duty, and as a reward, you should join us for a drink later," he said affably.

"Perhaps, but I've got to get back to the comms room." She sounded evasive and turned to go.

"Just a moment," I said. "I haven't seen you around here before, have I?"

"No, I'm new — just started with the squadron, in fact. Quite a bit of drama for my first day." With that, she smiled and walked away.

Jonty nudged me on the shoulder. "Looks like your next conquest, Skipper. She obviously likes you, for a start."

"Stop it!" I admonished him.

We watched her disappear from view.

"I just came to tell you how brave you are," he said in a falsetto voice.

"Jonty, no!" I wasn't about to embroil myself further. I already had Barbara to contend with.

"Really?" He looked surprised but then added brightly, "Never mind, I shall compose you a suitable ode, a paean to your bravery. A song that will go down through the ages, speaking of the feats of Scottish Angus."

Willie groaned. "Please, please don't."

"It shall be done forsooth, and the naysayers shall be silent!"

"I'll give you silent," Willie replied.

"Come on, children! Back to the hut, the pair of you," I said.

"Yes, but does *he* have to?"

"Let me tell you of the ballad of the Scottish flyer brave, and the Kiwi warrior pilot whose life he did save…" Jonty began to sing lustily.

"Oh please, spare me, for the love of God…"

I chuckled as I followed the two of them, while Willie complained vociferously about Jonty's singing.

The rest of the shift passed without incident, and it was late afternoon when we were about to head off home. I suddenly noticed Tomas, all togged up in motorbike gear. Where was he going? On the spur of the moment, I decided I would try to follow him. As luck would have it, Gordon was nearby.

"Ready for home, sir?"

"Yes and no."

"Oh?"

"I want you to follow Tomas," I said without preamble. There wasn't time to explain. I didn't want to involve the batman, but it couldn't be helped; his was the only jeep to hand.

"Follow Tomas, sir?"

"Yes."

Tomas was getting on his bike and kicking it into life. At any moment, he would be off.

"I need you to do it, and don't ask questions. I can't tell you why," I said. Gordon was trustworthy, I knew that much. After all, he knew of my liaison with Barbara.

"OK, what about the others?"

"They can find their own way back. Come on, and follow discreetly."

"As you wish, sir."

Tomas started off and we watched his motorbike head out of the airfield. Gordon put the jeep into gear and drove after him. We managed to keep him in view for several miles around some winding lanes until we reached a small hamlet not far away. I hoped he hadn't seen us or realised we were following him. We drove on past a large white building set back off the road behind a white picket fence and saw his motorbike parked outside.

Gordon, who was perhaps more skilled at this than me, drove on for a mile or so and then turned back, driving slowly and parking a short distance away. "What now, sir?" he enquired.

"I suppose I'd better go and see what he's up to."

Gordon pulled out his sidearm and handed it to me. "Then you'd better take this."

"What?"

"Sir, I'm not supposed to know a lot of things that I know; ask no questions, tell no lies, sir." He shrugged.

"OK, thanks." I took the weapon from him, although I had one of my own, as all pilots had to have one for obvious reasons. It was perhaps his way of telling me he knew exactly what was going on.

I decided not to enquire further and began to wonder who else was aware of my mission. There wasn't time to worry about it. I walked slowly towards the building, keeping an eye out in case I was spotted. There wasn't any cover to speak of, but the place seemed deserted. There was nothing to indicate what the building was or why Tomas would be going there. I went through the white picket gate and up the path. I kept the revolver close by my side and decided to creep around the back. Perhaps there was a window, and I could peer into it. As I rounded the corner, I came face to face with Tomas. He had his own sidearm raised and pointing at me. I responded in kind, and we were in a stand-off.

"Why did you follow me, Scottish?" he demanded.

"Why are you here?" I shot back. "What are you doing?"

"Is my business!"

"Oh? And what business is that?" There was nothing for it but to face him down. If he shot me, then he would most definitely be the spy, but on the other hand, I would be dead.

"You tell me why you followed me," he said, sounding a little hysterical.

It didn't sound like something a spy would do. They would surely be far more composed, whereas he was visibly upset. I decided there was nothing for it but to tell him. If he was really the spy, he might give himself away.

"Put that down, at least, and I'll tell you," I said.

"OK, OK, I will put it down."

He lowered his weapon, and I did the same.

"Look, I'm not supposed to tell you this, or anyone," I began, "but I needed to check if you were a spy."

He looked at me with an incredulous expression, and then he burst out laughing. "A spy? Oh, Scottish! Oh, that is a funny one. A spy!"

"This is a serious matter," I told him.

"Yes, is serious for sure, but me? A spy? Come on! I would rather shoot myself than become a spy for the Nazi pigs."

"OK," I said, starting to believe him. "But what are you doing here?"

"Ah, well, come, I will show you." He holstered his weapon and walked up to me, putting an arm around my shoulder. "A spy, Scottish? Me? Come on."

We rounded the building, and I saw Gordon watching me anxiously from the jeep. I gave him the thumbs-up and we went up some steps to the front door. There was something I had missed: a plain cross above the door. I began to get the feeling that Tomas definitely wasn't a spy after all.

He opened the door and ushered me in. As I had guessed, I appeared to be in a church. There were pews and an altar at the front. A priest was standing in front of the altar, possibly in the act of leading a prayer. Kneeling among the pews were several people, who all turned to look.

"This my religion, Scottish. I come here to pray."

It dawned on me then. Habits. This was his habit. He wanted to practise his own religion and was doing it here, though it was not obvious that the building was a church from the outside. They were evidently being discreet.

"So, now you can tell me why you think I was a spy, no?" he said.

I knew I was going to have to do so, in spite of strictures not to. Perhaps it could be to my advantage to have some help.

"Is there somewhere we could talk, privately?"

"Yes, for sure. We can sit here, at the back — no one here can speak English. Tell me and I will help you, if I can."

CHAPTER SIX

For a few moments, I looked at the goings-on in the church while collecting my thoughts. Tomas was watching me patiently, with a smile playing on his lips. He was quite a handsome chap really, in his thirties, with fair hair, brown eyes and a well-defined, square jawline. He was older than me and probably wiser.

"Look," I said at length, "if I tell you what is going on, then you can't tell a soul."

"Who am I going to tell, Scottish?" he laughed and gestured expansively. "I'm in a house of God."

"OK, but you must swear, because Bentley will have my guts for garters."

"Come on, Scottish, I give you my word. I swear it on the Bible, on my mother's life."

I laughed too, and somehow this exchange engendered a form of trust between us. "Right, well, apparently there is a spy in the squadron, and I've got to find out who it is." I sat back, awaiting his response.

"A spy, OK."

It was clear he did not entirely credit it, so I continued, "Bentley himself told me and has ordered me to track them down. Then I had a visit from two chaps from MI6…"

"Yes, I see. It sounds serious."

"It is. Deadly serious. Bentley says he thinks the spy has been giving away our movements to Jerry."

"Bloody bastard," he said under his breath. "If I catch him, I will…"

"Do nothing but turn him in to the authorities," I said at once. The last thing I needed was Tomas gunning down the spy in cold blood. MI6 would want him alive to interrogate him — or her, I corrected myself. There was no saying the spy wasn't a woman.

Tomas held up his hands as if surrendering. "Fine, fine, OK." It was his turn to be silent, thinking it over. Then he said, "But tell me, Scottish. Why did you pick on me?"

I coughed, feeling embarrassed. "Well, it's these two Johnnies from MI6, they said…" I paused. There was nothing for it but to be honest. "They said I should look at the foreigners first."

This revelation didn't seem to faze Tomas at all. He simply rolled his eyes. "This does not surprise me. It is the same everywhere in this country of yours."

"I didn't… I wouldn't… I don't think like that," I hastened to explain myself.

"No, Scottish, not you. I know you. You are not like them. But the others. To them I am just that strange foreign chap, the foreign Johnnie — it must be him, he's the jolly spy all right." He mimicked a perfect cut-glass British accent, and I could not help chuckling. He grinned. "Why do you think I am in the Mavericks, hmm?"

It was an unwritten rule that we never asked anyone how they'd got into our squadron. We just assumed they'd been chucked out of the others for some misdemeanour or other. If someone wanted to tell you, that was another matter.

"I don't know," I said.

"Well, I'll tell you. The last squadron, the CO, he did not like me because I am a foreigner. He always grounded me, made me sit out the war when I just want to kill Germans. So, one day I said to him. 'Why do you not let me fly?' He said, 'How do I know you can even fly properly? You weren't trained in this country. You are a foreigner.'"

I listened sympathetically while abhorring his CO's prejudice.

"So, I said to him," Tomas went on, leaning forward, "I said, 'If I am good enough to die in your bloody war then I'm good enough to fight in it, so put me in a bloody plane and let me fly. I can fly better than you; I was there when Hitler invaded our country. What did you think I was doing, sitting on my arse in an office drinking tea, you stupid bastard?'"

"What happened then?" I asked with interest.

"I get sent to the Mavericks."

We both laughed again. Tomas seemed almost indefatigable. I could not imagine what he had been through. In the Mavericks we didn't care about his nationality, just how good a pilot he was, and he was very good indeed.

"Listen," he continued, looking grave, "this is nothing new. There are bad things happening in my country, very bad things. I hear, from my friends." He jerked his head at the congregation. "I hate these bastard Nazis. I want to kill every one of them. Every … one."

I saw his eyes grow cold as he said this, and I knew for sure he was not the spy.

"Tell me what you need, and I will help you," he said.

"The thing is, I don't really know," I admitted. "I'm no spy catcher. I'm making it up as I go along. Those men told me to look out for people with habits, and that it would be the one I least suspected."

"Yes, yes, I see." He pondered this for a moment. The ceremony in the church seemed to be drawing to a close. "Tell you what we can do. I will think, and you will think, and then we will think together."

"Sounds like a plan."

"Yes, but now I have to..." He indicated the priest.

"Of course, we'll talk again."

"We will, Scottish, we will."

He shook my hand warmly and I left him as he made his way to the front of the church, presumably to receive his blessing or something. I returned to Gordon, who had been patiently waiting.

"Everything OK, sir?" he asked as I clambered into the jeep.

"Tomas is in the clear, so yes," I said, handing him back his pistol.

"That's excellent news he's not the spy," said Gordon, and then realising his faux pas, he shot me a guilty look.

"Does every man in this damn squadron know about the spy?" I demanded.

"Oh, no, sir, not at all. I make it my business..."

"To know." I finished the sentence for him and shot him a wry smile.

"Are we ready to go home, sir?" He shifted the conversation, evidently thinking discretion was the order of the day.

"Yes, I'm famished. Hopefully there is something nice for dinner."

"There will be, sir — for you, at least. Lady Barbara..."

"Oh, right." I sighed. It was to be another tête-à-tête with Barbara, I gathered. I had been hoping for a quiet night in, but it would be far from that. Barbara wasn't particularly quiet, and it was a good job her rooms were far away from anyone else's.

"Shall you be joining her?" Gordon asked as the jeep bowled along.

"Do I have a choice?"

"There is always a choice," the batman said sagely. "Some choices are best not taken."

"Precisely, Fred, precisely."

Barbara was attired in her negligée in her boudoir. Supper was served on a small table in the rather amply sized bedchamber. The fact she was already dressed for bed was a good indication that she was more than comfortable with our relationship. I was her lover, and this fact was pretty much cast in stone. For how long, I had no idea. I had no thoughts past a few months or even weeks. Tomorrow I might catch that bullet and I would be no more. Just a footnote in the annals of the Air Force.

"There you are," she purred. "I was thinking you would never come."

She rose swiftly and enveloped me in a kiss. I had to admit that every time she did so, I was lost. I had started to experience 'feelings' with respect to Her Ladyship, although perhaps I did not recognise them as such. I had never had those kinds of feelings before. Not really. Love was foreign to me.

"I do have a job to do, stopping Jerry from invading our country," I told her with mild acerbity when she finally released me.

"I know." She sighed, ignoring my sarcasm. "If only I could have you all to myself."

"I'm pretty much at your beck and call as it is," I objected with a smile.

She inclined her head in acknowledgement and resumed her place at the table. "Come here then and sit beside me."

"As my Lady wishes."

Her voice had taken on a teasing tone, and she was completely irresistible in almost every way. I imagined this would be what had attracted her husband to her. I pushed the thought away and joined her.

She lifted off the silver cloches to reveal a roast chicken, roast potatoes, cabbage and parsnips. On the table was a gravy boat. A veritable feast, and still warm too.

"A whole roast chicken!" I exclaimed. This was something of a treat. Chickens were quite precious and needed for laying eggs. To kill one for the dinner table might be seen as profligate by some. I was certainly not about to mention it outside of her bedroom.

"Only the best for my love," she replied, smiling.

"Shall I carve?"

"Of course."

The dinner was delicious, and I indulged myself a little royally on that fowl. I felt a pang of guilt, but then one must not look a gift horse in the mouth. Besides, I knew I would need to keep my strength up for later.

"Did you have a good day?" she asked me.

"Apart from running out of fuel and having to glide home, and then going on a wild goose chase, yes."

"Oh!" she pouted. "You need to take better care of yourself, running out of petrol like that — something could have happened to you!"

She was admonishing me as if I had done it on purpose. I found it amusing rather than irritating.

"I'm here, aren't I? Those are the risks we take."

"I wish you didn't have to."

"No, but I *do*," I replied pointedly. It was no use bemoaning fate. What had to be, had to be. I had chosen this path and I had to see it through. It was, after all, for King and Country, meeting adversity with the British stiff upper lip. All of us knew what was at stake if we lost the battle in the air.

She put down her cutlery and pushed away her plate. "Have you finished?" she asked me, letting the silk fabric fall provocatively away from her bare skin.

"Yes, have you?"

"I haven't even started."

Creeping back to my bed in the early hours, I felt dead tired. One of the drawbacks of this nocturnal existence was the lack of sleep, which was down to Barbara's insatiable appetite. She could not get enough of me, it seemed, and I let her, because in truth the feeling was mutual. I could not see how it could lead anywhere at all but at the same time, I couldn't stop myself either. I crept under the covers and slept. As luck would have it, I wasn't on the early shift for a change, so I slept in and finally appeared in the breakfast room for what might be described as brunch.

"Ah, the sleeping beauty awakens. Where did you disappear to?" Willie demanded when he saw me.

"Oh, well…"

"Don't tell me, I can guess." He smiled. I had hoped my nocturnal meanderings were secret but then again, Willie could be trusted with whatever he knew. "I had to listen to Jonty's bloody paean to your bravery all by myself and for that, I won't forgive you."

We laughed and at that moment Jonty also arrived.

"My name being taken in vain, is it?"

"No, it's bloody not. I had to listen to your infernal row for most of the evening, so I'm entitled to complain."

"It was an epic song of heroism. Didn't you like it?" Jonty at once assumed an air of one most aggrieved.

"No!" Willie replied shortly.

"Philistine."

The day passed without incident, although we had several runs out to meet bombers or fighters. Jerry was certainly starting to throw his weight around, but for the most part, we showed him we were not to be trifled with.

A few more days ran by, each much the same as the last, while I continued to think about the spy. Bentley was bound to ask me soon, and I needed to have something to tell him at least. Currently, I was out of ideas.

One afternoon, when I was walking out to check on my plane, Tomas came up to me. He seemed to have something on his mind.

"Tomas?" I prompted.

"Scottish, I have been thinking."

"So have I, but it hasn't got me anywhere."

"Never mind," he said. "I have thought of someone we must check."

"Who?" I became interested at once.

"You will not like it."

"Go on, who is it?" I said eagerly.

He hesitated and then said, "Lawrence Calver."

"What? Ace? Are you mad?"

"No, listen, come over here where nobody can hear us." He practically dragged me to the edge of the field.

"Why on earth do you think it's him?" I asked.

"Because," he said urgently, "like you say, it is the one you least suspect."

"Yes, but even so — I mean, Lawrence Calver! He's dyed-in-the-wool British from an upper-class family."

"But don't you see, that's just it. His kind, they are, how you say, not always loyal!"

"What do you mean?"

"Some of these aristocrats, you know, they like the bloody Nazis."

"What?"

"Yes, people know this. I read the newspapers. I know people who know…"

"OK." It wasn't entirely news to me. I was aware of such sentiments by some in the upper crust, naturally. I did not like it, but I was aware of it.

"But Ace is the best pilot we've got with the most kills," I objected.

"What better cover than to kill many Germans? Then nobody can suspect you. You are, how do you say it, untouchable, no?"

I stared out across the field, watching the breeze ruffling the trees, and pondered his theory. It was now early September, and the leaves were beginning to turn brown, ready for the autumn fall. I wondered if I'd see the winter or even Christmas. Such maudlin ideas would get me nowhere.

"Is that all you've got to go on? Just because he's part of the aristocracy?"

"Well, you suspected me because I am a foreigner, no?" he shot back, but he wore a cheeky grin.

"Touché." I acknowledged the hit. "Even so, how on earth are we supposed to discover if Ace is the spy or not? He doesn't exactly go creeping off on his own, or does he?" I looked at Tomas in case he knew something I didn't.

"No, no, but we can search his room."

"Search his room?" I must have looked aghast at the idea. Searching a fellow officer's room was taboo. It was crossing some very clear lines of etiquette, among other things.

"Oh, Scottish, your face!" He burst into a peal of laughter.

After a moment or two, I saw the funny side and joined in. We continued in this vein until I recovered myself a little and had another thought. "Yes, but we can't just go searching his room. I mean, what if he catches us?"

"We must search when he is flying in the air," the Czech pilot said practically.

"Right, but we're always on the same shift as him, pretty much."

He shook his head enigmatically. "You worry too much. I will arrange or God will arrange for us."

"And how, exactly, are you, or even he, going to do that?"

Tomas just raised his finger to his nose and tapped it confidentially. I frowned, feeling no good could come of it, but he simply smiled and strode away.

There was no further time to think about it as pilots came pelting out of the hut at a run, making for their aircraft, and I automatically followed suit.

Techie spun up the prop and I was soon airborne with Jonty and Willie on my wings. I cast an impatient eye around to check where Lawrence was. Blasted Bentley, and here I was thinking of searching Lawrence's room. I put my attention firmly back on the job.

"What's the crack, Kiwi?" I asked, having not been in the hut to hear the clarion call.

"Jerry heading in force, as usual — bombers, most likely," Willie said.

"Red Leader, this is Blue Leader. We're heading for the coast; apparently Stuka dive bombers are attacking some of the fleet. We had a call for help from Fleet Command." Judd possibly overheard our conversation and decided to enlighten me further.

"Roger," I said.

"Now you know," Willie said dryly.

"I feel this could be another good day for a ballad," said Jonty.

"Oh no…" came a groan from my antipodean colleague.

Stuka dive bombers were something of a strange beast. They carried a payload of bombs, and they dived straight down to drop them. The Stuka always made a screaming noise as it dropped, which anyone who had been in a raid would certainly remark upon. It was a plane that struck fear into the hearts of many when it commenced ground and sea-based attacks. The Stuka had a rear-facing gun for defence, since they were vulnerable to enemy planes when diving. However, due to their delivery method, the bomb dropping was quite accurate. The last thing we needed was Jerry sinking our ships.

The coast shortly hove into view, and we could see a flight of Stukas, circling around and dropping for the kill.

"Break, break! Take them down as quickly as you can," came Judd's voice.

"You heard him," I told my section.

We peeled off left and right, and I made for the nearest diving plane. I fired two bursts before it could drop its deadly cargo. It went into a steep dive. I heard Jonty yelling something at me and looked in my rear-view mirror.

"You've got a 109 on your tail! Break right, break right, Skipper!"

The intelligence penetrated and I did as instructed. Tracers whizzed past me and I kept on banking, hoping to come around on him. This pilot wasn't to be shaken so easily, so my zigzag manoeuvres didn't work. Wondering how to get rid of him, I pulled up sharply, looping over and feeling the g-forces kick in hard as they always did. Next thing, I blacked out.

When I came to, all I could hear was Willie shouting, "Pull up, Scottish, for God's sake pull up! Scottish! Scottish!"

My Spitfire was dropping out of the sky and was on target to hit the water at maximum speed. I would be a goner and no mistake. Instinct took over. Somehow, after wrestling with the stick and then throttling it up, I got control of the steep dive and flattened it out just a few feet from the water. The plane skimmed over the waves. At last, I was able to pull it into a climb. I remembered the 109 on my tail and looked wildly around, but it was nowhere to be seen.

"If you're looking for that yellow nose, I took it down for you," came Willie's voice, flooded with relief.

As I levelled off, the Stuka attack was over, and the planes were all gone.

"All sections return to base, show's over," Judd cut into my thoughts.

"Let's go, chaps, Red Section on me," I said, starting to regain my composure.

"What the hell happened?" Willie asked me once we were en route for home.

"I don't know, I must have blacked out for a moment. Too much g-force, I guess."

"It was a hell of a climb, I'll give you that."

"And a hell of a scare you gave us too!" Jonty cut in with feeling.

"Yes, but I'm all right now. Happens to the best of us."

If I'd thought the matter could be shrugged off lightly, I was soon disabused of the notion when I landed. Almost as soon as I jumped down from my plane, I saw Judd striding toward me.

"What on earth happened out there?" he demanded as soon as he came abreast of me.

"I don't know, sir. I think I just overdid the g-force in that loop."

I attempted to snap a salute, but he said irritably, "Never mind that blasted protocol now. You are grounded until the doc has examined you and cleared you for flying again."

"But..."

He didn't let me finish. "No buts, Angus, I'm serious. You don't get back in a plane until you've been checked over. It might be as you say, but I have to be sure. You are one of my best pilots and I can't risk losing you or your jeopardising..."

He did not have to finish. I knew exactly what he was talking about. If there really was something wrong with me, then I would be a liability to those flying with me. I cursed under my breath.

"Yes, sir."

"Very well, let's hope it's nothing. Keep me posted," he told me before leaving abruptly.

"What was that about?"

Willie and Jonty were at my side almost as soon as he had departed. Willie looked at me expectantly.

"I'm grounded, chaps, until the doc says I'm OK. You'll have to fly without me for a while. Willie, you can take over the section, maybe get Tomas on the wing."

Neither of them questioned my authority and just nodded in acquiescence.

"I'm sure it's nothing, just a blackout, old man," said Jonty sympathetically, clapping me on the shoulder.

"You'll be fine," said Willie.

"I hope you're right."

"How about a snifter to chase the blues away?" Jonty ventured.

"I think under the circumstances..."

"No, perhaps not," he said sadly. Then, brightening up, he added, "A song then, to cheer you up."

"No!" said Willie emphatically. "If anything, that's guaranteed to make him practically suicidal."

"Well, I say!" Jonty looked aggrieved.

"Perhaps another time, Jonty. I'm not in the mood for songs."

He seemed a little mollified by this. "Yes, of course. Well, better get you off to the doc, then."

The two of them insisted on accompanying me to the medical unit, where they left me, making me promise to report the prognosis later.

Doctor Vivek Ramachandran was our medical officer. He was originally from India but had settled in Britain after his medical training and joined the RAF. He was in his fifties, a mild-mannered, distinguished-looking man with grey hair and a beard. He wore round gold-rimmed spectacles and gave the air of someone who was knowledgeable in their field.

I sat across the desk from him while he took down some details.

"Have you ever had any blackouts like this before?" he asked when I had related the circumstances.

"No, never. Surely this is just a one-off, due to the g-forces — I just overcooked the loop, didn't I?" I asked, willing him to agree.

"Yes, normally I would imagine this the most likely case, but I have to examine you nevertheless."

"All right, and then will you sign me back on, assuming I'm all right?"

He laughed. "It's not as easy as that, Angus. Indeed no. I will need you to have some X-rays and a blood test just to make sure there's nothing else."

I made a face, and he looked on in sympathy. "Fine, and how long is that going to take?"

"I see you are impatient to get back to putting your life on the line," the doctor said with some amusement.

"It's my job, my section needs me."

"I'm sure they do, but they can do without you for a day or two while we do our investigations. Then, if all is well, you'll be back in action soon enough."

With that, I had to be satisfied. I acquiesced somewhat meekly in the end while Doctor Vivek did what he needed to do. I would have to go to the local hospital for the X-rays, which meant another delay, but there was nothing I could do about it and Bentley would certainly back up Judd if I tried to get around it.

As I was leaving the medical unit, a figure peeled itself off the wall outside and appeared at my side. I looked down to see a keen pair of brown eyes searching mine in a worried fashion.

"Angelica?" I had not seen her since that day on the airfield.

"Sir, I … are you all right?"

"What?"

"I heard about your blackout, and I wanted to see if you were all right."

I looked at her curiously. I had only met her once, yet here she was taking a very keen interest in me. "Well…" I began.

"Yes?"

"The doc says I have to have some tests."

"Tests?"

"Yes, he wants to make sure I'm OK before he signs me back on."

"Oh, so he doesn't think there is anything wrong?" I heard the anxiety in her voice and wondered still more why this woman who barely knew me should care.

"He didn't say, but he just wants to be sure. Personally, I think I overcooked the loop and that's what happened."

"Right," she smiled.

"So, I'm grounded." I sighed.

"Oh, well…"

"Well, what?"

"Well, then you can take me for a drink." Angelica gazed at me with an impish expression that was far too endearing for my liking.

"I … you're very forward," I blurted out.

"So I've been told." Her smile was dazzling, and it took me quite aback.

"By whom?"

"People, people who know me," she informed me airily.

"Oh, right."

"So, are you?" she persisted.

"Am I what?"

"Going to take me for a drink, silly!" Her laughter tinkled melodically in my ears.

"If you like, er … when?"

"Now is as good a time as any. I'm off shift…"

I shrugged as the sage expression 'might as well be hanged for a sheep as for a lamb' sprang to mind. "In which case, let us go thither."

I started to walk towards the jeep, where I could find Gordon to drop us at a local pub. Angelica caught up to me and tucked her arm in mine. I looked down in surprise. She was acting as if she'd known me for years and it had been less than five minutes.

"Splendid," she said, smiling still.

The thought occurred to me, quickly squashed, that Barbara might not quite approve. However, I told myself, in the way that one does, it was just one drink. Surely one drink could do no harm?

Gordon said nothing when I handed Angelica up into the jeep and sat down beside her. However, his look spoke volumes. I was not entirely sure if I had incurred his disapproval, although he was a very fair-minded man.

He drove us to a local pub that was not my usual haunt. The Black Swan was not known as a forces pub, and I supposed he felt there was reason to be discreet. We tended to congregate at The Nun's Habit, which was something of a misnomer considering the goings-on that particular establishment had witnessed.

"Oh!" said Angelica when the jeep pulled up in the forecourt.

"Is something wrong?" I asked her.

"Are we going here?"

"Well … yes."

"Oh."

My mind raced for some ready excuse as to why I, or rather Gordon, had chosen it. For once, my wits were functioning as I replied, "I thought you might like somewhere quieter, where we could talk, get to know a bit about each other."

Gordon kept his eyes firmly facing the front, although I was sure he would have shot me quite a glance if he could. I helped Angelica down from the jeep and noticed her hand was trembling in mine just a little.

"I'll just tell Fred when to collect us," I told her, and she nodded.

"Give us a couple of hours, would you?" I said to him.

"Of course, sir. I'll make sure to have some dinner set aside for you."

"Thanks."

He smiled before dropping his little bombshell. "By the way, His Lordship has returned home on leave. Just thought you would like to know."

"Ah, yes, thank you."

With that intelligence delivered, he drove off. It perhaps could not be more fortuitous that Colonel Lord Amberly had come home. Barbara should certainly be too preoccupied to miss me, and I had the perfect cover for my illicit drink. I chided myself: this was all above board and, in any case, why shouldn't I have a drink with a colleague, albeit an attractive young lass, if I wanted to? I was making excuses to myself, I knew. I felt guilty and that was all there was to it.

"Are we planning to go inside, you know, for that drink?" Angelica asked me politely.

"Oh … yes … sorry, I was miles away."

"So I see."

"Perhaps a day or two's rest will do me good," I prevaricated.

"Perhaps." She didn't seem convinced, and I wondered why I got the feeling she could see right through me. "Come on then, slowcoach, I'm parched."

We sat together in what I felt was a less conspicuous spot. I nursed a pint of bitter, while Angelica took a half pint of lager.

"I know, you probably think I'm common for having a beer instead of something ladylike such as a sherry," she said, before downing a good swig.

"Not in the least," I demurred. I refrained from saying it seemed a tad unusual, but perhaps this was just my upbringing. In the circles in which I had been raised, the ladies did not drink beer.

"This is the war, Angus; times have changed, and they are still changing. Women are doing many things they weren't perceived capable of before."

"So I see."

She smiled enigmatically at me. I felt unable to read her thoughts in return.

"Tell me about yourself," I said, wanting to move the subject on, and from a genuine desire to know more about her.

"Isn't that my line?"

"You first."

She was easy to talk to and ready with a quick rejoinder or a joke when needed. I felt my own history was fairly dull. I was a favoured son born to a laird, who would inherit the estate and everything in it, though now the war had intervened. I had been brought up to enjoy the finer things in life, although we were never what was called 'high society'.

Angelica came from different stock. She hailed from the south of England and her parents were not well off. She'd joined the Air Force to find adventure and to help with the war effort. Prior to that, she had worked as a telephone operator, and that was perhaps why she'd ended up in comms.

"So now you know," she said, with sparkling eyes. "I'm just an ordinary girl."

"I wouldn't say *that*," I began, and then caught myself about to indulge in flattery.

"Oh? What would you say?"

Feeling that now I'd started, flattery was perhaps in order after all, I continued, "I'd say you're more than ordinarily pretty, for a start."

"Oh!" She blushed and lightly touched my arm. "Does that mean you'd like to take me for a drink another time?"

"I wouldn't say *that*," I quipped and then demurred. "I'm joking, I'm joking."

"You are very…" She punched me gently.

"Very?"

"I cannot be unladylike. My lips are sealed."

I burst out laughing at this and some people looked around. "Why not? We could have another drink, some other day," I said.

"Done, and I will hold you to it."

"I never renege on a lady."

She smiled. It was almost a smile of satisfaction, as if I had passed some kind of test. It was time to go, and Gordon was waiting outside. He dropped Angelica off in her road, and I helped her down from the jeep once more.

"Such a gentleman. I can get down by myself, you know."

"I'm sure you can, but I was brought up properly," I told her.

"Let's hope not too properly." She shot me a saucy glance and walked away quickly, leaving me pondering this remark.

"A live wire, that one," said Gordon as a resumed my seat.

"Oh?"

"Oh, yes. She's a sparky little thing for sure."

He said no more, and I wondered where on earth he had gleaned this information from, but I didn't like to ask.

"How are things at Amberly Manor?" I asked him, changing the subject.

"Ah, well, let's say perhaps a little tense, sir."

"Meaning?"

"Her Ladyship remarked upon your absence at dinner."

"Oh. But surely her husband…?"

"It was perfectly innocently said, sir, but even so. Her Ladyship was not in her usual spirits."

"Ah."

He shot me a kindly glance. "Tread lightly over soft ground, sir, that's the best advice I can offer you."

I nodded, taking this in. Barbara wasn't going to be happy about my absence after all, it seemed. "I'm probably going to have another drink with Angelica," I told him, though why I felt it necessary to explain myself I was not sure. Perhaps it was because Gordon cut a rather fatherly figure to us younger pilots.

"I expected no less, sir," he replied.

I was left to contemplate the cryptic nature of this latest utterance on the journey home. Was it an admonishment? A commentary on my character and morals? I wasn't sure and didn't want to ask, in case the answer was not to my liking.

I ate my dinner alone and went to bed. With some relief, I turned off the light and pulled up the covers, when the door to my room softly opened and closed.

Before I could say anything, Barbara slid naked under the covers and snuggled up to me.

"Is that you?" I asked unnecessarily.

"Of course it's me, darling, who else would it be?"

"But … what about the colonel?"

"What about him?" she purred in my ear.

"Well … won't he miss you?"

"He's fast asleep, my love. It didn't take long to service his needs."

"What?" I was quite astonished at this brazen reference to their private life and the fact she'd come to my bed directly after being in his.

"Hush." She put a finger to my lips. "That means nothing to me. You mean everything. And I missed you at dinner. Where were you?"

I could almost feel her pouting in the darkness.

"I felt it perhaps prudent to make myself scarce, under the circumstances."

"Silly boy, my silly darling boy."

Her hands were now rendering thought impossible, and her lips were setting mine on fire. I realised I had got myself in the deep end, yet again. Even more so now there was Angelica, and whatever was I to do about her? Further musing on the subject was postponed, as Barbara made her immediate requirements perfectly clear without uttering another word.

At breakfast I watched the others depart for their shift while I ate a little desultorily. I wanted to be going with them and I couldn't.

"Take care of Jonty, Kiwi," I said as Willie got up to leave.

"Don't worry, I'll make sure he gets home safe."

"Are you taking Tomas on your other wing?"

"I'm not sure. We'll see what Bentley wants. Don't fret yourself, Scottish. We'll be fine without you."

"Oh, now I'm superfluous."

"Idiot," said Willie affectionately.

"That's no way to talk to a senior officer!"

"Idiot, sir," he said, and we both laughed.

The room was empty after all of the pilots had left, and I was finishing my plate of eggs when Tomas appeared in the dining room.

"Tomas, aren't you supposed to be…?"

He wasn't quartered with the rest of us, although I didn't like to ask why. Apparently, he was staying with a widow in the village. Until that moment, I had not thought that perhaps he might prefer it. Perhaps the widow was the attraction.

"Yes, sure, I am going, but, Scottish…" He dropped his voice to a whisper.

"Yes?"

He looked around in case we were overheard. "Now is the time to, you know…"

I regarded him blankly.

"You know … search the room…"

"Oh!" The penny dropped. "Are you sure?"

"Yes, because Ace will be with us, in the air."

"Ah, yes, but is this really the best idea?"

"Of course, Scottish, of course." He clapped me on the back.

"Right."

"What can go wrong? It's easy!" He spread his arms wide. "It's a perfect time, because you are grounded."

"Yes, I know, but you're not the one who has to do the searching."

"It's going to be fine, Scottish, really."

"If you say so."

I was still not convinced and was certain somehow that if something could go wrong, it would.

"Don't worry about anything. I told you, God will arrange it and he has," Tomas said as he left the room.

"Easy for you to say," I called after him.

I sat there for a long time, nursing my tea and accepting a further cup that was offered to me by a maid. The entering of a fellow officer's room was taboo. Yet, Bentley himself had ordered me to find the spy, so perhaps that gave me the right, if I suspected someone. I was sure the MI6 Johnnies wouldn't have the slightest compunction about doing it. And yet, much as I disliked Lawrence, he still did not seem like a spy to me. Whichever way I looked at it, it just seemed entirely wrong. Finally, after a good while, I decided it would be best to get it over with and then get out of the house. Barbara might discover I was still there, and that would mean she would waylay me once more.

Like a guilty schoolboy, I tried to walk nonchalantly past Lawrence's room and then back again. I did so several times, each time trying to steel myself to do the deed and not quite being able to. Eventually, I took myself back to my own room and gave myself a stern talking-to. This was no way to carry out my duties. Having done so, I marched back to Lawrence's room and this time put my hand on the handle. It turned easily enough, as none of us locked our doors. The door swung silently inward. I stepped in and quietly shut it behind me.

The room, which I had never seen before, was spacious enough. Unlike mine it had, to my annoyance, a private bathroom and a much larger bed. I wondered why he'd got a better room, but this was no time to be distracted. There was a dressing table, chest of drawers, and wardrobe. In fact, rather a lot of places to look. I wondered where to begin and what I hoped to find. Electing to start with the chest of drawers, I went through each drawer carefully, feeling under the clothing and finding nothing particularly untoward. That was until I discovered a sheaf of magazines in the bottom drawer. They bore titles such as *Frolic*, *Titter* and *Bizarre*. A quick flick through and a glance at the covers revealed them to be what were euphemistically titled men's interest publications. They seemed also to contain quite a lot of naked men, not just women. I thought little of it since there wasn't time and I was still afraid of imminent discovery, even though Lawrence would be at the airfield.

"Well, I never," I said under my breath, replacing them carefully. These were hardly incriminating evidence of spying, amusing though it was to think Lawrence wasn't quite whiter than white after all.

I closed the drawer and headed for the wardrobe as my next port of call. There was nothing on the top of it, and I was just about to open it when who should walk into the room but Lawrence himself?

For a few unnerving moments, we stood staring at each other.

"What the hell are you doing in my room?" he demanded once he'd recovered his composure.

While he had hesitated, my mind had been frantically searching for a plausible explanation. I also fleetingly wondered why he wasn't flying with the squadron, but it wasn't the time to ask. Unable to think of anything clever, I decided to go for something approaching the truth and make it up as I went along.

"Answer me, damn you, or I'll…"

He balled his fist in a threatening manner. This did not, however, frighten me. If he wanted to engage in fisticuffs, I was more than his match, having learned to box at school. However, it wouldn't do to be brawling with a fellow officer, and we'd both end up in Bentley's office on the carpet if we did.

I decided to be bold and said, "If you must know, Bentley asked me to search your room and … and other rooms too."

He looked somewhat taken aback but did not lose any of his aggressive demeanour. "Oh? And why exactly would Bentley do that?"

My mind was in a whirl, searching frantically for a reason, and so I said the first thing that came into my head. "Because … the general told him someone has been stealing his vegetables."

I shot him a triumphant look. This was a masterstroke, I felt, and now I was ready to elaborate upon the most ridiculous-sounding reason anyone could have come up with.

Lawrence most certainly looked incredulous at this statement. "His vegetables?"

"Yes, his vegetables. You know, the various things he grows in his garden — they've been going missing, and he is convinced it's one of the pilots who keep buzzing his house."

Although Lawrence's expression was somewhat sceptical, he did appear as if he might actually believe me. "I see. And Bentley thinks it's me, does he?"

His irritation was now more directed at Bentley than myself, I was glad to see.

"Well … you did rather snap back at him when he mentioned about not barnstorming the general's house anymore."

This struck home, but he still wasn't completely convinced. "And why would I hide the vegetables here in my room, assuming I had taken them?"

Since I couldn't think of a good answer, I opted instead to play Bentley as the trump card in the argument. "I'm not sure, but Bentley was insistent."

Lawrence's ire was now up, and Bentley was the object of his wrath. "Damned nonsense, that's what it is! I'm going to see bloody Bentley and tell him a thing or two."

"I wouldn't do that if I were you."

"Oh? And why not?"

"Because then he'd suspect even more that it was you, because you obviously know about it."

I definitely wanted to put him off talking to Bentley, because I had no idea what Bentley would say. He probably wouldn't twig I was searching Lawrence's room in case he was the spy and would claim it was a prank. Worse still, he'd haul me over the coals for playing said prank.

"But you just *told* me."

"Ah, but he doesn't know that."

He thought about this for a moment. "I see, I see, and so you think you can just..."

"Bentley's orders," I reminded him, feeling I now had the upper hand.

"Have you searched any other rooms?"

"Well, no, not at present."

"Fine, then let's search them now. I'll come with you, in fact, and find these bloody vegetables myself."

"I don't think that's wise."

"Oh, you don't? I see. Well, fine, but you can jolly well tell Bentley I've never seen the general's damnable vegetables, and I'll be damned if I'm called a thief."

"I'm sure he didn't..."

Lawrence was in full flow. "As for the bloody general, I'm going to barnstorm his house every chance I get. I'll barnstorm his bloody vegetable garden too. See how he likes that!"

"I'm not sure he will take very kindly to..."

Lawrence made an exasperated noise. "Just go, will you, please?"

I edged around him gently and eased open the door. "Shouldn't you be up with the squadron?" I ventured, feeling slightly reckless.

"It's none of your damn business if I am or if I'm not! Now, will you please get out?"

"Right, yes, I'll just..."

I made my escape with alacrity and a massive sigh of relief. The whole episode had been a complete nightmare from start to finish. The most surprising thing was how my vegetable story had suddenly become very plausible. I congratulated myself on being so quick-witted. I had no doubt Lawrence would mention something about it to the others. If Bentley tackled me on the subject of the general's garden, I would deny everything.

I avoided running into Barbara and passed the rest of the day pleasantly enough taking a long walk, breathing in the country air. I was waiting for word from the hospital as to when I could go for my tests, and in a way, I was grateful for the small amount of respite I now had from the constant exigencies of combat. As I returned through the village, I happened upon Tomas arriving on his motorbike.

"Scottish!" he called out, pulling off his helmet.

"Tomas," I nodded, coming up to him. "How's things?"

"Ah, it was the usual stuff, Jerries come, we try to shoot him, we come home."

"Did we lose anyone today?" This was the question on everyone's lips every day we went into combat. Inevitably there were losses, and with the hard-fought battles of late, there had been quite a few across all the squadrons.

"No, today we were lucky. God smiles on us." Tomas smiled too. "Come, come inside for some tea."

He indicated a small cottage next to us, and having nothing more pressing to do, I followed him as he wheeled his motorbike through the gate. The cottage was rather picturesque, though small. He introduced me to Ruby, a dark-haired woman who said very little but served us some tea and crumpets in the kitchen. The glances she and Tomas shared spoke of something more than him simply being a tenant, but I didn't enquire further. If he wanted to, he would volunteer it. I didn't feel I knew him well enough to ask.

"So," he said, stirring his tea, "how did the searching go? Did you find anything?"

I buttered a crumpet, ladled jam on it and related the story to him. He roared with laughter until tears ran down his face.

"Thanks," I said, feeling slightly aggrieved at his reaction. "I don't see what's so…"

"Oh, but it's funny. Come on, Scottish, it's funny."

He definitely had quite a sense of the ridiculous. The laughter was infectious, and I chuckled.

"I suppose it is really. Yes, you should have seen his face when he found me in his room."

"Oh, I wish I had seen this, I wish so much."

I couldn't help joining in the mirth, and before long the two of us were practically crying with laughter. Ruby put her head around the door to see what was going on and then disappeared as soon as I looked up.

"I thought it was bad idea," Tomas admitted when he could finally speak.

"What? You said it was an excellent plan … and you let me go through with it!"

He held out his arms as if I'd caught him out. "I know, Scottish, but it was funny, no?"

I sighed. "Yes, yes, it was, but it hasn't got us any closer to finding the spy."

"No, that's true, and I don't think we should do the room searching again."

"It was *me* searching his room, by the way, not *we*. I was the one who was caught."

"Yes, and … and oh…" He burst into peals of fresh laughter while I pursed my lips a trifle. "Ah, Scottish, you know. Sometimes these plans, they don't work."

"I'll say they don't work."

He became serious all of a sudden. "So, what are we going to do?"

"I thought you were the clever one," I retorted.

"No, Scottish, you are the clever man, that's why Bentley has chosen you."

"I'm not doing a great job so far."

Tomas made a noise as if he demurred. "But you've found two who are not spies."

"Yes, that's true."

"So, we just have to check the others."

I nodded and became a little more practical. "OK, so I am pretty sure it's not Willie and it's not Jonty. I'm close enough to them to notice if it were either of them."

"So…"

"So that just leaves the rest of the pilots."

"Fine, I know what we do. We make a list and then we tick them off one by one. We must be detectives, no? Find out more about them."

"I really thought this would be easier than it is," I said.

"If it was easy, then we should know who it is, no?"

"Yes, you're right."

"I will get the paper."

I leaned back while Tomas disappeared and returned with two notebooks, one for each of us. What Bentley made sound simple was really very complicated. I would certainly rather have been flying aircraft, and I couldn't even do that.

"OK," said Tomas. "Let us begin."

There was another briefing the next morning, and even though I wasn't flying, Bentley had ordered me to attend.

"Now then, chaps," he said when we were all assembled and looking grim. "I'm sure you are all aware that Jerry is doing his level best to flatten London to rubble, focusing much of his attention on it."

There were angry murmurs of agreement at this.

"I don't like it any more than you do, but that's what we have to deal with. They are flying in night and day at the moment, and we are severely stretched."

He paused for effect and looked around at us. The squadron wasn't usually the first into action, as it was at the back end of the queue. This was no doubt due to the reputation of its pilots — some of which was deserved but, on the other hand, we had some of the best pilots in the RAF and they showed their mettle.

"Are we to fly night sorties, sir?" Charles Forster piped up. He was a young, quite aristocratic man with reddish-blonde hair and blue eyes. We called him 'Foxy' on account of his hair. He was quite handsome with it. He had an almost perfect English accent and I put that down to him having been to public school.

"No," said Bentley firmly. "We shall not, because our Spitfires simply aren't performing well at night, and the bombers are flying too high and out of searchlight range. It's different in the daytime. We have to leave the night fighting to the Hurricanes."

There was a collective groan. Much rivalry existed between the Spitfire and Hurricane pilots. Some had even almost come to blows in the pub when one over the eight, due to disagreements as to which plane was the better one. Personally, I liked my Spitfire, but had I been asked to fly a Hurricane instead, I would have done so without demur. It was simply a job in many ways, and the plane was a means to an end.

"All right, all right, settle down," said Bentley crossly. "I don't want any more of this anti-Hurricane tomfoolery. We are all on the same side and believe me, some of you have probably had your necks saved by a Hurricane pilot before now, so let's hear no more about it."

There was silence after this admonishment.

"Right, well, anyway," he continued, satisfied he had successfully quashed things for the moment. "Our squadron is going to be playing a bigger part and this is going to mean multiple sorties. Land, refuel, load up and fly again, perhaps three or four times, even."

This was met with further silence. Up until now, we'd had it easy. Fly a sortie, then return to base while other squadrons took over. However, we all knew that our pilots were getting shot down and squadrons were being depleted. Finally, the Mavericks were being called on to play a bigger part. At the same time, the pressure of multiple sorties would take its toll in pilot fatigue and potential errors of judgement. It was going to be tough.

"So, unless anyone has any questions?"

"When is this going to start?" It was Jean Tarbon.

"Immediately."

We all exchanged glances. Lives were on the line more than ever before from this moment onwards. Nobody had anything more to ask. Bentley ended the meeting and then, to my surprise, I found him standing over me.

"I'd like a word, Angus," he said.

"Oh."

"In my office."

"Now, sir?"

"Yes, now, might as well come back with me."

"Yes, sir." I stood up and accompanied him to the main building.

"Are you fit to fly yet?" he asked conversationally.

"I am having tests tomorrow, I believe, so hopefully after that."

"Good man. Well, this shouldn't take long."

I wondered exactly what it was that wasn't going to take long, while we strode along in silence. Bentley took rather large strides, due to his legs being somewhat longer than mine, and I found myself almost running to keep up. We arrived at his office in no time, and he took a seat behind his desk. Then he reached for his wretched pipe. Audrey was typing away as usual and shot me a smile when Bentley wasn't looking.

"Sit down, Angus, there's a good chap," he said.

"Sir."

I took a seat and waited to see what Bentley wanted. He tapped his pipe, scraped out the bowl and filled it without saying a word. I waited on tenterhooks for him to say something. Instead, he lit the damnable pipe and puffed out the noxious smoke.

Without warning, he suddenly launched into it without preamble, pointing the stem of his pipe at me as if it was an inquisition. "What I want to know, Angus, is what the hell is Lawrence going on about? He was mumbling something about General Grimthorne's vegetables of all things? Hmm? What's it all about?"

The squadron leader had a most disconcerting way of staring one down when he wanted to, and he was doing so now. However, I was made of sterner stuff, having endured more than one carpeting by Bentley in my time. Most of the pilots had incurred his wrath on occasion.

"I really don't know, sir," I said at once.

He looked very much as if he didn't believe me in the slightest. "I see, is that so? Well, the man was absolutely raving at me and telling me he's not a thief. So, if there's something I need to know about it, then you had better tell me."

I remained silent, deciding discretion was the better part of valour.

"And you've no idea at all why he would be doing that?" He favoured me with another very hard stare that indicated he thought I had everything to do with it.

"No, sir, I really don't," I lied, hoping it sounded convincing.

"I see," he said, still fixing me with a beady and suspicious eye. His next utterance disabused me entirely of the notion that he was convinced of my innocence. "I know you don't like him but nevertheless, making up stories about vegetable-stealing just to discompose the poor chap isn't on. Do I make myself clear?"

"Perfectly, sir, and if I hear anyone doing that, I shall certainly admonish them on your behalf." I returned his gaze with what I hoped looked like steely resolve.

"Yes … well … you'll be the death of me, the lot of you with your carrying on. The number of complaints I've had from the publican of The Nun's Habit are legion, I tell you, legion. It's not as if there isn't a war on and I've got a job to do… You've just heard how we are going to be stretched to the limit, and the last thing I need is ridiculous tarradiddles about Grimthorne's blasted vegetable garden. I've enough problems from that quarter as it is."

"Yes, sir," I said. The vegetable incident had evidently hit a nerve.

He visibly relaxed then, having got matters off his chest, and puffed on his pipe reflectively for a few moments. I tried desperately not to cough as the smoke swirled around the office. "Anyway, what's happening with the mission I entrusted you with? Any results?" he said at length.

"We're … erm … I'm working on it…" I said quickly.

"You said *we*," he shot back, picking up on this at once. "Who is 'we'? I told you explicitly that this was top secret."

Having nearly dropped a clanger, I made a quick recovery. I couldn't tell him about Tomas Jezek, as he'd probably hit the roof. "Me and the MI6 Johnnies, sir, that's what I meant."

Once again, I came under his disbelieving gaze for a few more moments before he stuck his pipe firmly between his teeth and looked down at his papers.

"Well, work on it a bit harder, will you, Angus? And, for the record, I don't want to hear about vegetables again, anybody's vegetables. The only place for vegetables is on my dinner plate, is that understood?"

"Yes, sir, perfectly, sir."

"Good, dismissed."

I stood up, snapped him a salute and left his office, breathing a sigh of relief. As I made my way to the main entrance, Audrey caught up with me.

"Don't mind him," she said sympathetically. "He's not himself lately."

"Why's that?" I asked her.

"His dog died. A heart attack, apparently."

"Oh, right, I see. I didn't know." I'd had no idea Bentley even had a dog.

"Nobody is supposed to know about it; he's a very private man. Not at all as bad as you lot think he is. He was very fond of the dog, and his wife is distraught."

"Ah, yes. Yes, of course."

"He'll be in a better mood soon, I'm sure." She smiled reassuringly.

I had pets myself, but they were all up in Scotland and I probably wouldn't see them for quite some time to come. The death of a pet could definitely affect one's temperament.

"You know…" Audrey said suddenly.

"Yes?"

"Well … Angelica … she really likes you."

This was the last thing I was expecting. "Oh."

"No, she *really* likes you, sir." She looked at me meaningfully.

"I see. Well, thank you for the information."

Her eyes softened a little just then, and her lip trembled as if she felt quite emotional about the whole thing. There were obviously hidden depths I had not perceived.

"She's a lovely young woman. We all adore her. Please don't break her heart."

With that, she turned on her heel and left me staring after her, dumbfounded. For all of my affairs, I was no nearer to understanding women than I had ever been. I wasn't sure why she had said it, other than perhaps she was looking out for her colleague. Did people know about my affair with Barbara? Or was it that I came with a reputation, and not a very good one at that?

I had no particular intentions towards Angelica, although I did like her and felt drawn to her. Was I supposed to stop seeing her? I didn't feel inclined to do so, but should I try to keep my distance, emotionally? I sighed. Why did everything have to be so complicated? Or rather, why did I have to be so naïve about it? Besides, Angelica had asked me out for a drink, and she seemed most persistent. It wasn't entirely up to me.

On which thought, I filed it all away for the moment. I had developed the ability to do that. Perhaps it was because of the war that I could think less about the consequences of my actions than I normally might. We were all grown-ups, I reasoned, and we knew the risks.

I did not go back to the hut. It was painful to watch the others being able to fly while I could not. The hospital appointment was the next day, and I hoped I'd be cleared to fly again shortly after that.

As I was looking around for Gordon to take me home, the object of Audrey's concern came up to me, almost skipping with delight as she did so.

"I thought it was you!" Angelica said, grinning broadly. "I managed to grab a quick break to come and see you."

"And now you are," I replied, smiling.

"Well ... I'm still waiting for the invitation?" She made a mock pout.

"Oh, and what invitation is that?" I teased.

"You know very well!"

I laughed. Her joyous mood and ready smile were infectious. "Would you like to come for another drink?"

"Yes, I'd love to, and I thought you'd never ask!"

The die was cast, and although Audrey's words echoed dimly in my mind, they were lost in the audaciousness of the girl she so wanted to protect.

"I'll pick you up later then, around seven?"

"Yes, that would be lovely."

"Fred knows where you live. I will see you then."

"Indeed you will."

She turned and fairly danced away with pleasure. As I watched her go, it was hard not to be carried along by her evident enthusiasm for life.

I returned home for an early dinner, as I did not want to be late for Angelica. In fact, my spirits were considerably lifted by the idea of spending another evening with her. This was an interesting development for me, emotionally. I wasn't sure what to make of it and decided not to refine upon it too much.

At dinner, Lady Amberly was quiet and subdued. The colonel held forth in what one might consider to be slightly forced enthusiasm. He spent a good deal of time describing some of the various foreign climes he'd seen and pronounced that he was glad to be back in Blighty. All of us wanted to keep on his good side, particularly me, so we showed we were suitably impressed by his tales.

Finally, dinner was over, and just as I was getting up to leave, he spoke to me. "Stay a moment, Angus, if you will? Come and have a glass of port with me in my study."

Port was the last thing I wanted to have at that moment, and my mind was very much elsewhere, on a young lady with brown eyes. However, hoping it was going to be short, whatever it was, I did not demur.

"Of course, sir, whatever you wish."

"Splendid." He smiled, a smile which did not quite reach his eyes. He stood up and led the way out of the dining room. His wife's anxious gaze followed us both, but I dared not look at her.

Once in his rather spacious study, complete with ornate desk and ornaments from various parts of the world, as well as a large number of books, he spent a not inconsiderable amount of time pouring two glasses of port.

I was chafing but made the appearance of one completely nonchalant and with all the time in the world. His demeanour was starting to unnerve me, and I began to wonder if he knew about my affair with Barbara, and, if he did, what was about to ensue. It would not be the first such conversation I'd had with an irate husband. He handed one glass to me, kept hold of his own, and motioned to an upholstered leather armchair.

"Sit, there's a good chap." It felt almost as if he was addressing his dog by his intonation, and this perhaps did not bode well.

He drank a goodly swig of his port in a most ungentlemanlike fashion while I took a sip of mine. I had to fleetingly acknowledge, as I did so, that he kept a very good cellar.

"I know all about you and my wife," he said suddenly, almost conversationally, as if he was talking about the weather.

I started slightly at his utterance, not knowing quite how to respond. This wasn't the usual way these conversations went. "What? Oh."

He nodded sagely and without rancour. "Yes, oh yes."

I waited, somewhat filled with trepidation at what might come next. The prospect of being sent to a foreign posting seemed as if it was about to loom large in my future. I had fallen into the same pattern again. I wanted to kick myself for doing so, but he was speaking, and it cut into my tangled musings.

"Yes, old boy, I know all about it. You're probably thinking my wife is discreet, but thankfully some of my staff at least are loyal to *me*."

"I see." Still not sure where this was leading, I felt that the less I said, the better.

There was another silence while he downed the rest of the port and poured himself another. "Don't worry, I'm not about to get you chucked out of your squadron, if that's what you're thinking."

"I assure you, I..."

He cut me off. "Your reputation precedes you, old chum. Yes, indeed. People talk, and I know all about your little peccadillos. My wife is just another in a long line."

"I…"

He stopped me again by the expedient of putting up his hand. I fell silent: this was very much his show, not mine.

"I don't want to know anything about it, not a thing. It's not that I don't care, but my wife has needs. Needs which, let's just say, are perhaps beyond me…"

I could hardly imagine what must be coming next after this little disclosure.

"No, I was a young man once, but no more. Apparently, Barbara has a penchant for young men, of which you are simply another."

"Right, well I…"

Hoping he was done getting this off his chest, I sat forward as if to go, but he wasn't entirely through.

"I'm not finished," he told me in the voice of one used to command.

I remained seated and waited. He ruminated for a bit, fixing me with an unreadable expression. It seemed almost as if he wanted to hit me but at the same time could not be bothered with the effort of doing so. I had no doubt I was not his favourite person at that moment.

"I just want you to disabuse yourself of any notion that you are anything more than a small dalliance. If you harbour any thoughts of something more permanent in your future, you are out. There has never been a divorce in my family, and nor will there be. Barbara is not for the likes of you. Do I make myself clear?" He spoke quite forcefully then, in a manner quite dismissive.

"Perfectly, sir." There really was nothing more I could say.

"Good, now you can get out of my sight. At least you had the good grace not to deny it."

He turned away from me then, no doubt expecting me to leave. After a moment I decided discretion was the better part of valour. He had apparently given me carte blanche to sleep with his wife, but to expect nothing more. I didn't expect anything more; all of those expectations were from her. However, I doubted he would credit it if I told him. I left the room and headed back to my own, glancing at my watch and noting I was already running late, only to be waylaid by the very object of Lord Amberly's torment.

"What did John say to you?" Barbara hissed, catching my arm.

"I … I can't tell you here."

"Fine, we'll go for a drive, and you can tell me. Come on."

"What, now?"

"Yes, of course now!" she said urgently.

In no state to deny her, I shelved my plans for the evening, but I had to somehow let Angelica know. "Fine, but I have to speak to Fred."

"Whatever for?"

"I had some business to do for Bentley, but it will have to wait. I just need to tell Fred."

She stared at me as if I was mad to be running errands at night for the CO, but she didn't question it. "All right then, meet me at the garages as soon as you've done that."

"OK."

She rushed away and I went to discover Gordon's whereabouts. As luck would have it, he was in his room, which wasn't far from mine.

"I imagine you're not going to meet your friend?" he said diplomatically. I wondered if he had somehow been party to everything that had lately transpired. He seemed to have an infinite capacity for discovering everyone's secrets.

"No, I can't, something has come up." I shrugged. There was no need to explain further, since he had evidently divined what was occurring anyway.

He nodded sympathetically at my predicament. "I shall let the lady know you were unavoidably detained by the colonel," he said.

"Thank you, Fred, you're a treasure."

"I do my best, sir."

Whatever he thought of my antics, Gordon had my back. I knew he would lie for me if needed. I had in fact now lied to two women, and I wasn't sure what that made me. I didn't want to think about it, really. It wasn't who I was at all, but events seemed to have overtaken me. I turned away quickly with a muttered word of thanks and went to join Barbara.

We headed out into the countryside in her Rolls-Royce. She told the chauffeur to let me drive it and I did, with her beside me in the passenger seat looking like thunder. It was a beautiful car to drive, and I enjoyed that part of the experience immensely. I pulled the car up in a secluded spot overlooking a golf course. There was nobody around at that time of night.

"Go on! What did he say?" she demanded once we had come to a stop.

I gave her the gist of the conversation.

"How dare he? How dare he treat me like a common chattel?" she said angrily.

"I would have thought it was the least of your worries."

"I am *not* his to command and give out to others, unless I choose to do so!"

"But you have chosen to. He's just not objecting to it," I said reasonably.

"Yes, but even so!" If her eyes could have shot sparks out of them, they would have.

"Would you prefer it if he got me chucked out of the squadron and sent to God knows where — Africa, most likely?"

She softened at once. "No, no, of course not, no. That would break my heart."

"Then, isn't it better this way?"

She sniffed and a tear rolled down her cheek. "I suppose so." After a moment, she said, "It's not for him to say that I cannot have you, all of you."

"Sure, but he's an angry man and he has his pride." I shrugged. This was a conversation I definitely didn't want to have at that moment.

"I suppose you're right."

"Are we to just go on as before, then?" I asked her, assuming the answer would be in the affirmative.

"Of course we are. What a silly question. In fact, get into the back of the car."

"What?"

She was smiling now, teasing. The old Barbara was back again, the irresistible Barbara whom I couldn't deny. "I need some light relief."

"Is that what I am to you? Light relief?"

"No, darling, you know you're not, but come on … now … please, I want you, I *need* you."

She opened the door, and I did the same. I had no idea how this was going to end, but then I never did know how these things would end. Besides, she still thrilled me, and I couldn't think of letting go, not yet. So being none the wiser as to the future, I began to unbutton my clothes.

CHAPTER SEVEN

I was rather glad it had been a balmy autumn evening, recollecting the frantic nature of the previous night's rendezvous. The stress of the situation seemed to have unleashed a torrent of passion in Barbara, and she was like an unstoppable force. When I drove her back, she had a smile on her face, at least. She kissed me in the Rolls before leaving me at the garages to go upstairs alone to her boudoir. Had His Lordship not been at home, no doubt she would have taken me with her.

I had plenty of time to ponder over my perfidious nature before going to sleep and then again after breakfast, waiting for Gordon to take me to the hospital.

"We always think the worst of ourselves, sir. We are our own harshest judge and jury," said Gordon, almost as if he was reading my thoughts.

"Yes, perhaps…" I wasn't ready to put away the sackcloth yet.

"Don't be too hard on yourself, sir. There are far worse things in the world."

"I suppose you are right," I sighed.

"As they say, sir, it'll all come out in the wash."

Gordon seemed to have a vast panoply of sayings for every occasion. To be fair, some of them were very apt. He did cheer me up and I bore the exigencies of the hospital tests stoically, hoping that they would all simply prove I had blacked out and nothing worse. I came from hardy stock, and my family history was a remarkably healthy one. My parents were hardly ever ill, and I hadn't been a sickly child.

Having been subjected to more procedures than I had ever had in my life, I was finally released and told that my doctor would inform me shortly of the results. With that, I had to be satisfied.

I ate lunch in town, and Gordon picked me up. I was expecting him to take me home, but instead he drove me to the airfield.

"Why are we here, Fred?" I enquired with interest.

"The good Doctor Vivek has requested your presence."

"The doc wants to see me? So soon? That can't be good."

At once dire melancholy thoughts entered my mind. By the time we had arrived at the medical unit, I had practically run my entire funeral attended by my grieving family in my head. I was no hypochondriac, but in situations like this one often anticipated the worst.

"Ah, Angus," said the doctor, greeting me with a friendly smile as soon as I was ushered into his office.

I sat waiting expectantly while he fiddled around with his papers.

"I have the results of your tests. I asked them to expedite them and send them post-haste." He pulled out a manila folder and began to study it intently.

"Right, well..." I decided to take the bull by the horns. "If it's bad news, then give it to me straight, please, Doctor."

He looked up sharply. "Bad news? Who said anything about bad news?"

"Well, I thought, you know, the urgency of this meeting and..."

He roared with laughter and cut me short. I wasn't sure if this was how doctors were supposed to treat their patients, and I was somewhat put out.

"I knew you wanted to get back to flying, you silly chap," he chided me. "So, I asked them to get a jolly move on, and they did."

"Oh, I see." Relief began to flood my whole frame.

"There's nothing wrong with you, I'm pleased to say, so I conclude it was indeed just a g-force blackout."

He smiled triumphantly and I smiled back, immensely glad I wasn't about to die from a brain tumour or some such.

"Yes, you're fit as a fiddle, fighting fit, in fact, and I'm happy to declare you fit for active duty." He wrote furiously on a pad and handed me a piece of paper with a flourish.

"Thank you," I said. "No, I mean it, thank you very much."

"Don't thank me, thank whoever gave you those strong genes. Now, off you go and try not to get yourself killed."

On this happy note, I thanked him again and fairly danced out of the office, slap bang into Angelica. "Is it your habit to lurk outside of the medical unit?" I demanded, still in high spirits.

"Is it your habit to stand up ladies you've asked out on a date?" she countered, not in quite so high spirits.

That brought me down to earth. "Oh, that, yes — I'm so sorry. Something came up and I…"

"No need to explain. I give a chap at least three chances before I give up on them," she said.

"So, I've got another two?"

"Oh, you've probably got a few more than that." She grinned. "But don't take it as an invitation."

"Oh, no, I won't. Look, I promise to take you for that drink soon."

"All right, done. And no, I don't lurk outside the medical unit generally, to answer your question. Only when people I'm interested in are in it."

"Right, I see."

It was fascinating how she said quite a lot without actually saying anything directly. It was certainly a talent of hers.

"So, what was the news? Good, I assume, considering the way you waltzed out of there."

"The best! I'm on active duty once again."

"Oh good, so you can go and be reckless with your life all over again."

I looked at her, and she suddenly seemed serious, emotional, in fact.

"Oh, don't mind me," she continued, composing herself at once. "And I'm giving you forty-eight hours."

"For what?" I said.

"To ask me for that drink!"

"And if I don't?"

"Then I'll ask *you* and you'll know you have failed the test of a proper gentleman."

"What?"

She laughed and her eyes sparkled. "You really have to learn when I'm teasing."

"And how am I supposed to do that?"

"Spend more time in my company. It's the only way."

She set off before I could answer and quickly walked away. I stared after her, never having encountered a woman like her before. She intrigued me, made me laugh. I definitely did want to spend more time in her company, even knowing that I was potentially digging myself into something it would be very hard to extricate myself from, if indeed I wanted to extricate myself from it.

I went straight away to see Bentley.

"Ah, Angus," the squadron leader said as I flipped a crisp salute. "What's ailing you?"

"I've been cleared for action, sir," I said, trying not to gloat while placing the paper from Doctor Vivek on his desk.

"Good, very good," he said, handing the paper to Audrey without even looking at it. He seemed preoccupied with files open all over his desk. "Well?" he added, noticing that I was still waiting.

"Aren't you pleased, sir, to have your ace pilot back in action?" I said, slightly aggrieved at his lack of interest.

He glanced up at my slightly sarcastic tone and then down again to his paperwork. "Pleased? Of course I'm pleased. But as you can see, I've a damnable lot of work to do. It's excellent news. Now shove off and report to Flight Lieutenant Judd, there's a good fellow."

"Yes, sir, thank you, sir." I saluted once more and left the office, only to find Audrey on my tail once more. It seemed to be becoming a habit.

"Don't mind him, sir," she said. "He's very pleased really. Fighter Command is pressing him to fly as many sorties as possible. He's worried about you all. We all are."

"Right, I see," I said. This was a little sobering, since it certainly meant some of us would not return from those sorties.

"And thank you." She lightly touched my arm.

"For what?"

"For being nice to Angelica."

"Oh…"

She walked away, leaving me to wonder if everyone knew my business. Surely not? I made my way to Lieutenant Judd, who signed me on and told me I would be on the first shift in the morning.

"What's it like, sir, with all these sorties?"

"Do you really want to know?" he asked me.

"Yes."

"We're all dog tired, worn to the bone already and it's pretty much hell." He smiled at me wryly.

"Right."

"Go home and get some sleep. You'll need it." He patted me on the shoulder.

Getting sleep would be more easily said than done if Barbara had anything to do with it. I found Gordon and got him to drive me back to Amberly Manor. My life seemed to be becoming awfully complicated. Perhaps being shot down was the better option. I banished such negative thoughts immediately — it wouldn't do. I needed to get through the war, however long it lasted. We all did. Each of us thought we would make it, and many of us had not. I hoped to be one of the lucky ones. I also had to turn my attention to the spying issue. I needed some calm reflection before the action kicked off once more.

Calm reflection did not last long. After dinner, my door silently opened and closed once more, and Barbara's needs overrode any idea of meditating on things. I did, however, manage to persuade her to allow me some sleep, though she wouldn't return to her own bed. In the morning she was as rapacious as ever, but I still managed to make it for a hearty breakfast before setting off in anticipation of flying once more.

I was not to be disappointed. Within half an hour of arriving, we were scrambled to intercept yet another bombing raid on London.

"Clue me up on how this goes," I had said to Willie before the call came in.

"We go in, we hit them hard, we come back, we fuel up and replenish the ammo, and then we go again."

"Right, I see. I think I can manage that."

"Of course you can. Just try to stay alive in the process."

"I'll do my best."

We both knew that underneath the banter was the acknowledgement of the serious possibility of dying. We lived with it every day. I would be devastated if Willie was killed, or Jonty. We had become quite close.

Once more airborne with my section on my wings, I felt somehow released, reprieved. The adrenaline was coursing through my body. It felt exhilarating to be back. In the back of my mind was the puzzle of the spy, and the thought that I had to keep one eye on Lawrence Calver. This was easier said than done, as he was in a different section. Bentley had laid the stricture on me and at times it felt like a curse.

The flight of bombers was bigger than any I had yet seen. I let out a low whistle as they hove into view.

"Quite a sight, is it not?" said Willie over the radio.

"I'll say."

"That's what it's been like while you've been off."

"I'll be damned," I said.

"We will all be damned if you lot don't watch out." It was Blue Leader, Lieutenant Judd. "Now, let's get down to business. Get in fast, take them down and get out, all right?"

"You heard the man, break, break, and watch out for the fighters," I said to my section.

We peeled off along with other planes in the squadron and swooped in for the kill. I couldn't see their escort, but it surely wasn't far away. I picked a target, fired and pulled away just in time to see the ME109s dropping down on us from a great height.

"Bandits, bandits, twelve o'clock," I said urgently, banking away from the main flight of bombers. My instincts were always to watch the squadron's back, and so I climbed in order to intercept the 109s.

"You trying to take the whole lot on your own?" said Willie, who appeared on my wing.

"Hey, leave some for me. The 109s are much more fun," said Jonty, arriving on the other wing.

"Is that what you call nearly getting shot down?" I admonished him.

"All in a day's work," he laughed.

Further conversation was cut short, as we broke left and right, and went into the attack. As luck would have it, I got a 109 in my sights almost immediately and fired a burst, then another. It turned sharply but smoke was pouring from its engine. Willie had given chase to another fighter, and Jonty was hallooing like an idiot while looping round to try and catch the rest of the 109 pack.

Down below, I could see at least two of our chaps had copped it from the Heinkels' returning fire. I saw one bail out and the other crash in a ball of flames. There was no time to dwell on it, as yet again I saw Lawrence being run to ground. With Bentley's admonishments in my ear, I gunned the throttle and screamed down towards the German fighter. He must have seen me, because his aircraft turned away sharply and disengaged. Then almost as quickly as we had come, Lieutenant Judd gave the order to go.

"Mavericks, disengage. That's enough. Return to base and refuel."

We flew away from the bombers, and I saw another squadron take over the fray. This was the new tactic: sending flight after flight to try and diminish the bombers before they hit London. Naturally, they still got through and we knew that many parts of London were being heavily bombed. It made me feel thankful that we were stuck out in East Anglia.

"Did you hear that Binky Norman bought it?" said Jonty sadly as we flew homeward.

"I think I saw him go down," I replied.

"He was a good sort."

We fell silent until the airfield appeared below. The devil was in me that day, and I said, "Shall we take a pop at the general, give him a start?"

"Better not." To my surprise, it was Willie, who was usually game for anything.

"Really?"

"Bentley's threatened to ground any pilots who do it, old boy," said Jonty. "Apparently Ace has become overzealous in that department, and Bentley has had enough of the general in his ear."

Since I was partly responsible for Lawrence's actions, I did not demur. "Ah, well, I suppose best not, then."

"No, don't, otherwise I'll be forced to play second fiddle to that blasted Kiwi again," said Jonty.

"Oh, and what's wrong with that?" Willie retorted.

"Shall I sing you a song about it?"

"Emphatically no!"

I couldn't help cracking up with laughter at the pair of them. Denied our little bit of sport, we landed, taxied to our standings and jumped down. The turnaround time was apparently around twenty minutes or so to refuel and replenish the ammo on the Spitfires. It was just enough time to have a cup of tea and something quick, like a slice of toast, before heading back out to the fray.

All in all, we flew about four or five sorties before we were stood down until the next emergency. Each one was much the same and we went at it with gusto, though as Lieutenant Judd had told me, fatigue started to kick in. Fatigue was a killer, because when you were tired you made mistakes and your reactions slowed down. Bentley had to nurse the squadron carefully and tread a thin line between overdoing it and making sure we had enough airtime to continue the sustained attack on the enemy planes.

By the time the shift came to an end that first day, it was getting dark and I was hungry. We were not only flying more sorties but also working longer hours doing it. As we weren't doing any night sorties, everything ended once the sun began to sink. I was thinking very much of a hot bath, a meal and bed as I walked over to the main building. I was not really sure why I did that, other than perhaps some subconscious desire to see if Angelica was in evidence before I left for Amberly Manor.

As I neared the main building, I suddenly noticed, over by the Nissen huts where various stores were kept, a shadowy figure at one of the windows. At once I drew into the wall and melted into the shadows. The person had not seen me and proceeded to lift up a window. They climbed in. I crouched down, wondering what to do. Was this the spy in action? Had I caught them red-handed?

Just as I was considering various options, including drawing my sidearm and confronting them, there was a tap on my elbow. I spun around to find myself facing Angelica, who was crouching down next to me.

"Hello," she said quietly.

"Hello, and I wish you wouldn't do that!"

"Sorry, did I startle you?"

"Yes, you did."

"Oh. Anyway, what are we doing?" she asked me.

"*We* are not doing anything," I said quickly, not wanting to involve her in this affair. Besides, Bentley's attitude when he'd nearly discovered I had told someone else was certainly not understanding.

"Oh, come on," she replied, still smiling in the encroaching darkness. "I know something is going on. You are watching someone, aren't you?"

How on earth she had worked that out, I didn't know, or maybe she'd been there earlier, unseen.

"Maybe," I replied evasively.

"Oh, fine." She tilted up her chin defiantly. "If you are going to be like that and you don't trust me, then…"

She made as if to go and I lightly touched her arm, making her hesitate.

"Look, wait. It's not like that. I can't tell you. I'm not allowed to. But you're right."

"Who is it?"

"I don't know, and I'm not sure what to do because … wait … hush."

The figure suddenly reappeared and jumped down from the window. They appeared to be carrying something and walked swiftly in our direction.

Without thinking, I launched myself from my hiding place and ran towards them, shouting, "Hey, you, stop!"

In hindsight, this was probably not the best thing to do, because without warning they broke into a run and headed straight for me. Before I knew what was happening, I was shoulder charged and bowled over onto the ground.

"Hey, wait, come back! I order you to come back!" I shouted as they pelted off into the darkness and towards the airfield boundary. Since it wasn't fenced off, it would be easy enough for them to disappear.

Angelica leaned down and offered me a hand up. "Are you all right?" she asked me anxiously.

"Yes, yes, I'm fine but damn it, that was a stupid move on my part."

She helped me to my feet and dusted me down. "I don't like to say anything, but it probably wasn't the wisest thing you could have done."

"No, but anyway, I'm going to go in the direction they went to see if I can see something. You'd better go back."

"Oh no, I'm jolly well not going to miss this," she retorted.

"Fine then, come on." I was starting to realise that Angelica was quite determined, and if she wanted to do something she wasn't going to be easily deterred from doing it.

"What exactly are we looking for, and who was that man? I suppose he *was* a man?" she demanded as I tried to lead us in what I hoped were his footsteps.

"It certainly felt like a man — he hit me like a ton of bricks."

She laughed and it tinkled through the night air melodiously. I had not noticed before how pleasant the sound was. "You can tell me, you know. I'm cleared for top secret communications," she said as we continued walking.

I sighed. "If this carries on, the whole squadron will know and it won't be top secret anymore."

"If what carries on?"

"The number of people who know about the spy," I said, letting it slip without realising.

"Oh, that. I've seen the intelligence on *that*," she scoffed.

"What?"

"I told you, I have clearance."

I stopped dead and looked at her. "Maybe you're the spy."

"Sorry?" It was her turn to be taken aback.

"Well, how do I know you've got clearance? You could be lying. You could be the spy and are trying to find out what I know, and then there's the fact you were out there at the same time as that chap who was sneaking into the Nissen huts..." I trailed off.

"Good work," she said. "Are you going to arrest me now or later?"

There was a tense moment before I managed to discern in the darkness that she was grinning at me.

"OK, I was joking. I don't think you are the spy at all."

"If I was the spy, don't you think I would be off seducing the CO or something to get his secrets?"

"Well, how do I know you haven't?" I quipped.

I was treated to a punch on the arm for my troubles.

"Ow!" I complained.

"Sorry, I spent too many years around boys when I was young; it's a natural reflex."

"Well, it's a pretty sharp one at that," I said, rubbing the place where she had hit me.

"Are we even, then?"

"What do you mean?"

"You stood me up, I punched your arm."

"Has anyone ever told you how incorrigible you are?" I asked crossly.

"Frequently."

"Oh, I give up. You've got an answer for everything." I turned and started walking again. She was funny, attractive and now, I discovered, infuriating all at the same time. My mind was on the spy, however, and I didn't have time to ponder this combination.

"You shouldn't give up so easily." She caught me up and walked beside me.

"Shouldn't I?"

"No, and not when I don't want you to."

In spite of the flirtatious nature of this remark, I was about to frame a pithy retort when I noticed a light in the distance. It was seeping out of a barn in the middle of a field next to the airfield.

"Look," I said, our banter forgotten.

"What?" she hissed dramatically.

"That barn, there's a light coming from it. Maybe that's where the spy went."

"How do you know it was the spy?"

"How many other people sneak around breaking into Nissen huts?"

"Good point."

I made up my mind to investigate. "Come on and keep behind me."

I drew my sidearm, and we cautiously approached the barn in the darkness.

It was a sizable stone building with a thatched roof and a big door at one end. I could see some light very softly shining around the edges of a small door set in the main doors. It smelt as if someone had lit a fire and from the interior was a murmur of voices. I gently put my hand on the door handle.

"OK," I whispered. "This is it, ready?"

Angelica nodded.

I supposed I should have told her not to come in with me, but now she was involved, the thought never crossed my mind. Besides, it gave me some sort of moral courage to have someone with me while doing something that was doubtless utterly foolish.

"Now!"

I thrust the door inward with a bang and burst into the barn, brandishing my pistol.

"Right!" I said loudly. "I am arrest—" I stopped.

Staring at me open-mouthed were a number of gentlemen and ladies of Indian descent in traditional garb. They were sitting on the floor, which had some sort of large mat or carpet laid out. In the centre of the mat were plates of food, while off to the right was a makeshift stove, on which some pots were evidently cooking something. Standing up and about to take a mouthful of whatever they were eating was Pilot Officer Arjun Sharma, in his uniform, gazing at me dumbfounded. However, ever the officer and gentleman, in spite of my bizarre entrance, he spoke with great affability.

"Scottish," he said, smiling. "How nice to see you."

I could hardly credit the nonchalance with which he greeted my appearance, and since he was the only person likely to have been in the Nissen huts I wasn't about to let things go that easily.

"Sharma," I replied. "Where were you a few moments ago?"

"A few moments ago, I was right here," he said. He eyed my pistol with misgiving, as I had not elected to drop my aim.

"So, you weren't breaking into one of the Nissen huts?"

"I'm not sure what you are talking about," he said.

"And you didn't run through me and knock me to the ground."

"I … no…"

His hesitation made me all the more suspicious. His smile was a little apprehensive now. He was obviously hiding something, and I was determined to discover what it was.

"Won't you put that pistol down?" he asked.

"I'll put it down when you start telling me the truth," I said, perhaps a little too aggressively.

He regarded me for a few moments longer and then set down his delicious-smelling plate of food. "OK," he nodded. "Come over here and I'll tell you."

He moved to the side of the diners and motioned for me to join him. I did so but kept my distance, and a grip on my pistol.

"Well?" I demanded.

"Look, OK, it was me, but it's not what you think."

"And what do I think?" I asked him.

"I wasn't stealing anything. It's just that I … I was keeping some food supplies in there, for a special occasion."

"You were what?"

"Supplies, things like chapati flour — it's special flour to make our chapatis, a form of flatbread. You can see them over there, on the plate."

I stole a look and there was indeed a plate of round white slices of something resembling bread. While it seemed a little odd, it somehow made sense, but I wanted to investigate his story a little further.

"Oh, I see … but why do you keep it in there?"

"To keep it safe, away from the rats and so forth. I can't keep it here, you see."

I digested this explanation for a moment, before another thought occurred to me. I glanced at Angelica, who had been taking in this exchange with interest.

"Why did you run into me like that?"

"You startled me. I'm sorry, I didn't know what to do. Nobody knows I keep things there, and nobody really goes in there, so it's the perfect place."

"Couldn't you just have told me, instead of running off?"

He laughed. "You can see how it looked and I didn't want to get into any trouble, so I ran for it."

"You gave me a hell of a scare, if I'm honest."

"I'm sorry." He looked contrite.

I sighed. It was most unlikely he was the spy. Why would he be? He was here on secondment from the Indian Air Force, or at least that is what I assumed. I could hardly imagine him being a Nazi sympathiser. After all, the Nazis were certainly known to be ostracising other races and worse.

"Fine, I believe you, God knows why. But anyway, what are you doing here, in this barn?"

"This is where we have communal food sometimes. We can't cook it properly at the place we stay, not for so many people. Today we are celebrating Diwali, the Festival of Lights. It's not actually Diwali, because that is between October and November, but because of the war I may not be here then." He shrugged.

None of this made much sense to me, but I felt I had to simply accept it as an explanation. Sometimes the most unlikely explanations were the real ones.

"Anyway, look, we've plenty of food. Why don't you and your lady friend stay and eat with us?"

It was tempting, but the British politeness ingrained into me made me say, "Oh, I couldn't possibly impose…"

"Well, I could and that food smells jolly nice. Besides, I'm famished," said Angelica, cutting in.

"Looks like you've been overruled," said Arjun, laughing.

I looked at Angelica, who had something of a martial light in her eye, and I elected not to test her resolve. I was also hungry, and the food did smell rather inviting.

"Seems so. In which case, we accept your kind invitation."

I holstered my sidearm and took a seat on the mat beside Angelica. I pondered upon the bizarre nature of sitting eating curry in a barn in the middle of a field and decided that the war had made the extraordinary quite ordinary. So, I stopped worrying about the whys and wherefores, and decided to enjoy it instead.

"These are members of my family," said Arjun casually. "But the lady is hungry. Let us eat first. I will make introductions and explain."

A plate was given to each of us, laden with rice and small portions of several dishes. Cutlery was procured for Angelica and myself, although I noticed the others were eating with their hands.

The next thing I knew, Angelica was doing the same. With a shrug, I put down my knife and fork and joined her. The curries were incredibly delicious.

Arjun came and sat beside us, introducing us to his various relatives, some of whom apparently lived in the farmhouse where he was quartered. They were various aunts, uncles and cousins who were directly or indirectly related to him. Those not residing with Arjun had come from their abodes in London for this special celebration.

"How did you come to be serving in the Air Force over here?" I asked him between mouthfuls of something called dhal, which was made of lentils. I was not a curry aficionado and much of it was quite new to me — mostly vegetarian, too.

"Ah, it's a long story…" he began.

"Go on."

"My mother is Indian, from the Brahmin caste. My father, well, he's British in the RAF, very high up in the RAF. So, we can't talk about that. He brought me here and sent me up to Cambridge, and my family too. He's been … good to us. I'm actually a British subject, for my sins, and thanks to my father."

I was much struck by his story. He wasn't on secondment after all; he was a commissioned officer in the RAF.

"Things are not always as they seem," he said. He was certainly right about that.

"Your father must think a lot of you," said Angelica.

"Oh, I wouldn't say that. It's rather he thinks a lot of my mother. He wanted to fulfil what he saw as his … obligations. They were very much in love, but he was already married, you see. And in any case, he can't marry a woman from another race, I'm afraid. You know how it is."

I received a sharp look from Angelica at the mention of an extramarital affair, but it was there and gone in a flash.

"How did you come to join the Mavericks?" I asked. "I mean, surely your father…"

"You know how it is, Scottish. I've got the right accent, the right skills, but the wrong colour skin. My father made sure I got a commission in the RAF, trained as a pilot, and here I am. His influence over such things is not infinite." He laughed dolefully.

I shook my head. I had never been able to understand this type of prejudice. "All of us are on the wrong side of somebody, I'm afraid," I said.

"Why are *you* here, Scottish? You seem like a decent fellow."

"Me?" This was the last thing I wanted to discuss in front of Angelica — my numerous affairs and falls from grace. "Oh, you don't want to hear about *that*. I'm just not very good with authority."

He seemed to accept this a bit too readily, but thankfully didn't enquire further.

"So, you live in the farmhouse? All of you?" I asked, glad to change the subject.

"Yes, yes, we do. The farmer was one of the few people who would take us."

"What will happen to your family, if you … you know?" I asked him. It was a question we all had on our minds.

"I don't know. They'll get my pension, but perhaps they will have to return to India. It depends on how benign my father really is."

"You best keep out of trouble, then."

We both laughed. Trouble was something a pilot was constantly in while airborne. It was unavoidable. We talked for a while longer and were served a spicy Indian tea called 'chai' along with more food until we were full. At length, we thanked our unlikely host, took our leave and made our way back to the base.

As we were walking up the main drive, Gordon pulled up beside us in his jeep. He seemed to have the genius for being in the right place at the right time.

"I was looking for you, sir," he said.

"Well, you've found us, and we could use a ride home."

"I thought as much. Hop in."

I wondered if he'd been driving around for a while searching for me, but I forbore to ask him. I helped Angelica into the back and got in beside her.

"As it happens, we had an impromptu dinner with Arjun," I told him.

"Ah yes, in his barn? Interesting fellow old Arjun is, sir, yes indeed."

I realised at once that Gordon would, of course, know all about it and for all I knew was invited to eat there too now and then.

We drove in silence, the stars shining down on us, and before long we were at Angelica's lodgings.

I walked her to the gate, while Gordon jumped down from the jeep and, turning his back on us, lit a cigarette. He was, as always, the soul of discretion.

We stood facing each other, and without thinking I leaned in for a kiss. It seemed only natural, but instead of responding she pulled back and shook her head.

"No," she said softly.

"Oh, I'm sorry … I…" I was a little flustered, embarrassed even. I should not have presumed.

She was smiling. "It's not that I don't want to. It's just … it's not the time."

"It's not?"

"No."

"Right then… OK … well…"

She cut in quickly, "I'll tell you when I know it's the time, Angus."

"Right."

"Why were you sent here to the Mavericks?" she said suddenly.

This was the last question I was expecting and also the last one I wanted to answer.

"I…"

"I'll get it out of you one day," she said with a twinkle in her eye.

I said nothing. Surely the truth would put her off for life, and that would be the last thing I wanted.

"Goodnight." She turned away and went through the gate.

I watched her go. She was a strange one indeed — intriguing, and I had to admit beguiling. I was beginning to be hooked, and if that was her intention, it was working.

Returning to the jeep, Gordon was waiting.

"She's a good sort, that lass," was all he said.

"Yes, I do believe you're right."

We picked up speed and Gordon turned off for Amberly Manor.

"Her Ladyship was asking…"

"Where I was?"

"Yes."

"And you said?"

"I said I believed you were on official business, which in a manner of speaking you were."

"I'm not sure where I'd be without you, Fred," I said, and I really meant it.

"That's kind of you to say so, sir," he replied. "I do my best."

"That you certainly do, Fred. That you certainly do."

"Where have you been?" Barbara asked, as she slipped once more into my bed. I had become used to her nightly visits and had almost come to expect them.

"I had something to do."

"Are you sure that something is not another woman?" she said archly.

"What makes you say that?" I was finding it difficult to know if she and Angelica were serious or joking at times. It was most disconcerting.

"Oh, nothing, darling, nothing."

She kissed me then and the fire lit immediately. This was what made it so hard to end it, even if I had wanted to. She was everything I desired in so many ways, but she wasn't Angelica. I quashed the thought as quickly as it had arrived.

"Doesn't your husband miss you, coming down here every night?"

"Oh, no. I see to him first, and then I see to you," she said.

"So really *you've* got another man," I retorted.

"Oh, stop it, I only have *one* man. The other, well, I wish he'd shove off back to wherever he's been posted."

She was very dismissive about her husband, I felt, callous even. She had, after all, acquired her station in life through him and the prospect of never having to do anything but be a lady of leisure. If he was killed, she would no doubt be a very wealthy widow. That idea, however, did not particularly draw me to her, were it to happen. I was already the heir to a large estate in Scotland. Besides, I could never wish any man's death on him. What figured for me was love, the most elusive thing. The one thing I never really had. Feelings were stirring within me that I didn't recognise. Nor, when I thought about it, were they confined to one woman.

CHAPTER EIGHT

I caught up with Tomas the following day. Barbara returned to her own bed in the early hours and left me to sleep. I was grateful for that, and I slept quite well, though it didn't seem sufficient. While we were waiting for the first sortie, he asked me to look at something on his plane. I followed him out to the airfield and over to where the Spitfires were parked.

"Have you found out anything?" he asked me. "Since we last spoke?"

"Yes, Arjun is not the spy." I related the story of the previous night to him, and he nodded wisely.

"I didn't think it could be him," he said.

"No."

"But should we check, about this flour in the Nissen hut?"

"No, let's leave it. He's a good sort, he has a family to look after, and I can't see a family man like that being a spy. What possible reason could he have?"

"No, you are right. We must look at the others … although…"

"Although what?" I looked at him suspiciously.

"I still think we should check Lawrence Calver again."

"Oh, no. I'm already in enough trouble over that last time. What do you think he'd do if we started something else?"

He grinned. "Yes, but I still think it must be someone like him."

"Public school and all that jazz?"

"Yes, he is an aristocrat, no?"

I laughed. "Hardly that. He's from the upper classes; his parents are well-to-do. He went to a posh school, but he's not going to become a lord or anything."

"Exactly! That is what spies do: they become part of society, accepted, and then they can do their dirty bastard work."

"You seem to know a lot about it," I said with interest.

"Yes, I do. I know because I had friend in secret police in my country, before the Germans. He told me many things. He knew many things. But now also he's dead."

"Ah, I see. I'm sorry."

"The Germans." He practically growled the word, so deep was his loathing of the Nazi regime.

"Even if Ace does fit the bill, I don't think it's him."

"Shouldn't we follow him? Spy on him?"

"Are you mad? He's paranoid enough as it is."

He laughed. "OK, Scottish, you have it your way. We must find someone who is like him, then."

"Well, maybe, or maybe it's just someone who seems quite ordinary, who knows?"

"Yes, who knows?"

Just then, the other pilots came running for their planes.

"Looks like we're on," I said. "We will discuss this later."

"For sure, take care."

"You too."

My kite was a few steps away. I jumped in, strapped in and we fired her up. She purred like the beautiful machine she was, and I taxied her out for take-off.

"Here we go again," said Willie as he settled on one wing.

"Tally-ho and all that," said Jonty, joining our section on the other wing.

"What's the crack today, Kiwi?" I said to Willie.

"Bombers."

"Right."

The bombers were formed up in three waves. We attacked the first wave, but I could see we'd have to come back. It was going to be another long day. To make matters worse, it was something of a cloudy day and the bombers were using the cloud cover to their advantage. It was thick and impossible to fly in, let alone start opening fire.

"What are we going to do?" said Willie as we circled around, trying to find some inroads into the clouds.

"Nobody is to fire until I give the order." Flight Lieutenant Judd's firm tones came over the radio.

"Wilco, Blue Leader," I said.

"We are just going to follow them. They have to come out of it at some point, or they can't see their target. Stay in formation until I say."

We flew behind them, watching our backs for ME109s, but these were also not in evidence and probably concealing themselves too. Our squadron and one other stayed under the clouds. There were shadowy glimpses of planes above, great hulks, but not enough to let loose a burst or two.

This stand-off continued for several minutes until Jonty said, "Look up ahead! There's a break in the clouds."

Indeed there was. This would be our chance.

"Wait for Blue Leader to give the word," I told him, but Jonty wasn't listening.

He suddenly broke ranks and throttled up his kite. He took off from the main squadron and hurtled away.

"Stop! Stop that, man! Stop, I say! I order you to stop!" Judd practically shouted over the radio, but to no avail. Jonty wasn't going to have anyone spoil his fun.

"Come on, chaps, what are you waiting for?" he said merrily.

"Sir, there's a break in the clouds," I said frantically to Judd. "Permission to break formation."

"Blast and damn you! Yes, break, break, take what you can get."

"Now we're in the basket," said Willie.

We split off from the main pack immediately and flew in Jonty's wake. The bombers burst out of the cloud cover, which was highly dangerous since we were below them. Their guns in the bottom fuselage faced backwards and we were in the line of fire. This, however, did not deter Jonty and without warning, he flipped his plane upside down and flew straight up at the mass of bombers. Naturally, tracers started flying everywhere but Jonty fired several bursts and one of the Heinkels exploded, sending shrapnel out in a cloud of smoke and flame. It set off a chain reaction and the bombers nearby swerved to avoid it. There was a collision and two more went down. By this time, we had closed the gap and sprang into action.

I elected with Willie to move sideways out of range, and then to circle inwards to fire on the outliers. We both hit one of the Heinkels together, and it started to pitch and roll. Jonty had flown straight up through the shrapnel without a care and was now well above the bombers. He dived and fired again.

Just then, a cry of alarm came over the radio.

"Bandits, coming in fast, behind the main pack," said Jean Tarbon frantically. I looked back and indeed there were several 109s screaming in.

We turned our attention to those Messerschmitts. Jonty must have spied them, because I heard him shouting "Tally-ho!" as he dropped down to fire a burst at the leading 109. As luck would have it, he shattered the cockpit, and the plane went into a straight down dive. Despite his reckless behaviour, he'd claimed at least three kills.

The fight was fast and furious. I got on the tail of another 109 but he was nimble, twisting and turning like a running deer. Then, as rapidly as the gap in the clouds had appeared, the cloud closed in and the bombers were gone, no longer visible along with their escort.

"Disengage, we'll have to leave them for the other squadrons," said Judd at once. "Return to base."

Never was I happier to hear that command and as Jonty settled back on my wing, I knew this would not be the end of it.

"I think you overstepped the mark this time, old boy," I said to him as we made our way homeward.

"But did you see how I shot that Heinkel down?"

"I saw it, Jonty…" I said no more. I wasn't happy at all with what he'd done. He'd jeopardised his own life and ours. The upside-down flying stunt was a bridge too far.

I was expecting Judd to come over and admonish us, but he didn't. This surprised me, but I suspected things had escalated a little too much, even for him.

We were in the hut waiting for the next scramble when Audrey appeared in front of me.

"Bentley wants to see you and Pilot Officer Butterworth in his office, sir," she said.

"Right." I sighed. "Now, I suppose?"

"Yes, sir, right away. I wouldn't advise keeping him waiting." Her expression told me all I needed to know.

I stood up. "Come on, Jonty, I believe it's time for the reckoning."

"Oh, blast, really?"

"Come on."

We accompanied Audrey back to the main building.

"On a scale of one to ten, just how angry is he?" I asked her casually.

"Oh, I'd say at least a twelve, or maybe as much as a fifteen." She smiled.

"Right, I see."

"Time for the exercise book down the trousers," said Jonty airily.

"Jonty, try to rein in your sense of humour, would you? I've a feeling this won't be a pleasant experience."

"Just what our Headmaster Judkins used to say when we came into his study," he laughed.

I shook my head. When Jonty was in this mood, there was no reasoning with him at all. I then saw Willie catching us up at a run.

"Where are you two off to, may I ask?" he said.

"Another spell on the carpet in Bentley's office," I told him without enthusiasm.

"I'm coming too."

"Why? He didn't ask for you."

"Moral support, and I'm as much part of this section as you two."

"I see," I said. "All for one and one for all, is it?"

"Something like that."

"Well, if you don't want to miss the fun, come on then. I suppose Bentley might as well shout at three of us, rather than two."

Audrey looked over at me sympathetically, as if she knew what was in store. We had reached Bentley's office by then. She opened the door and then stood aside to let us through. We filed in and she closed the door behind us.

Bentley got up from his desk and came around the front of it. Audrey made as if to go, but he said, "No, Audrey, you can stay."

"Sir."

She went and sat down at her desk and began shuffling her papers. I guessed this was some form of humiliation for us to be dressed down in front of a junior rank.

We were standing easy when Bentley suddenly barked, "Stand to attention!"

This had the desired effect and took me back to my parade ground days of yore.

"Sir, I…" Jonty began, a tad unwisely.

"Did I invite you to speak?" Bentley roared.

"No, sir."

"Then don't bloody well speak!"

We stood like that for several minutes while Bentley regarded us with a fiery expression. The dam of his wrath must surely burst soon, I felt, and it certainly did.

"I have just been apprised, by Flight Lieutenant Judd, of what transpired on your last sortie," he said with barely controlled fury.

We remained silent, as I knew this was only the beginning.

"Never in the history of this squadron — and there have been some pretty appalling incidents — have I heard of such absolute profligate tomfoolery as I've heard of today." He came and stood in front of Jonty as he said this. "*You* were seen flying upside down while attempting to engage the enemy. What the hell do you think I'm running here, a bloody flying circus? And don't answer that!"

Jonty, realising he was indeed in deep water, kept his eyes firmly straight ahead — something I was eternally thankful for.

There was only one thing to do in a Bentley type storm, and that was to let him blow himself out.

"Not only that, but you also disobeyed a direct order from a senior officer not to engage. You took it upon yourself to break ranks and have a go at the enemy without permission to do so. Then you disobeyed a command to return to the flight and continued on one of the foolhardiest pieces of bravado anyone has attempted. You do realise your actions endangered the entire squadron, let alone your own life?"

It was a rhetorical question.

"Were you born stupid, or have you studied for it?" he demanded furiously. "Do you have no respect at all for military protocol? Senior officers? What on earth is wrong with you? Don't you think I have better things to do than to waste my time remonstrating with officers who cannot obey a simple order?"

Jonty looked as if he would open his mouth in the face of this verbal assault but thought better of it.

Bentley whirled on me as his next target. "And as for you, Mackennelly, Butterworth is in your section, isn't he? Are you incapable of controlling your own crew? What on earth is the use of those insignia if your juniors are going to ignore them? I am grievously disappointed in you, grievously so." He then addressed Willie. "And you! I don't know what you're doing in here, since I never asked for you to come. I suppose it's some misplaced sense of loyalty to that reprobate over there." He pointed at Jonty.

I noticed the heat had gone out of his tirade slightly, and thankfully he seemed to be calming down.

"Let me tell you this, all of you. The only reason I put up with your ridiculous antics is because we need you as pilots. If not for that, I'd see the lot of you off to Timbuktu for all I care. You are a constant thorn in my side, the lot of you. Just because you are called the Mavericks does not mean you need to behave like it round the clock, do I make myself clear?"

"Yes, sir," we said in unison.

"I never, and I do mean *never*, want to hear of another escapade like this again. You *will* obey orders, Pilot Officer Butterworth, or I shall have your guts for garters, is that understood?"

"Perfectly, sir," said Jonty.

"Good, well, see that you remember it next time you want to put on a bloody dog and pony show in one of my aircraft."

"Yes, sir," we said again.

Bentley seemed, like a proverbial volcano, to have burnt himself out. He left us standing there and made us wait while he very carefully emptied his pipe, scraped out the bowl, filled it and lit it. He took several puffs while we tried not to cough.

"Anyway," he said, "I hear that you at least shot down some Jerries, so that is some consolation — a very small one, mind you."

We were too sensible to answer this and waited for what seemed an age before he let us go.

"Right, you are dismissed. Get out of my office, the lot you."

We saluted as one and left his office smartly, making haste to get out of the building.

"Phew," said Jonty. "That was a bit of a blinder."

"A well-deserved one, Jonty, you idiot," I said without any rancour.

"And please don't make a bloody song about it," said Willie.

"I was just considering the first verse, actually," Jonty replied cheerfully.

"Please, for God's sake, can't you order him to stop?" Willie pleaded.

"I can't order him to do anything, and that's why we ended up on the carpet," I said.

Jonty stopped, because there was a serious tone behind my sarcasm. "Skipper, I'm sorry. I was at fault and I got carried away. Sorry you got caught in the crossfire, so to speak."

"You should know better, Jonty, you really should," I said mildly.

"I won't do it again, I promise," he vowed.

"Best not. I don't think it's good for Bentley's health, and you don't want his death on your conscience," Willie quipped.

"No indeed," said Jonty, much struck by this line of reasoning.

The problem was that Jonty was prone to do foolish things. We all knew it, but sometimes he went too far. I thought the world of him, but even I could understand why Bentley had gone off the deep end. Jonty had crossed the line and then some. Hopefully, he wouldn't be quite so stupid in future, though chance would be a fine thing.

As we were walking back to the hut, I was hailed from behind.

"Hey!"

I looked around and it was Angelica.

"Aye, aye, bandit at six o'clock," said Jonty.

"And a pretty one at that," Willie added.

"Stop it," I admonished them. "You go ahead. I'll catch you up."

They walked on while I turned to face Angelica, who came running up to me.

"Are you all right?" she said.

"Shouldn't I be?"

"I heard Bentley hauled you over the coals," she said. "I wanted to check up on you."

"You seem extraordinarily concerned about my welfare." I smiled.

"Someone has to be." She poked her tongue out at me.

"I'm fine. Most of his ire was directed at Jonty."

"Oh dear, what did he do?"

I related the events of what was probably by now the infamous upside-down flying incident. She tilted her head back and laughed.

"Oh, I wish I had seen it."

"I can assure you it wasn't funny then, though in hindsight…" I chuckled. A thought occurred to me all of a sudden, and on impulse, I asked her, "Would you like to see what it's like up there?"

"What do you mean?"

"I mean would you like me to take you up for a spin, in the trainer craft?"

"Would you?"

"Why not? Nobody needs to know."

She regarded me seriously. "Are you sure? You only just got into trouble. I wouldn't want you to get into any more."

"I'm more discreet than Jonty," I laughed.

Her face cracked once more into that radiant smile. It floored me every time she gave it. "Well, if you think it's all right, I'd love to."

"Fine, I'll arrange it and let you know."

"In the meantime…" She trailed off, prompting me.

"In the meantime, how about that drink?" I finished the sentence for her.

"Oh, that would be lovely, as long as you're not going to stand me up."

"As long as you are not going to punch my arm," I retorted.

"I promise." She shook my hand. This time when she touched me, I certainly felt a little spark. My attraction to her had been creeping up on me.

"I hold you to it," I said, smiling.

"As will I."

Then, once more, she left abruptly. It seemed to be her habit, and I was starting to wish she wouldn't because I wanted her to stick around. I liked her company, and I liked *her.* I was able to admit that much, at least.

Whatever else I might have thought about was lost as another scramble ensued, and we were airborne shortly afterwards. Flying once more into the face of danger, I hoped that this time Jonty would behave, Lawrence would stay out of trouble and maybe I'd have a brainwave about who the spy was. A tall order, by any stretch of the imagination.

Fortunately for my peace of mind, and Willie's too, I suspected, Jonty was the soul of discretion for several days thereafter and did not put a foot out of line. I breathed a sigh of relief and waited eagerly for a rest day so I could take Angelica up in the trainer. On the appointed day, I kitted her out with a life vest and parachute for our little sortie. Thus garbed, she walked beside me, full of expectation and positively bubbling over with enthusiasm, until we came to a stop in front of the Tiger Moth. Then she gaped at it, somewhat incredulous.

"Are we going up in *that*?"

"Yes."

"But … I thought it would be one of the Spitfires or something."

I laughed, although she seemed quite disappointed. "I'd love to take you up in one, but they don't do a two-seater version."

She continued to eye the unfortunate aircraft somewhat askance.

"It's perfectly safe; we all train in them when we first start," I told her.

"But … isn't that from the Great War?" she demanded.

"They did use them then, but this one's a bit younger than that. It wasn't made in 1918, at least."

She seemed hesitant still, and I thought perhaps she might want to back out.

"If you'd rather not, after all…" I shrugged my shoulders and turned as if to go.

"No, wait, it's not that. It's…"

"What?"

"I'm scared of heights, and I don't want to fall out."

I started to crack a smile at this. She wouldn't be the first to have such apprehensions.

"Don't laugh! It's true!"

"You'll be strapped in, don't worry, and I won't loop the loop or anything."

"I should hope not."

Redwood, who had been standing by the Tiger Moth patiently waiting, came over. "Would you like some help to get in, Miss?" he asked.

Somehow this seemed to do the trick, and she made up her mind. "Yes, thank you, that would be lovely."

Angelica poked her tongue out at me and followed him to the aircraft. He strapped her in, and I checked her harness too before jumping into the pilot's seat in front.

"Spin her up, Techie," I shouted.

"Aye, aye, sir."

The prop turned and very soon we were taxiing out to the runway.

"Are you all right back there?" I asked her.

"Yes, perfectly fine at the moment."

"Well then, here we go."

I opened up the throttle and we took off in a lazy climb while Angelica screamed with delight in the back.

"Are you still all right?" I asked anxiously on hearing this.

"Yes, yes, it's marvellous, wonderful, I love it," she said breathlessly.

For a happy half an hour, I treated her to a flight around the surrounding countryside while she made suitable noises of appreciation. I then went up as high as I dared, dived down, and treated her to some low-level flying before levelling off at the end.

"Oh my gosh," she said. "I can see why you love doing this."

"Yes, there's nothing like it. Shall we head back?"

Both of us had probably had enough, I felt.

"Yes, if you like."

As we were approaching the airfield, Angelica suddenly said, "Isn't that one of your chaps?"

I looked down and there was, indeed, someone who looked as if they might be in RAF uniform. They were walking away from a small white hut. The hut was perhaps a mile or two from the airfield and not far from a large expanse of woodland. The figure appeared to be carrying something as they crossed the field in the direction of the woods. It seemed rather odd.

"I don't know, maybe. I can't see who it is, though," I said.

Just then the figure looked up, but we were still too far away to discern their features. As soon as they saw us, they broke into a run.

"What's he doing?" said Angelica.

"I don't know, but let's go in for a closer look."

It definitely did look suspicious, and I thought I had better investigate.

I banked the Tiger Moth and started to close in, dropping down so I could see him better. He was heading for the wood at quite a lick, but I thought I could still catch him before he got there.

"Do you think that's the spy?" Angelica asked, echoing my own thoughts. It was the first thing that had crossed my own mind on seeing him out there.

"I don't know, but..." Whatever else I was going to say was lost.

Without warning, the figure pulled out what appeared to be a pistol and aimed it in our direction. My combat reflexes kicked in and I banked away sharply. Just in time, as it happened, since they fired once and then again.

"Was he shooting at us?" said Angelica, alarmed.

"Yes, he certainly was. Had to take evasive action."

When I turned the Tiger Moth again, the figure was gone, no doubt into the woods.

"Damn it," I said. I circled around the wood for a while, but it was no use; they weren't likely to break cover while I was doing so. In the end, I reluctantly turned back to base.

We touched down and I taxied the Tiger Moth back to its standing.

"That was fun," said Angelica, once we were standing on solid ground.

"Indeed, now you know what it's really like to be a pilot in combat."

"I enjoyed it anyway, in spite of —"

"Sir," said Redwood, coming up to me looking concerned. "Has someone been taking potshots at you?"

"Why?" I asked, deliberately being non-committal.

"Have a look at this."

He led me to the lower wing, and there was a perfect bullet hole right through it. The blighter had not missed us after all.

"Oh," I said, examining it.

Redwood waited politely, not saying anything further.

Angelica came up behind me and said, "Good God, is that where that chap shot at us?"

Redwood gave me a speaking look.

"Fine," I said. "Some lunatic, probably a poacher, took aim at us and I had to weave a bit to try to avoid being hit. We were lucky that I did; it might have got one of us otherwise."

"Oh, ah, yes, I'm pretty sure it was a poacher," Angelica put in, catching on fast.

"That's not good, sir. Shall I inform the MPs?" said Redwood.

"Ah no, best not. If you do, then Bentley will find out and I'm not his favourite person at the moment, due to Jonty's recent antics. There was no harm done, so it's better he doesn't know I took Corporal Kensley up, to be honest."

"Ah, yes, I see. We did hear about the … erm … yes." He stopped, evidently trying to be discreet, but I finished his sentence for him.

"You mean Bentley practically burning our ears off?"

Redwood laughed. "Yes, sir, I'm afraid word gets around."

"I'm sure it does."

"I'll get this patched up, and nobody will be any the wiser. Mum's the word." He tapped the side of his nose and winked.

"Thank you, Techie, I'm grateful for your discretion."

"Not a problem," he said.

"And thanks again for setting this flight up."

He smiled and nodded. I turned away and walked back with Angelica, who tucked her arm into mine. I had to admit that I rather liked her doing so. It felt comfortable. Right, somehow.

"Shall we go and look for him?" she asked me. "That gunman?"

"What? No. It's too dangerous and besides, he'll be long gone by now. I'll go another day with Tomas and investigate that hut."

"Oh!" She pouted a little.

"Look," I said seriously, "if something happened to you, I'd never forgive myself."

"Really?" She smiled at once.

"Yes, really."

"That's all right then." Perfectly pleased, it seemed, with my response, she said nothing more about it. "I'm sorry I rather put my foot in it with your aircraftman."

"No matter, I would have had to tell him anyway. He's a good sort, looks out for us chaps."

"Yes, it seems so."

"Shall we get that drink?" I added, as a rather pleasant afterthought.

"Yes, but can we get rid of the life vest and parachute?"

"Of course, we shan't go out in flying gear."

I borrowed some transport, courtesy of Gordon, who seemed to be able to arrange anything. It was one of the staff cars, but he said it would be fine and I believed him. Happily, he didn't inform me until later that it was the one Squadron Leader Bentley usually used. Had he done so, I might not have been so complacent about taking it.

We spent a delightful day venturing further afield and having lunch at a nice public house in a village a few miles away.

Afterwards, we took a stroll and sat for a while in the sun on a bench near a river, watching the lazy water drift by.

"I wish this war would be over," she said.

"I do too." I sighed. "But it seems as if it's only just begun. It may be a long haul."

"I know. But then again, if it wasn't for the war, I might not…" She stopped.

"Might not what?"

"Never you mind."

"Do you know," I said, turning to face her, "you are probably the most infuriating woman I've ever met."

"Well, at least that's memorable." She laughed.

"You are so infuriating I could kiss you," I blurted out.

She smiled again, and I wondered if she would allow it.

"You could, but you won't," she said firmly.

"It's not time, I suppose."

"No, it's not."

"Will it ever be time?" I asked tentatively and a little hopefully.

"We'll see."

I suppressed a sigh. I certainly had never met a woman like her. Most women I had been with were only too eager to be kissed, and it was a new experience for me to be denied it.

"Could I hold your hand, then?" I asked her instead.

"You may."

She placed her hand in mine. I looked down at its delicacy and perfectly shaped fingers. My fingers closed around it, and somehow that was almost as magical a moment as a first kiss.

"You really are very beautiful," I said to her simply.

She smiled and said nothing. She could be exceptionally enigmatic at times. However, the more she denied me, the more I wanted her. That, at least, I began to realise.

Eventually we returned to the car, and I drove her home.

"Thank you," she told me. "For a lovely day."

"You are welcome."

"I enjoyed it."

"So did I."

I watched her walk to her gate, then turn back, look at me and go in. I felt a pang of something like regret that she had to go. Somehow, she was creeping under my defences, such as they were. I had never been in love, but perhaps I had also shied away from it. I still wasn't sure this was it, and then there was also Barbara.

Back at Amberly Manor, I discovered the aforementioned lady in my room and looking displeased.

"Where were you today?" she demanded.

"I went out, if you must know," I said.

"Where?"

"Is this some kind of inquisition?" I demanded a little irritably, not wanting to have to lie to her again.

She retracted at once, as if she was afraid I would reject her if she pushed too hard. "No, I'm sorry. I'm just going crazy cooped up with … him." Naturally, she was referring to her husband.

"I'm sorry, what did you expect me to do?"

"I had some idea it was your day off, so I thought you might take me out." She gave me her best pout. It was quite effective. I sat beside her and took the kiss I had been denied by Angelica, and then several more. The kisses were sweet, but I still could not help straying to thoughts of another pair of lips.

"Should you like to go out?" I asked her at length.

"Yes, I should. We can take the Rolls."

"All right."

I wasn't averse to having another crack at driving her magnificent car. As we started off down the driveway, I thought I saw a lone figure watching us from one of the windows. I put the colonel firmly out of my mind.

Making sure to head in the opposite direction to the place where I'd taken Angelica, we took in a meal at a rather expensive-looking hotel in a nearby town. Barbara insisted on paying and said it gave her satisfaction to spend her husband's money on me.

She seemed so terribly bitter about her marriage. I wondered if she would be quite so against it if I was not part of the equation. Not that I wanted to give myself too much credit, but it was more than obvious Barbara had strong feelings for me. I, in turn, had feelings for her and I knew it. They were different, though, to the way I felt about Angelica. Angelica was joyous, full of life, and she buoyed me up. Barbara was melancholy and it seemed as if she did not relish life at all, although she liked to be with me. I seemed to have become something of an anchor for her. I could not blame her for that, since I had been an active participant. But it begged the question of where it was all leading. Gordon said it would come out in the wash, but I wasn't so sure. I wasn't convinced it would resolve quite as straightforwardly as he suggested.

CHAPTER NINE

It was impossible to go the next day to search the hut due to the exigencies of fighting Jerry. A couple of days later, though, during a short break in flying due to the weather, Tomas and I made our way out to the hut I had seen from the air. I had managed to pinpoint the approximate location on a map, and it wasn't too hard to find. It was actually only a short walk from the road. As we approached it, we both drew our sidearms in readiness.

The hut was painted white and made of stone. It had a tin roof, a door and small windows. It had possibly been a shepherd's hut at one time and now seemed abandoned and unoccupied.

Nevertheless, we were tense as we neared the door, and used only hand signals. Tomas held his pistol at the ready, while I put my hand on the door handle. With a nod from him, I thrust it violently inwards, and Tomas rushed in first.

"It's all right, Scottish, nobody is here," he said.

Inside, the floor was beaten earth. There was a table and what looked like signs of recent occupation. In one corner were some discarded cigarette packets, empty tins of bully beef and a bottle of beer or two. There was a small table and a kicked over chair. It was as if someone had left in a hurry.

"Shall we get those?" Tomas said, indicating the food items. "Maybe we can get the fingerprints?"

"It's an idea, but how are we going to get them from the pilots to match them? It would raise suspicions for sure, and Bentley won't want that."

"True, I suppose," said Tomas wistfully, not wanting to give up on his plan quite so easily. The practicalities of it, though, defeated us both.

"How do we even know the spy was here? It could have been someone else — though God knows who or what for."

"I suppose, Scottish, but look!"

I followed the direction he pointed to, the corner under the table. Something glinted, obscured a little by dirt. I reached down and picked it up.

"Well, I'll be," I said, looking at the object in my hand.

"That means it was a spy for sure!" said Tomas triumphantly.

It did indeed appear to be the case. The object in question was a small radio valve, most likely used in a portable radio. These were often disguised in other objects, like suitcases.

"I can't imagine anyone other than a spy needing this, not in a hut in the middle of nowhere."

"Yes, for sure. We know he was here and it was him you saw from the plane."

"You are right, but he was too far away, so I couldn't identify him," I said, feeling disappointed.

The opportunity had slipped past me because I could not get near enough. Then I remembered the bullet hole and how mortified I would have been if it had hit Angelica.

"Don't worry, it's life." Tomas clapped me on the shoulder.

"Yes, so near and yet so far."

We searched the hut for further clues but found none. I did pocket one of the empty packets of cigarettes, since it at least told me the brand they smoked. However, it was common enough and from that point of view, it could be anybody. The beer was similarly one that was served in many pubs and drunk by the gallon. In all the best detective stories the spy smoked a certain special cigarette, which led the detectives straight to him. In real life, we had no such luck.

Outside there was nothing of any consequence and so we elected to leave it. I thought it worth at least following the spy's steps to the woodland and we did so, until we were standing at the edge of it. The forest was predictably dark due to the tree cover, and extensive.

"Is it worth going in and taking a look?" I said to Tomas, hoping he'd agree it was not.

"It's too big and too dense. I don't think we can find anything."

"No, let's go back."

Thankfully we turned away from the forest and left it. I had never been fond of these places and perhaps it was due to the monster stories I had read when I was younger. Trees came to life and grabbed onto any unsuspecting traveller who ventured into the dark woods. The unfortunate individual was thus captured, only to be discovered years later as a wasted skeleton in the branches of the tree. The thought still made me shiver, even all these years later.

"I wonder why he moved from the hut?" I said to Tomas as we returned to the car.

"Ah, these spies cannot stay in one place too long. They must keep moving in case they are discovered. The spies will not stay still."

"Makes our job even harder."

"I know, Scottish, but look, this time you got lucky and saw him. Next time maybe will be the time we will get him."

"Yes, all right, and we will arrest him and bring him to justice," I said firmly.

We both laughed at this. I had impressed upon him more than once the importance of not letting his hatred of the Nazis override our mission to capture the spy.

We returned to the airfield to find that the squadron was still socked in. A blanket of fog had spread over us, and apparently for a long distance south. We were grounded until it cleared, since Bentley refused to lose his planes by some chance collision. It was bad enough being shot down; we didn't need avoidable accidents as well.

Later on, predictably, the familiar figure of Corporal Angelica Kensley appeared, walking quickly towards the pilots' hut as I was idly lounging outside of it. I went up to meet her.

"Hello," she said.

"Hello."

"Did you go and look at the hut?" she asked eagerly.

"Yes, we did."

"And?"

"We found the spy, arrested him and it's all over."

"What?" She looked genuinely shocked at this news.

I burst out laughing and she pulled back her fist.

"Oh no, please don't punch me. It hurt too much last time."

"You certainly deserve it, pulling my leg like that."

"I couldn't help it. The temptation was too strong."

"At least I am tempting," she said playfully. She looked at me in a considering sort of way, though I could not tell what she was thinking.

"Yes, well, anyway. We did find a radio valve in the hut, but nothing of more interest. We are almost certain the spy had been there."

"Oh, well, that's good, I suppose."

"There is more good news," I continued.

"What?"

"You can't be the spy, because you were up in the plane with me."

"Oh, you!"

This time the fist came flying, but I was ready for it and dodged it. I caught her wrist instead. She looked at me with an unreadable expression once more.

"Unhand me at once, Flying Officer Mackennelly," she ordered, though she made no move whatsoever to remove her wrist from my clasp.

"Not until you promise to stop trying to hit me."

"OK, fine, we can stay like this all day then," she shot back.

I shook my head and, laughing, I reluctantly let go of her. What I really wanted to do was to sweep her up into my arms, though I knew I could not. It was not the time.

"You're a…" I started.

"Handful? Is that what you're going to say?" she finished for me.

"Yes, it was… How did you…?"

"Know? Woman's intuition."

"Will you just…"

"Stop finishing your sentences for you? Well, I might, if you know the secret code."

"And what might that be?"

"Oh, another date, perhaps, would suffice."

I burst out laughing. "You are…"

"Impossible?"

"Yes, that's it. Fine, you win. Let's try to go to the pictures or something — what do you think?"

"That would be lovely." She was so delighted by the suggestion that it made me quite forget it was all her idea. It was definitely a knack she had.

"Perhaps in the next day or so we might manage it?" I said tentatively.

"Fine, I will wait upon your invitation. Goodbye, my dear pilot." She put her hand up and lightly touched my cheek, then left as quickly as she had arrived.

I wondered if I had her right. Had she just used an endearment? And the touch of her hand on my cheek was like an electric jolt.

"She likes you, that one."

I jerked around to see Willie standing next to me. "I know, and I am beginning to like her."

"Well, old chap, hopefully things will progress as you want them to, without too many obstacles in your way."

This was an oblique reference to Barbara, I was sure. But there was something niggling at the back of my mind. What if the feelings I had for Angelica were simply the thrill of the chase? What if once the sly fox was caught, she would lose her appeal? I'd had similar experiences before, when pursuing my quarry had been everything. Once they had ceased to run, I'd lost interest very quickly. I wondered if Angelica was the same. The truth was I did not know. A kiss would tell me all, if and when it happened.

"Don't fret so much, old bean. It will all come out in the wash," Willie said as we returned to the hut.

"Have you been talking to Fred?"

"No, why?"

"He says the same thing."

"Because he's a sensible man."

We both laughed and spent the afternoon engaging in idle banter and reminiscing.

"Where's old Jonty?" Willie wondered when the time came to go home. We hadn't been able to fly, and all of us were chafing just a little.

"No idea — perhaps he snuck off?"

He wasn't in evidence at dinner and finally appeared later, with no explanation as to where he'd been. I simply assumed it was one of his rendezvous and left it at that.

Where Jonty may have been became a little clearer the next morning. We were all sitting at breakfast when Lawrence Calver suddenly appeared in the room, carrying what appeared to be a large pumpkin. We all turned to look at this bizarre turn of events when he slammed it down with what I considered unnecessary force onto the table.

"I say, steady on," complained Henry Conway, another pilot officer, who was just about to take a mouthful of scrambled egg.

Lawrence glared at him, ignoring this interjection, and demanded, "All right, who the hell put this pumpkin in my room?"

Glances were exchanged and there was silence while everyone shook their heads. I wondered if Lawrence had started to lose his marbles.

Then Jonty said, "Is that the general's pumpkin?"

The truth about the pumpkin began to dawn on me.

Lawrence turned his ire on Jonty at once, who looked quite nonchalant about the whole thing. "No, it's bloody well not, and I don't care whose it is, but I want to know who left it in my room!" This last was almost a shout.

However, he was once more met with silence as he glared at us each in turn, particularly me. I regarded him blandly, since I knew he was bound to suspect me. I had begun the vegetable caper, which now looked set to get completely out of hand.

Fortunately, I was saved from further scrutiny.

"Where did you find it, Ace?" Pilot Officer Colin Bridgewater said with interest. He put down his cutlery momentarily and waited for an answer.

"What does it matter where I found it?"

Unperturbed, Colin pursued his line of questioning. "I was just wondering, old boy, that's all. I mean, it's a bit unusual keeping a pumpkin in your room, but each to his own."

Lawrence looked as if he was near to having an apoplectic fit at this remark. "I didn't … I just told you…" He sighed with exasperation. Colin was like a dog with a bone and once he was onto a subject, he wouldn't let it go. "If you must know, and I don't know why you should … but it was on the pillow in my bed. Someone had made it look as if a person was sleeping there, with the pumpkin as its head."

I could see now that there was a crudely drawn face on the side of pumpkin. Willie, who had been containing himself with an enormous effort, found this simply too much. He burst out laughing, and so did the others.

Lawrence was not amused. "Oh, I see, I see, you're all in on this, are you? Is that it? A mass prank on Lawrence day, is it?"

"I wouldn't eat that if I was you," put in Henry. "Terribly bland flavour, those, much tastier ones to be had. Now, if you take the acorn squash as an example — hard to get, mind, but worth the effort…"

"I am not interested in a discussion on the relative merits of pumpkins!" Lawrence shouted.

Henry was unperturbed by this display. "Technically, old boy, acorn squash ain't a pumpkin, as it happens…"

Lawrence expressed himself even more forcefully in an effort to make him stop. "I don't care, do you understand? I want to know who put the blasted pumpkin in my bed!"

"Well, you're out there," said Henry, imagining the remark was addressed to him. "I've no idea."

"Oh, really, is that so? Well, let me tell you that…"

He was cut short as just then the cook appeared, no doubt to discover what the row was about. She spied the pumpkin, uttered a shriek of delight and scooped it up.

"Oh, my gawd. I've been looking for this everywhere. It's part of 'is Lordship's dinner, is that. Fond of a bit of pumpkin soup, he is. Wherever was it?"

The appearance of the cook appeared to cool Lawrence's ire somewhat and he said lamely, "I'd rather not say."

Fortunately for him, the cook was now distracted by something else. "Oh look 'ere, it's got a face on it. Honestly, you boys, always up to some kind of lark. Whatever will you do next?"

She shot Lawrence a glance of deep suspicion, which seemed to discompose him somewhat, and bustled out.

In the meantime, I turned my attention to Jonty, who appeared to be the picture of innocence.

Lawrence had one more despairing look around at us all, but having been robbed of the evidence it rather weakened his case. "You haven't heard the last of this, you pumpkin pranksters, not by a long chalk, oh no!" he said in threatening tones, and with that, he stalked out of the room.

"Pumpkin pranksters?" said Jonty. "A rather excellent name, that."

We all burst out laughing. Lawrence's head appeared around the door; he glared at us for a moment and then disappeared, which only served to increase our mirth.

"Poor chap," said Colin. "All this flying has gone to his head. Addled his brain or something."

"I hope we're not getting that blasted pumpkin soup for dinner," said Henry.

"I must admit, I find the prospect less attractive," Jonty added. "I mean, take that pumpkin, for instance. You don't know where it's been."

"Indeed," said Colin. "A sobering thought."

We finished our breakfast and were driven by Gordon to the airfield. He always took me, Jonty and Willie by preference and then returned for the others, assuming they had no other form of transport.

"Jonty," I said, once we were underway, "it was you, wasn't it?"

"My lips are sealed," he retorted.

"Fine, but I know it was you."

"Oh, all right then. You've caught me red-handed." He sighed. "It was too good an opportunity to miss."

"Perhaps," I said earnestly. "But if you carry on like this, I'm going to be kicked out of here, and so might you."

He was silent for a moment and then replied, "Of course, I wouldn't want that."

"No, so lay off the pranks, would you? And lay off Lawrence — he's caused enough trouble as it is."

"Yes, sir." He flashed me a sloppy mock salute.

"And don't be impertinent." I smiled at him, though.

"Listen to the man. I don't want to be left alone to deal with you, I couldn't take it," Willie put in with feeling.

Jonty suddenly raised his finger, as if a grand idea had just occurred to him. "A ballad! A ballad must be sung at the next pub session — it will be called the 'Ballad of the Pumpkin Brave'."

Willie made a face.

"You will do no such thing. I forbid it," I told him at once.

"Nevertheless."

"God preserve us," said Willie, groaning.

"You will *not*, Jonty," I said severely. "And if you so much as mention a pumpkin again, Willie and I will force-feed you pumpkin soup until you burst."

"I say, that sounds a bit drastic. Not sure I even like pumpkin soup."

We all laughed. It was hard to be angry with Jonty. He was just doing what we all did: trying ease the pressures of the constant combat.

Gordon kept silent during this exchange, but I knew he was taking it all in, and it wouldn't have surprised me to find he'd had a hand in obtaining the pumpkin for Jonty.

"You're a hopeless case, Jonty. You know that, don't you?" I said.

"Alas, poor Jonty, we knew him well…" he began.

"No, no, no, no! No more Shakespeare, I beg you," Willie protested.

"Let me sing you a ballad of the pumpkin soup; it's a sad and awful tale. For the pumpkin once was in bed with croup, and that's where we set sail…"

Willie shook his head and looked at me imploringly. However, there was nothing to be done but to listen to Jonty's dreadful pumpkin ditty all the way to Banley.

Almost as soon as we arrived, we were scrambled for a sortie. As we throttled up into the wild blue yonder, it crossed my mind that this could be the last time for any of us. Every time could be the very last time. It was a sobering thought and one I quickly pushed away. However, everyone had off days, and I felt a little sluggish. Perhaps it was the late nights or the constant drain of the sorties, but slow reactions could kill you or someone else. I was also distracted, thinking of Angelica. On top of that, I had to keep a look out for Lawrence. Every time we went up, I remembered Bentley's very irritating orders about watching his back. I couldn't disobey that order, much as I might have liked to. It wouldn't do; I tried to get my mind focused on the sortie.

As usual, we headed for the south coast. The word was that yet another force of bombers was coming in, most likely to try and hit London again. The city was suffering under the constant assault of Jerry's bombs.

"Here we go again," said Willie as we spied the massive swathe of planes coming in over the Seven Sisters. I was amazed they kept using the same route — you would have thought they would vary it. It seemed Fritz simply felt they could bludgeon their way through by force.

"Yes, and this time they've got quite an escort," I said.

What looked like one or more squadrons of ME109s were flying on the flanks of the main force.

There was no time to think as Judd called out, "Break, break!"

It was the signal to attack, and we wheeled off to the left. Then we separated and went into action. As one, the fighters turned on us and headed in to engage.

If Bosch had painted an air battle, it would have been rather like the scene of pandemonium that ensued. Planes were flying everywhere, zipping across the front of each other in pursuits and counter pursuits. The risk was not only getting hit by someone who was attacking you, but by stray bullets from someone else. Friendly fire was always a danger, but here it was doubled or more. The air was thick with radio chatter too.

"I've got him."

"He's after me."

"Look out, look out!"

"Bail out, man, for God's sake, bail!"

I tried to focus on taking on one plane at a time. This seemed the best plan and shut out the rest of the noise. A 109 seemed to have decided I was to be their latest victim, and we were playing the air version of cat and mouse. I was weaving and banking while he stuck to me like glue. I couldn't get behind him, though I tried every trick in the book. This time there was no Willie to get me out of the jam, as he was in a heavy dogfight over to the right of me.

Suddenly, a plan formed in my mind. We were still near the cliffs and now had moved further along towards Beachy Head, which was over five hundred feet of sheer sandstone.

I flew a little way out to sea, narrowly avoiding getting hit, and then dropped low to almost skimming level over the waves. It was a tricky manoeuvre, because one false move and I'd be in the drink.

As I'd hoped, the 109 was still in my rear-view mirror and had followed me down. This was somewhat foolish, since he could easily have stayed above me and shot me to pieces. Apparently, though, this was some kind of deadly sport for him. I gained a fraction of height, just enough to turn, and then proceeded to fly straight towards the cliff face. One thing I knew was that the Spitfire had a tighter turning circle than the

109 and a faster turn rate. I couldn't compete with it in a climb, but that wasn't what I had in mind at all.

I was counting on him being too intent on following me to notice what I was doing, and I was right. There was a split second as the cliff wall loomed large in front of me, and then I turned almost too late. I had never been so perilously close to hitting anything as I was then. With literally inches to spare, I flipped my kite left and the engine screamed as I throttled it out of the turn. Behind me, there was a bang and a loud explosion. The 109 was taken by surprise and hit the cliff at full pelt. He'd had no time to react and had paid the price for it.

I rose triumphantly above the cliff, breathing a sigh of relief.

"Thank God for that." It was Willie. "I thought you'd bought it."

"So did I, Kiwi, so did I."

We had no time for a further exchange, as I saw another 109 sitting on Henry Conway's tail. I pulled back on the throttle to close in on the fighter. There were seconds to spare as I manoeuvred into a position to fire. That was when the fatigue suddenly hit me. It was almost as if my fingers went into slow motion. Perhaps it was the aftermath of the adrenaline rush from my near-miss at the cliff, but I fired just a second too late.

In that moment, the 109 ripped a burst that shattered Henry's cockpit, and I saw him slump forward. His plane went into a nosedive, and I knew he was probably already dead. In a fit of anger, I emptied my ammo into the 109, which had not seen me. I had, at least, the satisfaction of watching it also plummet to earth, smoking like a chimney.

But it was no consolation. I felt I had failed Henry. All the way back to Banley Airfield, I was silent and brooding about the fact he had died because of me.

I jumped down from the plane. Jonty came up to me, bouncy as usual.

"That was a bun fight if ever I saw one, wasn't it, Skipper?"

"Just give me a moment, Jonty, there's a good chap. I just need a moment."

I walked away from the planes and to the edge of the field, brimful of emotion. Behind me, I heard Willie say, "Leave him be, old sport. He'll come about in a little while."

Grateful for his diplomacy, I sat on a bench that looked out over farmland beyond. I rarely got choked up, but this time the grief was overwhelming. I was overcome, and tears flowed — tears of anger with myself for failing to save Henry. Then, as I sat with my head in my hands, I felt an arm go around my shoulder.

"What's wrong?" It was Angelica, with soothing tones.

"I … I … I just…"

I broke down and she said no more. She pulled me in tighter and put her head on my shoulder, giving me her quiet empathy. After a few moments, I started to come out of it and eventually she sat up.

"Do you want to talk about it?" she asked.

"I … it's difficult…" Then I told her, in halting tones, and felt better for having done so.

"You shouldn't blame yourself," she said, when I had finished. "You're a bloody good pilot, and you can't save everyone. That's just life."

"I should have been quicker," I replied, reluctant to forgive myself so easily.

"I remember once," she told me, "my father and I were walking home from a hockey match. We had lost. I blamed myself because I'd had an open goal, and I was just a split second too late. My father said, 'You did your best and that's all that matters. I watched you for the whole game and you tried your hardest. In that one small moment, things didn't go the way you wanted, but we are all human. We fail sometimes. Accept it and move on.'"

I listened and looked at her. "But nobody died," I said sadly.

"That's not the point, Angus. You are one of the best pilots on this squadron, I know it, everyone knows it. I've heard the other pilots talk about how you saved this or that person. So today you didn't. You're not God. You're just you."

I smiled. I felt better, surprisingly so. She smiled back.

"Well, then?"

"Well, you're right, I suppose."

"I know I am."

That made me laugh, and somehow I was able to shrug off the melancholy mood. "Did I tell you how I almost smashed into Beachy Head?" I said, my eyes dancing.

"What? Don't say so!"

"Promise not to punch my arm and I'll tell you…"

Shortly after that little interlude, we were called up again. Another wave was coming in and with the planes refuelled and our ammo replenished, we were ready to go.

"Take care of yourself," said Angelica, watching me leave.

"I'll try."

"Please don't fly into any cliffs!"

I laughed and broke into a run, giving her a cheery wave. As we took off from the airfield, I could not help thinking that perhaps Barbara would not have been so sympathetic. Or if she was, she would have approached it very differently. The two women were poles apart. For the first time, I considered the idea of giving Barbara up. Just the thought was enough to make me want her again. She was like an addiction. I didn't think I could let go.

A couple of days passed, and the death of Henry Conway faded. I felt the guilt for a while, but it was not something one could carry for long when people were dying every day in combat. Henry wasn't the only pilot we had lost or would lose. The exigencies of the situation swept away the past, leaving us with the constant dangers of the present. There was no time to think or have regrets when every day could bring a new one. Perhaps it was the short-term nature of it all that made it harder to think seriously of relinquishing my tenuous relationship with Barbara.

I told her about Henry, and contrary to my assumption she was very understanding. She took me in her arms, held me and kissed me like a child.

"I'm so sorry, darling," she said. "It's not your fault, my love, don't be sad. All of us make mistakes, and this is war. You can't be responsible for everything."

I kissed her then and felt as if I had melted into her lips. She was so incredibly beautiful in her nature at times. I felt something of a villain for having made unflattering comparisons.

"You shouldn't be afraid to tell me about the things that hurt you," she whispered. "I'm here for you. I'm always here for you, don't you know that by now?"

Words like that pierced right to the heart. I fell into her fierce and passionate embrace, feeling that she really did care about me. She wasn't as self-centred as I had started to think. All of that made it even more difficult to know what to do. The trouble was, I knew I wasn't being fair to either woman.

"Am I a cad?" I asked Gordon suddenly as he was driving me to the airfield one morning. We were alone. Jonty hadn't got up for breakfast, and Willie had gone to see to him. Apparently, Jonty had a rather bad hangover. Willie promised to get him in pronto. As much as Willie professed annoyance at Jonty's ballads, he was an extremely loyal friend and colleague.

"I beg pardon, sir?" Gordon snatched a glance at me in surprise.

"Don't play the innocent with me, Fred. You know what I'm talking about. I'm asking if you think I'm a damnable cad."

He said nothing for a few moments, as if considering the question. "I wouldn't say you were a cad, sir, no."

"That's a relief. What would you say?"

Again, there was a pause before he spoke. "I'd say, sir, that you haven't found the woman who can make you forsake all others. Or rather that you perhaps have not recognised who that woman is."

"Oh, I see." This wasn't quite the response I was expecting. "But surely what I'm doing is wrong, even so?"

"I wouldn't precisely say wrong. Perhaps it's unfair, but we're not schoolchildren, sir. There are two parties in any relationship, and each of them makes their own decisions. Besides, one of the ladies is also married, and yet she is consorting with you."

I thought about this for a while, and we drove in silence. "Yes, good point."

"You worry too much, sir, if I may say so. Besides that, you're already up to your eyes in it, so..."

I laughed. "That's one way of putting it."

"Just be careful it doesn't swallow you up, sir, like quicksand."

I nodded. What he said wasn't precisely helpful. I already knew I'd dug a rather large hole for myself.

"It will work out, sir, you'll see."

"A great believer in fate, are you?"

"I'm a believer in the triumph of the human spirit, sir."

I had not realised Gordon was quite so deeply philosophical. If nothing else, it gave me food for thought. We arrived shortly afterwards, and I noticed Audrey hovering about. As soon as she saw me jump down from the jeep, she hurried over.

"Bentley wants to see you, sir," she said.

"Oh, Lord." I groaned. "What have I done now?"

"I'm not sure you've done anything, sir. He seems in rather a good humour, if I'm honest." She smiled reassuringly.

"Let's hope so. My meetings with him recently haven't been all that pleasant."

"We'd best go, sir, if you want him to keep his sunny disposition."

"Indeed, lead on…"

In short order, I was once more sitting in Bentley's office, and it occurred to me I had seen far too much of it of late.

"Ah, Angus," he said, sounding at least half amiable.

Following which he began his routine with his pipe, emptying it, scraping out the bowl, filling it and lighting it. Then, puffing contentedly on it and filling the room with particularly pungent tobacco, he elected to get to the matter at hand.

"You're skating on thin ice, Angus, very thin ice indeed," he said. It seemed to be his habit lately to spring such surprises on me.

"Pardon?" I said.

Since he'd not supplied any context, I reasoned the statement could have applied to any number of things. Evidently, though, contrary to Audrey's assumption, I had done something he wasn't happy with.

"Yes, thin ice, my boy. This pumpkin incident is just the latest in a long line of childish pranks, and I've had enough of it."

"But, sir, it wasn't me!" I said, filled with indignation at being accused of something I actually hadn't done.

"Really? You'll pardon me if I treat that with the scepticism it deserves."

He puffed ruminatively on his pipe for a few more moments, while I seethed quietly.

"And there's another matter," he continued. "You're up to your old tricks again, I hear."

"Sorry?" The cryptic manner in which he chose to couch his complaints was beginning to annoy me.

"I ran into Colonel Lord Amberly. Need I say more?"

I very likely paled just a little. This was definitely something I didn't want brought up. "Oh, I see."

"I hope you know what you're doing, consorting with his wife."

Audrey, who was busy at her desk with paperwork, looked up sharply and then down again.

However, now it was out in the open, I wasn't going to go down without a fight. "He told me he doesn't want to know about it."

Bentley tapped the end of his pipe on the desk, before puffing on it again. "That's as may be, but is it the conduct of an officer and a gentleman? That's what you should ask yourself."

"Sir." There really was nothing I could say to that. I had asked myself the same question many times, but no matter the answer I still did it anyway.

Since I volunteered nothing further, he said, "Well, I'm turning a blind eye to it, but if this blows up in your face, then I'll have no alternative."

"No alternative to what?"

"Africa, Egypt…" He didn't need to elaborate. I knew exactly what he meant.

"Oh, I see."

He sighed, as if he was explaining something to a particularly recalcitrant child. "Look, I really don't want to get involved in this. It's your affair, so to speak. But take my advice and tread lightly, my boy, tread lightly. The Mavericks need you, and these larks of yours are not assisting your career."

"Yes, sir. I'll bear that in mind."

He searched my face for a moment to perhaps discern if I had taken anything he'd said on board. Then he sighed again, as if he was the rather disappointed uncle of a wayward nephew. "Fine, dismissed."

Sticking his pipe between his teeth, he picked up a file and began to study it. This was the signal to leave. I stood up and snapped a salute.

As I expected, I got no more than a few steps away from Bentley's door before Audrey came running after me. I stopped and turned, anticipating her question.

"Does Angelica know?" she asked at once.

"Should she?"

"Well, what do you think?"

"I think she's a grown woman and makes her own choices," I shot back, immediately on the defensive. I used precisely the reasoning Gordon had given me earlier.

"That's exactly what a man *would* say, and I was starting to like you!" Her eyes sparked just a little.

"Sorry." I shrugged. I didn't want to discuss Angelica with Audrey. Her friends were entirely too involved already for my liking. But Audrey wasn't finished.

"I do like you, though, that's the problem." She gave me a tight smile. "But Angelica likes you more, and she got in first."

"Got in what, exactly?" I demanded, nettled.

"Oh, you'll find out … eventually…" she said airily, walking off before I could enquire further.

She and Angelica had the same infuriating habit, I thought bitterly. Walking away before I could take them up on something when they didn't want me to.

At least Bentley hadn't thrown me out of the Mavericks. I had to be thankful for small mercies. I shook my head and renouncing all women for at least the next hour or two, I hurried off to join the rest of the chaps in the pilots' hut.

CHAPTER TEN

A couple more days went by, and our focus was wholly on either going into combat or returning from it. Jerry had decided to make an extra effort to entertain us with squadron after squadron of bombers. Fortunately, we returned unscathed from the multiple sorties we flew.

One morning, when we were on a short respite, Tomas came up to me while I was standing a little way away from the hut.

"Scottish," he said in an urgent undertone.

"Yes?"

"We must talk."

This could only mean developments in the spy business, which I had to confess I'd not been paying much attention to. Flying sorties against the enemy had taken almost all of my attention. Tomas was far more zealous than me, even though I was the one who had been given the task.

"OK." I walked with him a little further from the hut and out of earshot.

"We must look at Gerald," he pronounced in hushed tones.

"What, Gerald Haliday?"

"Yes!"

Gerald was a young pilot officer, around twenty-five years of age. He was quite lanky, though not particularly tall. He had black hair and some fuzz that passed for a moustache. There was nothing particularly striking about his features. I probably wouldn't have recognised him in the street.

"Why do you think it's him?"

"Because! He fits. He is an aristocrat, or aristocrat's son. He was a rich boy until he joined the Air Force. His father is a lord or something and is a friend of Edward, you know … that king."

"Edward the eighth who abdicated, yes."

Tomas folded his arms as if he'd made a hugely significant statement. "And this king, he was a friend of Hitler. Come on, Scottish, really? I mean, come on."

"Just because his father is Edward's friend doesn't mean…"

"Yes, but he is someone in the best position to not be a suspect, no?"

"OK, but apart from that, what have you got?" This didn't sound very plausible to me — in fact, quite the opposite. But I continued to hear him out.

"He sneaks."

"Sneaks?"

"Yes, he goes out and for a long time, usually at night."

"Every night?"

"No, maybe once a week … twice."

I perked up at this. Perhaps it did fit in terms of doing something as a habit, as the MI6 chaps had suggested. This made him far more likely a suspect. "Right, so you've been watching him?"

"Yes, I watch, yes."

"But you've not followed him?"

"No, but we can do that, no?"

"Right." I mulled this over. So far, my following anyone had not resulted in anything to do with spying. However, you could never tell when something might be linked. We were going to have to do what Tomas suggested. "OK, so when are we going to do this?"

"Tonight, he will sneak, and we will follow."

"Right."

"Just after last sortie, he will go, you watch."

"All right, let's hope this time it might lead somewhere."

"Yes, Scottish, I know, I feel it. This is the right one!"

I did not share Tomas's enthusiasm and thought it far more likely to turn out that Gerald was not a spy at all. He was a rather unassuming chap and it seemed farfetched. However, the MI6 chaps had said it would be the one you least suspected.

My attention was claimed by another call to scramble and from then on, the day was simply flying out and flying back with some dogfights in between. What should have been stirring stuff was almost becoming routine. It was very strange. Happily, I had no cause to bail out Lawrence and could focus on my own section's fights rather than his.

As we touched down for the last time and I jumped down from my kite, Tomas came up to me.

"OK, Scottish, when he takes off his life vest, he will go. We will do the same."

"Right."

The two of us shed the extraneous flying gear. We waited, hanging around the hut and idly chatting with half an eye on the unsuspecting Gerald. He took his time but eventually left the hut, nodded to us and strode off towards what I assumed was the main gate.

After a few moments, Tomas and I started to follow, keeping well behind him. The airfield was not far from a small village and some of the officers were quartered there. It was within walking distance. It wouldn't seem too amiss if we walked too. There was also a local pub. I bet myself ten to one that Gerald was simply going for a drink.

"I thought you said he sneaked," I said to Tomas after a while.

"Yes, of course, look, he is sneaking, look."

"Well, it doesn't look like sneaking to me. He seems to be just out for a night-time stroll."

Tomas scoffed. "Ah, come on, Scottish, come on. This is sneaking. He doesn't live in the village."

"Well, he could be going to the pub."

Tomas was undeterred. "This is sneaking, you will see … sneaking!"

I held my peace, since there was nothing to be gained from arguing about it. The proof would be in the pudding.

After several minutes of walking, the village could be seen in the distance, and shortly afterwards we were on the outskirts. We did not talk any further, not wanting to draw attention to ourselves. Gerald had not looked around once, which was a good thing. As we continued down the small main street, he suddenly ducked down a side road.

"Come on, Scottish, he must have seen us and is trying to run away from us."

Tomas seemed to have a flair for the dramatic and took off at speed. I had no option but to keep up with him. We jogged around the corner and there was our quarry, still walking but in the distance.

"He didn't get away!" said Tomas with satisfaction.

A few moments later, Gerald disappeared into a large building, which could have been an old warehouse or something similar.

"He's gone inside!" Tomas hissed, stating the obvious. "We must follow him. I bet he is going to send a message on his radio."

Tomas was now convinced that there was no possibility Gerald wasn't the spy and that we would catch him red-handed.

"Right," I said, trying not to cast a damper on what seemed to be, for him, the thrill of the chase.

We soon drew abreast of the building and since there was only one door, we went through it. It appeared to be abandoned or at least had fallen into disuse. From its appearance, it looked as if it might have been some kind of cotton or cloth manufacturer. There was a pile of bobbins in an alcove on our right, which would probably have belonged to a loom.

"What is this place?" whispered Tomas, looking around.

I kept my voice low. "An old mill, I think, though God knows what it's doing out here."

A corridor stretched ahead of us with various doors that probably led to offices.

"Doesn't matter, this is very good place for spy to be. Yes, very good. Come on."

No matter what misgivings I held, it didn't do to be complacent. Keeping one hand on the butt of my pistol, I noticed Tomas doing the same as we moved forward as silently as possible. The place was eerily quiet, almost deathly so. It certainly smacked of something out of a spy novel.

Then, just as we reached the corridor's end, there was a murmur of voices and light shining from under a shut door. Tomas gave me a significant look. He was wholly in his element now, ready to apprehend the spy in the act.

"This is it, Scottish," Tomas whispered triumphantly. "Now we catch him red-handed."

"Right."

He put one hand on the handle of the door, turned it and eased the door open. To our surprise, instead of finding Gerald hard at work on his radio, there was, instead, a large room with rows of chairs in it. At the end of what appeared to be an aisle was a man standing with his hands on a podium. Sitting near the back was Gerald. The man stopped speaking when he saw us. There were several others who were part of what I took to be the audience.

I was glad we had not drawn our sidearms, since this would undoubtedly have been taken amiss.

"Welcome, welcome, newcomers, have a seat, have a seat," boomed the man at the podium.

"Hello, chaps," said Gerald, getting up to greet us. "I didn't think you were coming *here*."

This indicated to me that our attempts to follow him in secret were unsuccessful. He obviously knew we were there the whole time.

"What exactly is here?" I asked him.

Tomas looked rather crestfallen that Gerald was not the spy after all.

"A temperance meeting, I thought you knew. I thought that's why you came," said Gerald.

"A temperance meeting?" I echoed, a little dumbfounded.

"Yes, I discovered it not long ago and cleaned up my act. I feel so much better too, without the demon drink."

Fearing I had stumbled into a pilot's worst nightmare, all I could say was, "I see."

"Why don't you sit down and listen? It's only just started. You might find it interesting. You might be the latest converts."

I looked at Tomas and he looked at me. Now we were here, it would be difficult to extricate ourselves without some kind of awkward explanation.

"Right, yes, sure, we'd be happy to, erm … see what it's all about."

We sat with Gerald, who listened to the speaker with a beatific expression on his face. It reminded me of the fact that there was no one worse nor more of a missionary than someone who had renounced something like drink or smoking. They became quite odious at times and made one long for their self-appointed halo to slip. I had not counted on passing the better part of an hour being lectured about the perils of alcohol. I'd certainly spent better hours than that. It was full of fire, thunder and brimstone. I was certainly left with the impression that I would discover myself in the fiery inferno of hell if I so much as touched another drop. Finally, and thankfully, it was over, and we got up to go.

"What did you think?" Gerald asked me.

"Can I be candid?" I said to him.

"Yes, of course."

Before I could continue, Tomas butted in. "You have lost your marbles, no? Isn't that what you British say?"

"I beg your pardon?" Gerald started to bristle.

"Yes, you have lost the marbles, giving up alcohol. This is not natural. In my country, we can never, *never* give up vodka!"

"Now, look here … if you are going to be insulting, perhaps you would like to step outside…" Gerald began, looking as if he would square up to Tomas. For all his abstention, he was evidently running on a short fuse.

I felt it was time to intervene. "Easy, old chap," I said. "Tomas here is just used to a different culture, that's all — isn't that right, Tomas?"

"I am used to a man taking his drink, like a man!" he said proudly.

"Right…"

Seeing this was only going to end one way, discretion seemed the better part of valour. "We must be going," I said to Gerald quickly. "Thanks for the lecture and all that."

"Won't you stay for tea and cake?" Gerald asked me, perhaps hoping he could still prevail upon us to renounce alcohol forever.

"No, we're off. Come on, Tomas."

"Yes, I will come on. I need drink after listening to *that*."

Without further ado, I hustled him out before the two of them came to blows, as they very well might have if he stayed.

"All right, Scottish, I'm coming, all right," he complained.

"Yes, well, since you nearly started a fistfight in there…"

"Ah, come on, Scottish. I was just telling my opinion."

"That's the trouble!"

"Ah, what use is it to give up drinking? You British are all crazy people."

"Don't include me in that."

"No, not you, Scottish. You are a sensible man."

"More sensible than you were moments ago," I admonished him.

"Oh well!" He shrugged. "You want to go for a drink?" he added hopefully.

"No thanks, I'm going to find Fred and go home for dinner."

"Me too, Scottish, me too. The little lady, she is waiting. She has the vodka."

"Right." My suspicions regarding the widow he was boarding with were now confirmed.

"I really thought he was the spy," he said sadly as we walked back to the airfield.

"Yes, it's a shame."

"But we are going to catch this bastard spy, you will see."

"I'm sure you are right."

We parted company at the airfield, and he went to get his motorbike. Soon after, Gordon appeared as if by magic and drove me back to Amberly Manor.

"Lady Amberly requests your presence, sir, in her boudoir."

I looked at him sharply. "But isn't she with her husband?"

"His Lordship has returned to the war."

"I see."

Barbara would no doubt be pleased, I thought. And I was right. Soon after I'd made myself presentable, I arrived in her chamber. The small table was laid once more with silver cloches. She was wearing the sheerest negligée and furry mules. Her attire left nothing at all to the imagination. She was smiling broadly as soon as I appeared.

"Darling."

She got up to greet me and slid her arms around my neck. I did not resist her searching lips and kissed her with as much fervour as she gave me.

"Now we can be comfortable," she said. "He's finally shoved off, thank the Lord."

"Was he called back to his regiment?"

"Yes, apparently something is afoot. Never was I happier to hear the news."

I was not sure I echoed her sentiments, as pleased as I was to see her in many ways. Now he was away, she would very likely become more demanding. I wasn't entirely certain I wanted her to be. Things had changed and were still changing, for me at least.

However, for the moment, I allowed her to lead me to the table and lift off the cloches to reveal the culinary delights underneath.

"What's that?" I asked her as she took the lid off a tureen.

"Pumpkin soup."

I laid my head back and roared with laughter.

In spite of Barbara wanting me to spend every night with her, I managed to get some time to take Angelica to the pictures as I'd promised. *Night Train to Munich* was playing, which seemed rather appropriate. It was an excellent spy thriller, which by coincidence involved Czechoslovakia as a setting. Angelica let me sit with my arm around her, and she laid her head gently on my shoulder. It felt comfortable, and more than that, it felt right somehow. It led me to wonder if I was simply hedging my bets with Barbara, in case things did not progress.

After the film, we ate fish and chips sitting on a bench on the village green. The night wasn't cold, and the moon cast a long, bright light over us. It was quite romantic, in fact.

"You'll be amused to hear about the latest in the pursuit of our quarry," I said, popping some fish into my mouth.

"Do tell," Angelica said eagerly.

I had dropped all pretence of keeping secrets about the spy caper with her. It was very likely true she had a higher security clearance than I did. I related the story of the temperance meeting, which she found vastly entertaining, indulging in a fit of the giggles.

"Poor Tomas," she said. "He sounds as if he was most put out."

"He was mortified. The idea that people actually believe in abstention was something akin to the work of the devil."

"Oh, don't," she laughed. Then she said more seriously, "What are you going to do about finding the real spy?"

"I don't know. I must admit I'm at *point non plus* over the whole thing. I'm not a blasted secret agent — I don't even have the training. I don't really know why Bentley even asked me."

"Perhaps he trusts you," she ventured.

"Trusts me? You haven't been in his office lately when I'm there, that's for sure. All he's done is read me a litany of complaints, and there was that carpeting the other day."

"Audrey says he thinks a lot of you, actually."

I bristled at this remark. "Oh, she does, does she? And why should Audrey have anything to say about it?" I demanded a little tersely.

"Because I talk about you to her all the time…" she said gently.

I digested this piece of intelligence and then said, "Oh? Oh! I see."

"We are like sisters."

"Oh!" This didn't sound good at all.

"Don't worry," she laughed. "I don't tell her everything."

"And what pray is there to tell?"

"Never you mind."

"You know, I'm beginning to wonder if I shouldn't start reconsidering you as being the spy. You are remarkably good at evasion tactics, for a start!"

"That's not because I'm a spy, it's because I'm a woman."

I shook my head. "I can't win, can I?"

"Only if I let you."

"Touché!" I had to acknowledge the hit. She bested me at every turn. I had no idea how she did it, but she seemed to be able to turn the tables on me every time the conversation became a little personal.

"Anyway, that was very nice," she said finishing off the last of her supper and rolling up the paper. I did the same. "I ought to be going home," she added, though a little sadly.

"Shall I walk you to your gate?"

"What do you think?" She smiled and got up. When I did the same, she tucked her arm into mine.

"What do you suppose you'd be doing if you hadn't ended up here and if we hadn't gone to war?" I asked her as we strolled together down the street.

"I don't know, I'd probably be working in a boring office somewhere."

"But don't you work in an office now?"

"Yes, but it's certainly not boring. Not with all the air combat going on."

"I am glad we keep you entertained, at least. I shall send your compliments to Hitler."

"Oh, you!" She laughed.

We stopped at her gate, and she turned to face me.

"I worry about you," she said seriously.

"Worry? Why?"

"I worry that one day you'll fly out on a sortie and you won't come back." Her voice broke a little.

I didn't know what to say. What could one say, in any case?

"I worry that I won't get to kiss you before that happens," she continued.

I laughed. "We can easily remedy your fears, if you like."

"No, it's not time. You will just have to not get killed."

"I'll do my best then, shall I?" I said with a grin.

"It's no laughing matter. I mean it, Flying Officer Mackennelly. If you get killed, I will never…"

"Never what?"

"I will never forgive you."

With that, she turned and went through her gate. She'd left me dumbfounded yet again. A most extraordinary woman indeed.

"Have you ever met a woman where it's all on their terms, Fred?" I asked him as we bowled along the next day, heading for the airfield.

"It's always all on their terms, sir," he said wryly.

"That's why I avoid women like the plague," said Jonty from the back. "Much safer that way."

He felt at ease with us, and able to let his guard down. For others, he might keep up the pretence of being a ladies' man, but we knew he wasn't. He knew we knew too.

Willie laughed. "I am surprised you haven't made a ballad up about it."

"Ah, well, you're out there," replied Jonty at once. "It so happens that I have."

"Oh why, oh why did I have to go and open my big mouth?"

"You should never date a woman if you can," sang Jonty. "You should never date a woman if you can. For a woman will possess you and God will never bless you. You should never date a woman if you can..."

"See what you've gone and done," I chided Willie with a laugh.

"Don't I know it," he groaned.

Jonty was well into the second verse and showing no sign of stopping. There was nothing for it but to endure it for the rest of the journey.

"Why on earth did you become a pilot, Jonty?" I asked him, jumping down from the jeep. "Surely you'd be better off in the music hall, or the entertainment corps."

"As a matter of fact, I did ask about that, but they wouldn't take me," he said sadly. "So, I joined the RAF instead."

"Listen, what do you need, a letter of recommendation? I'll gladly write one or several," said Willie.

"Alas, too late, that ship has sailed. The bird has flown. The chicken has left the coop. The fox is…"

"For the love of God, will you please…" Willie was saying in exasperated tones when the call went up to scramble.

As soon as there was a scramble on, there was no time to think. We ran for the planes, fired them up to go. Every minute lost would be a minute that the blasted Jerry gets nearer to their target.

That day we flew up into a very strong headwind, and thence into a heavy shower of rain. We had no windshield wipers, but the air stream from the propellors seemed to keep the windshield clear so we could still see out. The driving rain was difficult and pretty soon after that, we hit a thunderstorm. Lighting flashed around us and thunder crashed. It was quite spectacular.

"Wonderful," said Willie. "Are we supposed to fight in this?"

"I imagine so, but Jerry is stuck in it too, so it's quid pro quo."

"Talking of Jerry, here they are."

Another large force of Heinkels was flying below us and well above us, I spotted their escort.

"Bandits! Bandits twelve o'clock, break, break," I said urgently.

We peeled off the main flight and into the driving rain. The ME109s were heading down to us and we turned up to meet them. The height gave them the advantage, and there was nothing for it but to engage. Once within range, the bullets started to fly. The rain probably did impair their vision, which helped a little. I flipped sideways and dived, then came up under one of the enemy planes, firing into its belly. I found the target but didn't do enough damage to stop him. He carried on and sped away while I gave chase.

These cat-and-mouse manoeuvres were a skill of their own, and hard won in combat sorties. When it was raining like it was, it became even more difficult. The 109 pulled up into a climb, knowing I would not be fast enough to catch him. I stuck to his tail, however, so that he couldn't flip over and get behind me.

"Come on, slow coach." It was Willie.

"Well, you come and get him then, if you're so much better."

"No, no, I've got my own problems just now."

He slid past me so close I could see him clearly in the cockpit, and then a 109 screamed by in pursuit. I was now in two minds. I had to decide whether to let go of my own quarry and help Willie, or to keep going and let him sort it out.

As usual, I couldn't leave a fellow pilot in trouble and so I broke away, turning quickly. I was able to close in fast on Willie's 109 and fire a burst into his tail. As luck would have it, it ripped it to pieces and the plane literally dropped out of the sky.

"Nice shooting," said Willie, "and thanks… Uh oh."

He turned his plane almost on a sixpence and flew straight back at me. Before I realised what he was about, he flew over me and fired. The 109 I had been chasing had turned back and had decided to come after me. It was a little close for comfort.

"Thanks, Kiwi," I said.

"Just returning the favour, old chap."

In the meantime, the rest of the squadron had engaged the Heinkels and had been quite successful by all accounts. I looked around for Jonty and saw him returning unscathed. I checked for Lawrence's plane too; this was now becoming almost routine for me due to Bentley's damned orders.

"Disengage, Mavericks, return to base," said Judd.

We flew back in formation once more.

"Where did you get to, Jonty?" I asked.

"Went after a Heinkel, got a Stuka instead," he said. "Got chased by a 109, lost him, came back. Quite an adventure, in fact..."

"No, don't say it, just don't say it," said Willie imploringly.

"A ballad..." Jonty began.

On my return from the sortie, I found Audrey waiting for me. I sighed inwardly. It was either going to be something to do with Angelica, or Bentley wanted to see me again. I could not think of any particular transgression I had committed, though I racked my brains.

I wasn't kept in suspense for long.

"Sir, there are two gentlemen here to see you," said Audrey.

"Two gentlemen?"

"Yes." She didn't volunteer anything further, but as I walked beside her the mention of two gentlemen rang a bell.

"Have I seen them before?" I asked her.

"Yes, they came once before."

"Raincoats, hats, moustaches?"

"That's right."

"The Marx Brothers!" I exclaimed. With all that was going on of late, they had not figured particularly large in my memory but the idea of their resemblance to at least one of the Marx Brothers had stuck.

"Sir?"

"It's who they remind me of."

She laughed.

"For God's sake don't tell them," I implored her.

"Oh, no, I would never do *that.* How funny and how observant. That's exactly who they look like."

Now I had articulated the thought, I couldn't shake it off and it amused me. We arrived at the door of the same room I'd met them in before. She opened it and let me in, then shut it behind me. It was rather like déjà vu. There they were, with the same raincoats, hats, ties even. I wondered if they possessed wardrobes full of matching sets. It made me want to giggle, and that wouldn't do.

"Ah, Flying Officer Mackennelly," said blue tie. "Take a seat."

They were sitting at the table just as before, and I sat down opposite.

"I'll get straight to the point," said red tie. "Have you any information for us about the spy?"

"Yes, we were wondering, since we've not heard from you."

"No, we've heard nothing at all."

I hesitated. I would have to tell them the truth. The chances were they already knew anyway.

"Well, no. Although I've followed up some leads, none of them led anywhere, at least not to the spy … so to speak."

"We know," the blue tie put in.

This annoyed me, and I perhaps showed it. "If you knew, then why did you ask me?" I said, looking from one to the other.

I knew I would never know their real names, so I decided there and then, to dub the one with the blue tie 'Harpo' and the one with the red tie 'Chico'. It seemed rather to suit them and I had a penchant for nicknames. Thus named I would henceforth never think of them otherwise.

"We wanted to see if you would be honest with us," said Chico.

"Why on earth shouldn't I be?"

"Because…" said Harpo, standing up. "We have to be sure that our sources of information are, shall we say, clean."

"What?" I didn't like where this was leading.

"Yes," he continued, pacing the room. "You see, we know that the spy is in the squadron."

"Right? You already told me, though."

He stopped and raised a finger. "Ah, we told you that, but the fact is we weren't certain at the time."

"Hang on," I said, irritated all over again. "So, you've sent me on a wild goose chase, knowing there might not be a spy at all."

"Precisely." He seemed completely unperturbed by the idea he could have wasted my time.

"So, what makes you say there is one now?"

He sat down again, and Chico took up the tale.

"We very carefully supplied different fake intelligence to each of the squadrons we suspected. Then we waited." Apparently, he liked a bit of theatre because he paused for effect at this point before carrying on. "We did not have to wait for long. Our sources in Germany soon told us which of the fake intelligence had been leaked to German High Command."

"And?"

"It was the information we had planted in the Mavericks." He smiled at me a little triumphantly.

"Right, I see."

"So, we know for sure that the spy is here in your midst."

I sighed. "All very well, but I'm no closer to discovering who it is."

"Well, you need to get closer," said Harpo. "Every day the spy is not found is another day when vital information could get through to the Germans."

"If it's so damn important, then why haven't you got your own people on it instead of me?" I demanded. "You know I am trying to fight a war here. I'm a pilot, not a secret agent."

"And so are we, Flying Officer, so are we."

"Yes, well, I will redouble my efforts, if that's what you want to know."

"We want to know a lot of things, Flying Officer. Are you loyal to the King? Do you believe in the sanctity of marriage? Do you think consorting with officers' wives is wise? Talking of which, you've two women in tow since we last spoke, have you not?"

"What? How dare you!" My fists balled up on hearing this.

"We know a lot about you, Flying Officer Mackennelly. A lot more than you know we know," said Harpo, furnishing me with a meaningful look.

"Which serves you how, exactly?" I said evenly.

"It serves us to make sure you do the job you were asked to do."

"And if I don't?"

"Let's just say, you won't like your next posting."

"Why I ought to knock your…" I stood up with every intention of landing one on at least one or the other.

"I wouldn't do that if I was you."

Without warning, I was staring down the barrel of a revolver, which had appeared from nowhere. The whole thing was becoming quite bizarre.

"I could drop you where you stand," said Chico. "Nobody would question it. You'd be exposed as a traitor, and we would say we shot you in self-defence."

"Who the hell are you people?" I shouted.

"Sit down," said Chico, motioning with the barrel of the pistol.

Then suddenly he pulled the trigger and squirted me with water. It wasn't even a real gun. It was a water pistol. The two of them burst out laughing, and I began to wonder if I'd walked into some terrible nightmare from which I would hopefully wake up soon.

"Your face," said Harpo.

"A picture," said Chico.

"Look, I don't know what game you two are playing, but frankly I don't find it half as amusing as you seem to." I pulled out a handkerchief and wiped my face.

They suddenly became serious all over again.

"This is not a game. That was a test," said Harpo.

"A test of what?"

"A test of resolve, attitude, call it what you will, and to demonstrate to you that in this game nothing is as it seems. That could easily have been a real revolver and I could easily have shot you dead."

"Look below the surface, not what you see on top. Appearance, in our business, is everything. Appearing to be someone you're not. Your spy is here. You just haven't looked under the rug hard enough, so to speak," said Chico, a little kindlier.

I calmed down with a considerable effort, although the impulse to punch at least one of them remained stubbornly embedded in the back of my brain. "Right."

"We need you to find the spy, Angus," said Harpo.

"We can't put our man on it because that's what the spy will be expecting," said Chico.

"They won't be expecting you," said Harpo.

It seemed they were now engaging in a double act of alternating sentences.

"We are counting on you to find them."

"And to keep that hot head of yours under control and not shoot them."

"I wasn't planning on it," I said.

"Well, best you don't. We need to question them and get the information out of them," said Chico.

"Sooner rather than later would be best," said Harpo.

They stood up, and so did I.

"We'll be seeing you," said Chico.

"Toodle pip," said Harpo.

With that, they were gone. I sat pondering the whole thing. It was surreal, but in some way, it had impressed the urgency of the task upon me. However, in spite of that, I was no nearer to discovering who they were looking for. At least I knew there was a spy for certain. I would have been incredibly miffed to discover there wasn't one after all.

On top of which I wondered if they knew that Tomas knew, and also Angelica. Not to mention Gordon. They probably did and for reasons best known to themselves had neglected to mention it. They were dangerous people; I felt uneasy in their presence, as if I might also be guilty. I didn't like them, and part of me wished the spy business to the devil. The other part was filled with a sense of duty to King and Country, as trite as that might be.

The door opened and Angelica came in, closing it behind her.

"Are you my shadow?" I demanded. I supposed I was still ruffled by Chico and Harpo. It wasn't right to take it out on her.

"In a manner of speaking, but I can go if you really want me to."

She seemed a little hurt by my attitude, so I softened my tone.

"No, don't. Stay." I didn't want her to go; her presence seemed to calm me somehow.

She sat down beside me. "Audrey said you had some visitors."

"Yes, I did, but I can't tell you about them. They were from MI6."

"Oh Lord, I already know *that*!" she scoffed.

Something struck me about this, and without thinking, I said, "What if you really are the spy, after all this?"

The little water pistol demonstration had indeed impressed itself onto my brain. Nothing was what it seemed on the surface — that was what The Marx Brothers had implied.

"What?"

"Well, you seem very interested in everything I'm doing, and if you were the spy then you'd want to know what I'd found out. You could work to deflect my attention from you. You could have told me you were security cleared and it might not be true."

"You can check with Bentley if you want, or Audrey. She'll tell you; she knows everything."

"How do I know *anything* you are telling me is the truth?" I said suddenly and a little cruelly.

Her face fell. She looked as if she was about to cry. I had genuinely hurt her. I could tell it wasn't an act. "I … I was just interested because … because I'm interested in you!" she said, getting up.

"Angelica … wait…"

"No, if you don't trust me, then I'll leave you alone. If that's what you want."

Before I knew it, she had slammed from the room. This was new to me. I had never seen her upset or angry. She seemed surprisingly even-tempered and of a sunny disposition. I sat thinking about it for a long while. The meeting with the Marx Brothers had shaken me up more than a little, and perhaps I had become overzealous. Before I knew it, I would be suspecting everyone, even my friends, and that wouldn't do. My instincts were not that off.

It was true, Angelica could be the spy. I examined the case, for and against. If she was the spy, then surely she wouldn't make a beeline for me; she would stay as far away from me as she could. After all, the more she consorted with me, the more likely I would be to find her out. On top of which, I wasn't a particularly useful source of intelligence and she was already in a good position to access classified material. As I was still mulling it over, the door opened and Angelica returned. She was carrying a piece of paper, which she placed gently in front of me on the table.

I looked at it and saw that it was a memo granting her very high security clearance and signed by one of the top brass from Fighter Command.

"Now do you believe me?" she said quietly.

"Yes, and I'm sorry."

She picked up the paper, folded it and put it away in her pocket. "I'm never one to shy away from a fight or to give up on something I want."

"I shouldn't have doubted you. It was wrong of me."

She shook her head at this. "No, it was exactly what you should have done. I went away and thought about it. I allowed my personal feelings to override my common sense. What you said was true."

I admired her for making such an admission. I knew from my own makeup how hard it was sometimes to admit you might be wrong. "That's as may be, but I am still sorry."

"Then I accept your apology, nevertheless."

I stood up, taking her hands in mine. She did not remove them, but rather clasped my fingers softly.

"Can I buy you a drink later, to make up?"

"Yes," she nodded, smiling.

"And what personal feelings did you mean?" I picked up on what she'd said.

"I'll tell you one day, perhaps…" she said quietly.

"All right." I didn't want to argue again.

"Was that our first fight?" she asked me with a little twinkle in her eye.

"I'd hardly call it a fight."

"Then I'll try harder next time."

I laughed. "No, please don't. I like your sunny disposition; it lifts my spirits too."

"You're welcome. Anyway, I'd better get back."

"OK. See you later?"

"You can count on it."

With one last smile, she was gone. What an extraordinary woman she was, I mused, as I returned to the hut. The squadron had scrambled in my absence. It couldn't be helped. I sat and waited, hoping they would all return in one piece.

CHAPTER ELEVEN

The nights were starting to draw in, and this curtailed our operations a little. It would only mean less flying and combat time as we moved through autumn. We had flown a particularly arduous set of sorties and were clipping the edge of twilight when we landed for the final time that day. I was dog tired as always with these multiple sorties. After I had rid myself of my flying gear, I wandered over to the main building where Angelica worked. We hadn't made any plans, but it seemed as if I manoeuvred things to bump into her and she did the same. We were drawing closer together.

As I approached in the now semi-darkness, I noticed a shadowy figure near the door, so I stopped, acting on some sixth sense. At first, I wondered if it was Arjun, but the figure was hovering around one of the entrances to the main building and not the Nissen huts. Everything about them was furtive. Without warning, the figure opened the door and slipped inside. I didn't stop to think but followed instinctively, feeling that perhaps this time I was on the money.

I eased the door open and slid through the smallest gap I could. It was a corridor that I had never been in before, and I suspected it led to the comms and other rooms. At this time of night, it would only be a skeleton crew on duty. With my back to one wall, I moved slowly, pausing before each door. Some rooms had internal windows, but they were in darkness. The corridor itself was dimly lit. Up ahead and around a ninety-degree bend, I could see there was more illumination. Perhaps the intruder was close by.

Then, just as I was making my way very carefully along the corridor towards the light, another door opened and Angelica appeared from behind it.

"Angus, what are...?"

I put a finger to my lips at once to silence her. She looked at me a little anxiously. I flicked a glance up the corridor and she nodded, understanding something was up.

She took up position behind me as I knew she would. I was in no position to argue. As one we moved forward once again.

I turned back and whispered in her ear, "Is anyone else here?"

"No, just me."

This was good and bad. No surprises, but by the same token, the light was definitely something to do with the intruder. By this time, we had reached the bend in the corridor. I hesitated and my hand went down to my sidearm, only to find it wasn't there. I cursed myself inwardly. I had forgotten to put it on. That was what fatigue did to you.

Nevertheless, even unarmed I felt it was a chance I couldn't pass up. Whoever was around that corner was up to no good, and I was going to find out what exactly it was they were doing. I motioned to Angelica to wait, but she shook her head stubbornly. She was determined to be involved, no matter the danger. She was a game girl, I gave her that, but my natural instinct was to protect her — an impulse that she most certainly wasn't going to let me fulfil.

I peeked around the corner. The light appeared to be coming from one of the offices. My heart was in my mouth as I moved silently once more and into the danger zone. The door was open, and light was spilling through it. We closed the distance silently, until we were right next to the door.

There was definitely someone in there, and judging by the noises they were opening and shutting filing drawers. I debated on the best course of action. To jump straight into the room without performing some kind of reconnaissance? As I had no weapon, this might well be foolish. I elected instead to put my head around the door and hope I would not be seen. I could better decide then what to do.

A figure in a trench coat was standing in front of a desk in the office. In front of them were some papers spread out, and the desk lamp was pointed downwards on the paper to give it more light. I assumed by their appearance that the intruder was male. He was wearing a Fedora, which meant he might or might not be RAF. The trousers though looked as if they were RAF issue, and the black shoes too. In his hands, he had a small oblong silver object, which I recognised as a Minox camera. The man was taking photos of the documents.

This told me all I needed to know. This was the spy and we had caught him red-handed. I wasn't stupid enough to think he would come quietly, however. I eased back to the wall and mouthed to Angelica, "The spy."

Her eyes widened.

What was I to do? Leave him and get help, or try to apprehend him? There was only one possible approach open to me, and I took it.

Perhaps it was a little foolish, if not to say impetuous when I thrust myself into the room and exclaimed loudly, "What the hell do you think you are doing?"

I had thought perhaps to take him by surprise. Then, in that moment, I would close the gap and tackle him to the ground. Instead, events overtook me at an alarming rate. Without warning, he seized a heavy typewriter on the desk with both hands and hurled it, with a superhuman effort, in my direction.

I had no option but to dodge the very large metal object flying towards me at speed. As soon as he had thrown it, he ran for the door, barging me aside as he did so. The typewriter, which I successfully avoided, smashed into the wall and crashed to the ground, but I hadn't time to examine the damage. I recovered and rushed out of the office. Angelica was standing pointing down the corridor. I could hear the spy's footsteps receding.

I was no slouch when it came to running, and I took off at full pelt after him with Angelica in tow. He was almost at the outside door by then, when he turned around and levelled a pistol.

"Look out!" I shouted to Angelica, who was behind me. Without thinking, I threw myself in front of her to protect her. There was a loud report and the next thing I felt was something like a large wasp sting. The door banged and the spy was gone. I looked down and saw my left arm was bleeding.

"I've been shot," I told Angelica unnecessarily.

"Oh, God, God!" she cried out, reaching under her skirt. There was a ripping noise, and she produced a long piece of her petticoat. She proceeded to tie it around the wound very efficiently and tightly. "That should hold it," she said.

"Sorry," I replied as the world began to spin. "I feel rather faint." I slumped back against the wall and slid down it like a drunk.

Angelica bent down into my face. "I'm going to get help, and don't you bloody well die on me, Flying Officer Mackennelly, do you hear me?"

"You know, you're rather attractive when you say it like that," I told her through the haze.

Without warning, I felt her lips touch mine, ever so softly.

She whispered, "Don't you dare die. I can't lose you … I won't … lose you."

Then she was gone, and I lay there clutching at my wound and wondering how bad it was. I could certainly feel wetness through her makeshift bandage.

In a matter of what seemed like moments in my semi-lucid state, I felt arms lifting me up. Voices too, but I could not tell whose they were. Then I was lying on a stretcher, then in a bed. I felt the prick of a needle, after which I was completely gone.

I awoke to find myself in one of the patient rooms of the medical unit. I was lying on a hospital bed, in a room with white walls and a window. There were oxygen tanks, trays and things I didn't recognise. Doctor Vivek, in his white coat, stood looking over me.

"Ah, so you are back with us." He was smiling.

"What … what happened?" I asked him, struggling to remember.

"Well, you got shot. You were lucky. The bullet went clean through your upper arm and fortunately did not hit anything major, like an artery."

"Oh…" My memory was fuzzy, but bits and pieces were coming back to me. I glanced down at my left arm to find it heavily bandaged.

"I'm afraid we had to put you out, patch you up. It'll take a few days to heal."

"Then I…"

He put up a hand at once. "Don't even ask me about flying again until it's healed. You are officially grounded for at least a week to a week and a half at the outside."

I sighed. It was no more than I'd expected, based on my injury. "Thanks, Doctor, for saving me."

He laughed. "Don't mention it. You did me a favour, actually. I managed to put to use some of the battlefield skills I learned with my military medical training. At least we didn't have to send you to the hospital."

"I'm happy to have obliged you, then," I said weakly, attempting a joke.

"Oh, and you should thank that young lady who was with you. She did an excellent job of bandaging you up — she stopped the bleeding, pretty much. Quick thinking, actually."

"Yes, I should thank her too," I said.

"You won't have to wait long. She's been anxiously enquiring about your health for several hours."

"Ah."

"Rest up. You will stay here for a day or so, and then you'll be allowed home."

"OK."

He left me to it. There was nothing for it but to acquiesce. The memories were starting to return. I assumed the anaesthetic had clouded my thinking. The spy! That was it. I recalled a typewriter flying in my direction, the spy running out and then the bang. Then there was something else. Angelica. I smiled. The sweet touch of her lips.

I closed my eyes, went to sleep, opened them again and there she was.

"Hello," she said.

"Hello."

She smiled, but I could see her eyes were red, as if she'd been crying.

"Are you all right?" I asked her.

"I should be asking you. You reckless idiot — you could have been killed! Why, I could punch you … you…" She suddenly cut loose, perhaps visiting all of her anxiety on me.

"Well, don't punch *that* arm, if you please," I said, smiling weakly and glancing at my left one.

"Damn you, Angus Mackennelly, why did you have to make me like you so much?"

"I don't know, was it my good looks? My ace flying skills, my…"

"Oh, shut up," she laughed. "You gave me such a scare."

"The doctor said I should thank you, for the bandage…" Some wheels started to spin in my head. I remembered the ripping sound of a petticoat. "Wait a second, didn't you…?"

"You owe me a new petticoat, yes," she said. Her eyes were sparkling.

"I must thank you again for such a supreme sacrifice."

"Don't mention it." She eyed me speculatively. "What else do you remember?"

"Oh … it's all a little hazy at the moment…" I teased, not wanting to bring up the kiss.

"I see." She looked anything but convinced, so I changed the subject.

"The doctor has grounded me," I told her.

"Good, it will give you time to recover."

"Yes."

She stayed for a while, promising to return to see me later. Shortly afterwards, I was visited by Willie and Jonty.

"Hello, old chap, I hear you got into a bit of a scrape," said Jonty.

"Yes, I surprised a prowler, and they shot me."

"So, I see."

"I'm glad you're OK," said Willie, gripping my good shoulder for a moment.

"You'll have to fly without me again," I said to him. "You can lead the section. In fact, if this carries on, you should go for a promotion to Flying Officer."

Willie shook his head. "No, I don't want it."

"But then you'll have a section of your own."

"I don't want another section, Scottish. I want to stay in this one."

"Oh, well, I'm flattered."

"All for one, one for all, you know," said Willie.

"Like the Three Musketeers," said Jonty.

"Of course."

"Besides," Willie continued, "I don't need a promotion. This isn't going to be my career. When this war is over, I'm going back to New Zealand, buying a farm, and getting myself a nice woman. Just the normal stuff." He blushed.

"Just the normal stuff," I echoed, realising I was far from doing any of the 'normal stuff' myself in that regard.

"The Three Flying Musketeers," said Jonty, deep in thought. "I feel a ballad coming on."

"Please, spare the man! He's sick, he's been shot, and he doesn't need your paeans to ruin his recovery," Willie told him firmly.

"Ah, then when you're better, Skipper, you shall hear it."

"I can hardly wait," I said dryly.

"No, please wait, for as long as you possibly can," Willie implored me.

I laughed and after a little while, they left. Jonty promised to try and return with grapes, which, apparently, he felt were the thing people on their sickbed needed to have.

They had hardly closed the door when it was opened again, and Bentley strode into the room.

"Ah, Angus, glad to see you are at least alive," he said, pulling up a chair.

"Very much so, sir, yes."

He sat down and leaned forward in a conspiratorial manner. "Tell me everything that transpired. I assume this was the spy? Tell me it all."

I recounted the incident as far as I could actually recall it, and with the retelling, it became clearer. Since I wasn't sure what Angelica had said or not said, I elected to tell the truth about her being there. He didn't seem at all fazed by this.

"I see," he said, bristling when I had finished. "That's a blasted rum do, and no mistake. Yes, indeed."

"I'm afraid I didn't see who it was, sir," I told him.

"No matter, I shall be taking some action about this at least. Can't have people shooting my pilots, no, indeed. I shall be speaking to Fighter Command about making this base more secure. I shall be questioning everyone, without, of course, telling them about the spy — in case someone has seen something. This is serious, very serious. We are going to catch that blighter and no mistake."

"Yes, sir." I didn't share his enthusiasm at all but in my present state, I wasn't in a position to investigate things further either.

"Right then," he said. "No flying until the doctor says so."

"Sir."

With that, he stood up and left the room. I was starting to feel sleepy, but I still had one final visitor. It was Tomas.

"Bloody hell, Scottish. I mean, come on! You are being shot at by the spy? I mean, come on!" he said as soon as he entered the room.

I told him what had happened, and he was suitably angry. He promised to floor the man who had done this to me and swore vengeance. I then had to make him promise not to kill the spy all over again.

"Ah, I won't kill, no. But if his nose does break, well…" He shrugged.

I laughed. Tomas had a way with words. We talked a while longer and conjectured a little more on who it might have been. He left, vowing to avenge me for the wrong the spy had done me. I had to chuckle to myself. He could be quite melodramatic.

I finally slept, after all my various visitors, until supper time. I awoke once more to find Angelica sitting by my bed with my hand in her hand. When she saw my eyes open, she made as if to withdraw it. I tightened my fingers around it and stopped her.

"You're awake."

"Yes."

I felt her fingers relax in my clasp.

"Shouldn't you be going home for dinner or something?" I asked her.

"I shall go presently. I just wanted to check up on you."

"Thanks."

We said nothing for a while, just enjoying each other's company.

"Bentley came to see me," I ventured at length.

"Yes, there is going to be a fence built around the airfield," she said.

"Oh."

"Bentley wants to reduce the chances of people coming onto the airbase who shouldn't."

I nodded. "Assuming it was someone who shouldn't be there," I said.

We both knew that if it was indeed an inside job, as we suspected, then fences were not going to keep them out.

"He's also called a meeting of all the staff here at the squadron."

"Oh?"

"Yes, Audrey says it's to ask if anyone knows anything about the shooting."

"Ah!" I thought for a moment. "But who did people think it was? Do they know about the spy?"

"No, Bentley is going to say he believes it was someone trying to steal a typewriter. That's the story we have to stick to."

I laughed. "Really? And they swallowed it?"

"Yes, apparently they have."

"I can't imagine anyone is going to own up, nevertheless."

"No." She shook her head. "You'll be going back to Amberly, I suppose, in a day or two."

"Yes, the doctor said."

"I could come and visit you there," she offered in a tentative way.

I was horrified at the suggestion. Keeping her and Barbara away from each other was of paramount importance. I had no idea what would happen if they did meet, and I didn't want to find out. "On the other hand, perhaps you shouldn't. I'll be OK, don't worry about me," I replied, feeling terrible for putting her off like that.

"Oh … I see." She looked a little hurt, as if I had rebuffed her.

"Look, I don't want to sound awful about this, but it's mainly us chaps there, and I'm not sure how exactly it would go down if I had a lady friend in my room."

This was utterly cowardly dissembling on my part, since I'd had Barbara in my room on many occasions of late. Had I not been Barbara's cicisbeo, I was sure she wouldn't have cared two hoots who I brought to the manor.

"Oh, I see, yes." Angelica nodded, digesting this information.

"Ordinarily I'd love to have you, but…" I trailed off, hoping I had convinced her.

"No, all right." She smiled reassuringly, though there was a hint of something else, as if she knew more than she was letting on. Did she? I shuddered to think.

She said no more, and I wondered what Audrey had been saying to her and if that was some kind of test. If so, I had very likely failed it, I thought. It was becoming incredibly awkward, as I was now trapped in a bed of my own making. I needed to put my own house in order. Then I winced at the pain in my shoulder and immediately shelved the idea of doing so until perhaps I felt better.

We stayed together, holding hands for quite some time. It felt comfortable, nice. Nothing was said, but in a way, everything was said in those wordless moments. I knew sometime soon, things would have to come to a head with her, and with Barbara. I wasn't looking forward to it. I suppose I hoped fate would supply the solution, even though I was doubtful that it would.

Angelica visited me more than once a day while I remained in the medical unit. After two days, the doctor declared me fit to go home.

"You can get some bed rest for at least two more days, then you can get about. We'll see about when you might be able to start flying at the end of a week. I warn you, it might be a few days longer. I'm not letting you up there again until I'm sure it's healed, so don't go doing anything stupid."

"Stupid like what?" I enquired with interest.

"Well, don't go and play cricket like one young idiot who broke his arm. Took another six weeks to heal because of it!"

I assured Doctor Vivek I wasn't about to take to the cricket field, and in fact, I felt like nothing less than indulging in such a pastime at present. Angelica was there to see me off with Gordon.

"Take care of yourself," she said, smiling.

"As soon as I'm allowed up, I'll come and see you."

"I'd like that." She touched my cheek briefly. Then she watched us drive away.

"She saved your life, the way I hear it," said Gordon quietly as we drove back to Amberly.

"Yes, I believe she did."

"And she's been there every day to see you, and before that too."

"Where exactly is this leading, Fred?" I demanded, expecting some kind of homily was about to ensue.

"I should be asking you the same question, sir. About your intentions towards that young miss who is besotted with you."

I laughed. "You make it sound as if I'm the devil."

"Not precisely the devil, no, sir. It's just, well, you will rarely find such devotion."

"I'm not an object of worship and I don't want to be, Fred."

"I don't mean it that way, sir. I'm talking about love. Unconditional love isn't something you find every day. I can assure you of that."

"Oh."

I had not really experienced love as he described it, and so I didn't know how to recognise it. Perhaps that was what was missing?

"When love hits you, sir, you will know it. It punches you in the guts. You suddenly realise you could never be without that person, sir. You want to be with them every moment you can get. You miss them like the devil when you're not. And you feel it. Right here." He thumped his heart lightly. It was almost as if he knew I had been pondering the question.

"Right, thank you, Fred."

He inclined his head. Having given his smattering of advice, he fell silent for a few moments. "On another matter, sir."

"Yes?"

"Lady Amberly, when she heard you were ill, she wanted to come down straight away to care for you."

"Did she?"

"I took the liberty of informing her that the doctor had ordered you were to have no visitors who were not from your squadron on official business."

I couldn't help chuckling at this. "Did you indeed?"

"Yes, sir, it seemed for the best."

"By Jove, yes, thank you, Fred."

"You are welcome, sir."

When I arrived at Amberly Manor, I went up to my room to lie down, as the doctor had ordered. Not long afterwards, the door opened, and Barbara entered, carrying a tray.

"What are you doing?" I asked her.

"I'm taking care of my sick man."

"You are?"

"Yes." She sat down on the bed and placed the tray on the bedside table. She picked up a bowl of soup and a spoon.

"What's that?"

"It's a very nutritious broth I had the cook prepare for you. Now, open wide."

"You know I'm perfectly capable of feeding myself," I objected.

"I know, but I want to take care of you. Now, be a good boy and open wide. If you are a good boy and eat your dinner, then other good things will ensue."

I did not ask what these other good things were. I could imagine them quite plainly without explanation.

She sat there and gently spooned soup into my mouth, wiping my chin with a napkin if I dribbled it a little.

"Shouldn't you be wearing a nurse's uniform?" I enquired, taking in her fitted red striped satin housecoat, tied at the waist.

"This *is* my nurse's uniform. I'm a special kind of nurse."

"And what kind of nurse is that?"

"One who takes care of *all* your needs."

"What needs are those?"

"Finish your soup and I'll show you."

As I continued to imbibe the nourishing broth, she shot me a speculative glance.

"Am I your only nurse?" she asked me suddenly.

This caught me a little unawares. "Why on earth would you say that?" I prevaricated, wondering what she'd heard. I had not thought until now of the maids and other servants who might have seen me and Angelica together.

"Oh," she said lightly. "People talk, you know."

I accepted another mouthful and pondered a response. This was hardly the moment for such a discussion. She smiled faintly, fed me the last of the soup and laid the bowl aside. She then leaned forward, and our lips touched.

"I can get quite jealous, you know, about what's mine," she whispered, kissing me.

Before I was lost in her kiss, a fleeting thought passed through my mind. Was this some kind of warning? Did she indeed know about Angelica? I let it go as her fingers ruffled my hair, and the kiss deepened into something far more passionate.

Barbara stuck to my side like glue for two days, day and night. She brought me food and ministered to me in every way she could. She changed my dressing and tended to me in the bath. She read to me and entertained me in her usual style.

"You know," she said, as she soaped me down in a hot bath, "this is how I imagined a life together should be. Not like it is with John. I feel easy with you, relaxed in your company. I like taking care of you."

"Yes," I said, not knowing how to answer her.

For all Gordon had spoken of devotion, this was extraordinary devotion indeed. I was grateful and I enjoyed her company, all of it. Yet, despite that, I was beginning to realise the feelings I had for her were perhaps not love after all. There was an emotional attachment for sure, but not as Gordon had described it. Was it because I now had something to compare it to? Angelica? If I examined my feelings there, I could feel the spark of something, but I was afraid it was all just in the chase. I had trapped myself between them, and I didn't know how to move forward in either direction.

The doctor had said I was allowed out once I'd had my rest, and to Barbara's disappointment I went out alone. Although it was not precisely alone. It was with Angelica.

"Where are you going?" Barbara would ask me.

I would simply reply, "I am going out for a while. I need time to heal."

I could see the hurt in her eyes, but there was no helping it.

"You know that if we are seen too much abroad in each other's company, tongues will start to wag," I also pointed out. "You surely don't want *that*."

"I don't care what people think," she would reply.

"But you do, and you will. You are still Lady of the Manor, after all."

"You begin to sound just like John."

"You are still married to him."

She sighed. "Fine, go on, enjoy yourself without me."

Her possessiveness started to grate, just a little. It didn't occur to me then that it was simply because I would not give her what she wanted: my undying devotion and love. The more I pulled away, the more she tried to pull me back.

Angelica was different, easy, and not at all possessive. She found ways to be with me without making it appear as if she was trying to suffocate me. It was an unfair comparison and I knew it, but I made it just the same, looking for a way out of the mess I had created.

Not long after I was allowed out, Bentley called a meeting in one of the aircraft hangars. All of the squadron was assembled as he took to a makeshift podium. I was standing with Willie, Jonty and, naturally, Angelica.

"I've called you here today," the squadron leader said, "because as I'm sure you are aware, Flying Officer Mackennelly was shot in the arm while surprising an intruder. A thief trying to steal our equipment. This is a shocking turn of events, shocking!" He paused for effect, looking around and stopping to stare at one or two people in particular. "I won't have these kinds of goings-on on my airbase and in my squadron. That's one reason why you can see a fence being erected around the airfield."

There was silence still. Bentley seemed in a no-nonsense mood.

"Now, if any one of you knows anything about this incident or any other incident to do with incursions into this airfield, then I am asking you to come forward and tell me, in confidence."

There was a shuffling of feet at this, and it reminded me of a group of schoolchildren called up before the beak for some misdemeanour or other. This behaviour seemed to annoy him greatly, and he suddenly became very angry indeed.

"Let me tell you this!" he thundered. "I will be having this properly and fully investigated. If I find any one of you, any one of you at all has been withholding information, then I will throw the bloody book at you."

I could see a few people quailing at his tone. Having been on the receiving end of it many times before, I wasn't fazed at all. At least for once I wasn't under the microscope.

"Let me be clear: if there's something on your conscience, then speak now or forever hold your peace. Understood?"

There was silence.

"I said *is that understood?*" he roared.

"Yes, sir!" said the assembled parties in unison.

"Very well, then bear that in mind. No stone whatsoever will be left unturned. So, if you've seen anything untoward, heard anything, or know anything, then come and see me right away."

He glared at everyone one more time before saying, "Dismissed." He strode over to me, and my companions melted away.

"Turncoats!" I called after them; they laughed and walked faster.

I snapped a crisp salute as Bentley approached.

"Angus, how are you faring?"

"I'm not too bad, sir. Hopefully, I'll be fit to fly soon."

"Yes, well, you're not going up until the doc clears you for take-off, so to speak. I don't want you airborne until you are fully fit, and that's an order."

"Sir."

"Anyway, that little speech should put the fear of God into the lot of them. Let's see what transpires."

He seemed rather pleased with himself. I wondered if it had all been an act — feigned anger and so forth.

"Yes, sir," I said.

"Take care of yourself, and as soon as you can get on the case regarding you-know-what, let me know." He put a hand briefly on my shoulder, we saluted and then he marched off.

The others were waiting outside when I left the hangar.

"What did old Bentley have to say, then?" Jonty asked me.

"Just a pep talk, that's all, and I'm not allowed up without doctor's orders."

"For good reason," said Angelica.

"She's right. Me and Jonty are holding the fort with Tomas, never fear," said Willie.

"I know. I'm grateful."

"Shall we get a drink?" Jonty suggested.

"You should be so lucky. We are still on duty, old sport. Maybe later," Willie replied.

"I can go with you, though." Angelica looked at me meaningfully.

"For sure, why not?"

"Might see you later then," Jonty said, before departing with Willie back to the hut. I watched them go wistfully, wishing I was with them. Yet here I was with Angelica, and that felt equally good.

We stayed at the pub for a while, talking and laughing. Willie and Jonty did not arrive after all, and I assumed they were delayed or wanted to leave us alone.

I was taking it easy on the drinks, as I always did. Then, out of the blue, Barbara appeared just as I was about to sup my pint. I almost choked on it as she sat down.

"Hello, stranger," she said to me, full of affability.

Angelica looked at her curiously. I was now in a position where I had to make introductions, and I did so. In the meantime, my mind was racing back to that conversation while Barbara fed me the soup. This was no coincidence, I was sure of it, and my worst fears of the two of them meeting had been realised.

"Lady Amberly, this is Corporal Angelica Kensley. Lady Amberly owns Amberly Manor, where our lodgings are."

"No, really? Owns Amberly Manor? I'd never have guessed."

I looked at Angelica sharply. The cutting tone was something I'd not heard from her before.

Barbara smiled and seemingly ignored it. "I was bored at home and wanted to go out. I don't usually come to the public house, but then I saw you two and thought I would come in after all and say hello."

She knew how to play a part, I gave her that. She had evidently come looking for me. Nobody would suspect we had been intimate, or would they? I glanced at Angelica, but she had become the soul of congeniality. It seemed Barbara wasn't just passing through and so I played the good host.

"Yes, well, would you like a drink?"

"Gin and tonic, please."

I disappeared to obtain it, full of apprehension as to what might transpire in my absence. The bartender took rather a long time to fulfil my order but as it turned out, nothing of consequence had occurred. Barbara and Angelica were giving every appearance of chatting amicably when I returned with the round. I handed the G and T to Barbara, who took it demurely and continued talking to Angelica.

"So, you're new at Banley, are you?" Barbara was asking Angelica.

"Yes, that's right."

"And before you joined the Mavericks?"

"I was working for Fighter Command."

"I'm surprised," Barbara replied with a tinge of acidity. "I would not have thought they would take someone so young for such an important position. Experience counts for a lot." Barbara raised an eyebrow and there was no missing the undertone of her remark.

"Oh, I'm sure. But then they must have recognised my obvious talents." Angelica furnished her with a fulsome smile.

"Indeed. And a corporal already, I see."

"Yes, I've worked hard for what I've got. Some of us have to."

Barbara did not respond to this jibe but sipped her drink, surveying Angelica coolly, no doubt dreaming up her next exchange. I winced inwardly.

Although an observer might be fooled into thinking they were on friendly terms, you could cut the atmosphere with a knife. There were further such brittle exchanges between them couched in what one could only describe as fake smiles. It became an ordeal from which I prayed, in a most craven fashion, to be released.

Barbara then asked me about my injury and how things were going down at the squadron, as if she knew nothing about it. I answered her questions, but was relieved when eventually she said, "Ah well, look at the time! I must be getting home. I'm a little tired, almost ready for *bed*, in fact."

She pointedly made this remark to me before saying goodbye. Angelica didn't miss it, I was sure.

"She seems nice," said Angelica blandly, the ice now gone from her voice.

I did not like to ask her what they talked about, although I assumed they had not crossed any lines.

My conscience, however, got the better of me. I turned to Angelica and said, "Look, I, erm, perhaps owe you an explanation about…"

Her finger came up to my lips and shushed me. "You don't owe me anything, and please … please don't tell me. I can guess anyway. I'm not a fool. It wasn't by chance she came here. I don't need to know."

I suddenly didn't want to be denied the opportunity to come clean and tried again. "But I…"

"No, Angus, don't, because if you do then I'll be forced to acknowledge Daddy was right."

"Wait, what?" I was momentarily diverted by this statement, which came as something of a *non sequitur* to me, though it evidently made sense to her.

"Yes, Daddy said I shouldn't get mixed up with those pilot wallahs, as he calls you. He said that you were profligate liars, philanderers and charlatans who would sooner take a lady's … you know … than look at her."

"Well … I would hardly…"

She continued, cutting me off. "And he made me promise. He made me promise never to fall in love with one of them." Tears started from her eyes. "And I did promise, and now … I've gone and broken that promise and…" She stopped and sniffed, looking at me defiantly.

"Hang on, what did you just say?" I was a little bemused and wanted to know if I had heard right.

"I said that he said you were profligate…"

"No." It was my turn to interrupt. "After all the insults to my fellow pilots, you said something else…"

She was still evasive, perhaps having said more than she wanted to. "I said, I'd promised not to fall in love."

"And then you said…" I persisted.

"Oh, Angus, you are such a damn idiot!" She started to cry and ran from the room.

I followed her outside and saw her standing on the pavement with her head down, her shoulders shaking. I went up to her and put my hands gently on them.

"You're so stupid, you can't even see what's in front of you! You can't even see when somebody likes you…" she said, choking on sobs.

"Angelica, Angelica." My eyes were perhaps twinkling a little. After all, what man wouldn't want to hear that a woman was in love with him?

"You, you asinine idiot, you fool, you…"

I cut her short by the simple expedient of placing my lips on hers. She melted at once into my arms and into my kiss. I had kissed many women in my time, but this was different. It was explosive. It was as if fireworks were going off in my head and my heart was suddenly all aflutter. Her arms went around my neck and she clung to me, kissing me back harder. It seemed to go on for an age and for no time at all. All at once, she broke off, with both of us gasping a little. Emotions were starting to well up inside me that I had never felt before.

"Now do you understand?" she asked me. She was smiling.

I wiped the tears from her cheeks. She looked so beautiful, too, standing there like that. "Yes, yes, I do."

My mind was a whirl. This woman was in love with me. Did I love her, though? I was certainly not ready to say so. I didn't want to tell her something that wasn't true.

She waited a little longer and then a playful smirk played around her lips. "You can kiss me again if you want to, you profligate philanderer."

I chuckled at this, and there was no need to be asked twice. The kiss was just as incredible as the first, if not better. So different to anything I'd felt before. So different to Barbara, even. At least I knew one thing: it wasn't about the chase. If anything, now I had kissed her, I wanted her more.

She was nuzzling my lips, kissing my face. "You have no idea, do you, how much my lips have burned for this moment? But I don't just want you to kiss me, I want you to know that. I want you to be as profligate as possible with me in every way you can," she whispered.

It was a clear invitation. I was disconcerted. I had no idea she was so forward and not half as bashful as I'd thought. I also felt torn, between wanting her desperately and not wanting to take advantage. Her next words blew that right out of the water.

"I don't care if you don't love me," she stated baldly. "I want you, and I want you in every way, and I'm *going* to have you. I don't care what you are to Barbara, and I don't want to know. I want you, Angus. *I* want *you*."

Her lips were pursed in defiance. I was speechless, but trying not to laugh because the whole thing suddenly struck me as funny. Funny because of how I had deluded myself about her when the answer was staring me in the face. She'd given me an open invitation, an insistent one, even.

"I'm going now. I'll see you later." With that, she turned on her heel and left me standing.

"Wait, don't you want me to … walk … you … home?"

Clearly not, from the determined set of her shoulders and the purpose in her walk. She didn't lodge far from the pub in any case, so I felt she would be perfectly safe. I watched her go, bewildered and flustered. The words she had spoken echoed in my mind: *I want you, in every way, and I'm going to have you.*

I shook my head in wonder. What was going to happen? How was she planning to accomplish this feat? I had no doubt she was serious and apparently, I had very little say in it. With all this and more churning through my mind, I made my way back to the pub to find the ineffable Gordon and get off home.

I did not know what reception I would receive when I returned to Amberly Manor, but Gordon left me in no doubt that Barbara was going to have it out with me. He knocked on my door as I readied myself for bed.

"Her Ladyship has requested you attend her in her boudoir, sir," he said.

"Requested?"

"She summoned you, but I wanted to make it sound more reasonable." He smiled.

"Right, well…"

"Her mood is a little unpredictable, I fear."

"Yes, well, I suppose I had better accede to her request."

"I'd certainly advise it, sir."

I had not apprised Gordon of the events of the evening, but I most probably would not have to. He doubtless already knew some of it, if not most of it.

I entered Barbara's room, and she was standing looking out of her window into the darkness beyond.

"Barbara," I said.

"Do you love her?" she asked me without turning around.

There was nothing for it but to be honest. The game was truly up.

"I can't tell you," I replied truthfully.

"Or won't tell me…"

"No, I can't because I don't know. That's the truth."

She still didn't move. There was stiffness in her frame. She was full of tension. "And does she love you?"

"She told me so tonight, yes. I did not know before." There was little point in lying.

"I see. Then that makes two of us, doesn't it?" She turned to face me and walked towards me. She was wearing next to nothing, as usual, and even so, in spite of all that had happened, I couldn't help but be drawn to her. "And what about me, do you love *me*?" She was standing in front of me now. I could feel her closeness.

"I don't know. I have feelings for you, Barbara, but what use are those? You are a married woman. I don't know if it's love or not, because I've never really been in love."

Tears began to roll down her cheeks. Her arms came up and around my shoulders. I didn't, couldn't, resist.

"Don't leave me, Angus, don't desert me. I need you. I … I love you … even if you don't love me. Please, just not … not yet … at least… I can't bear it … please."

I couldn't resist *that*. I didn't know how to. I pulled her close and stroked her hair, and then I kissed her.

"Love me, please, love me, just for a little bit longer," she said softly, and so I took her to bed.

I did not want to hurt her, and yet I was hurting her by continuing it. Something in the back of my mind, a small insistent voice, told me I could not have my cake and eat it too. Somewhere along the line, there would be a reckoning.

CHAPTER TWELVE

While I lived with my dilemma between two women and waited for clearance from the doctor, events overtook me in other ways. The spy, who had shot me, was also uppermost in my mind. I was now more determined than ever to find him and have him put away. It had suddenly become rather personal.

Not many days after the incident with the spy, I was summoned to Bentley's office.

Gordon came to collect me from the manor. "Sir, Bentley's orders, I'm to take you to him," he said almost apologetically.

"Oh God, what has Jonty done this time?" I asked, rolling my eyes.

"Nothing, as far as I know, sir."

"Well, I haven't done anything, either. At least, nothing I know of."

"No, sir."

As we drove to the airfield, another thought hit me. "It's not about Amberly's wife, do you think?"

Gordon shook his head. "No, I don't think so, sir."

I decided to probe further, since the whole thing consumed me at times. "I know what you must think of me, carrying on with two women…"

"I don't think anything, sir. Well … nothing detrimental."

I nevertheless felt it was incumbent upon me to explain my actions. "She won't let me go, Fred. Barbara won't let me go. I can't hurt her by rejecting her, and I'm hurting her and also Angelica by not doing so."

He flicked me a smile. "It's a conundrum, for sure. But look at it this way, sir. Each of them knows of the other, but neither has rejected you."

"Well, I suppose not, but…"

"Time, sir. Time will sort the wheat from the chaff."

"So, you are saying I do nothing?"

"I am saying, sir, that sometimes things have to run their course. Whatever that course is."

I fell silent. More homespun wisdom from Gordon that didn't really make me feel better about myself. I could not rue the day I had met either of them, though. In the end, Gordon was right. I would have to choose, or they would. Or I could end up dying, up there in the blue yonder. Who knew?

"Sometimes, we think too much," Gordon cut into my thoughts.

"Yes."

We arrived at the airfield, and Audrey was visibly hovering about, no doubt waiting for me. I thanked Gordon for the ride and jumped down from the jeep.

"What does Bentley want this time?" I asked Audrey as we hurried towards the main building.

"I think it's good news, sir," she said.

"Oh, well, that makes a change, I suppose."

She said nothing more, and I sensed a hint of disapproval in her manner. I chose to ignore it.

Very shortly I was standing on the carpet in front of the CO, who greeted me quite jovially.

"Ah, Angus, Angus, Angus. Sit down, my boy, sit down."

Unused to this kind of reception, I took a seat with all my senses attuned for what I felt must be a catch that would very shortly reveal itself.

I would be obliged to wait, as Bentley was in no hurry to disclose what was on his mind. A few long moments passed while he performed the ritual of scraping, tapping, filling and lighting. Then the room filled with acrid smoke while he puffed away ruminatively, as if he was perfectly at ease with the world. Just as my patience and tolerance for his pipe smoke were wearing thin, he elected to reveal the reason for my summons.

"We've got him," he said, smiling broadly.

"Got who, sir?" I said, perplexed.

"Got who? Only the spy, Angus! We've got the bloody spy!"

"Pardon?"

He puffed all the more on his pipe before answering. The room now lay under a pall of smoke, rather like the remnants of a battlefield. "We've caught him and he's behind bars, old chap!"

"Really? How? When?" I could hardly imagine how they had apprehended the spy quite so easily, but it seemed to be the case.

"Yes, indeed. We received a tip-off, from MI6 as it were. Apparently, they had somehow located the source of the radio transmissions. MPs were despatched to an address forthwith, and Bob's your uncle. Job done!"

"I see, and where is the spy now?" I asked him.

"Oh, locked up safe and sound, don't you worry about that."

"Can I at least see them, what they look like?"

"If you want to, but I can't imagine why you would. It's all right and tight, and all of that." He seemed content to let the business pass.

"Well, can you at least tell me who it was? Was it one of the pilots?"

"Apparently no, it wasn't anyone like that. I believe it was a cleaner or some such. Not military personnel at all."

"Right."

This struck me as odd. It seemed to clash with what the Marx Brothers had divulged. They'd insisted it was definitely someone in the squadron.

"Anyway," Bentley went on, harrumphing a little at my lack of enthusiasm for the news, "the show's over, as far as you are concerned. Mission accomplished. You can stand down. There'll be something in this for you, mark you."

"But I didn't really do anything."

"You were in the right place at the right time. You took a bullet. That's all that matters. So, you'll take whatever the RAF chooses to reward you with and take it with good grace."

"Yes, sir, of course," I said, seeing his jovial mood was fading.

"I'd have thought you would be pleased at least, that we've caught an enemy of the King." His tone was somewhat admonishing.

"Yes, I am, sir. It's great news. I was just a little surprised, that's all."

"Yes, hmm, well, jolly good. Anyway, how's that arm of yours?"

"Feeling much better, I think."

"Good. When the doctor clears you for flying, then you get back on the job."

"Yes, sir."

"Excellent." He turned his attention to the paperwork on his desk. "That will be all."

"Sir."

I stood up, saluted and left the room. As expected, Audrey followed. I turned to face her.

"Look, if you are going to give me a lecture about my morals, then spare me," I said.

She seemed a little nonplussed. "I certainly wasn't, sir. No, Angelica knows her own mind. It's not for me to censure either of you."

"Oh, oh right. Well then, what is it?"

"Don't be too hard on Bentley. He's been worrying about the spy for weeks. It's a great relief to him."

"No doubt."

"You don't seem convinced."

"It seems too easy, that's all," I said. She had evidently known about the spy when she was not supposed to. I didn't point this out but sighed inwardly. Angelica had probably told her.

I left her and went to see Doctor Vivek. The visit was disappointing, as he examined my wound and said I'd need a few more days. I was itching to get back in the air, accepting that I could put the spying business behind me. When I came out of the medical unit, Audrey was waiting for me once again.

"Don't tell me, Bentley wants to see me again."

"No, sir, not Bentley. The two gentlemen."

"Ah."

In short order, I found myself in the room with the Marx Brothers, sitting once more at the same desk. I took a seat opposite.

"What can I do for you gentlemen?" I asked them, opening the bidding. "Surely nothing, now the mission is accomplished."

"Yes, indeed," said Chico.

"Except that it isn't," said Harpo.

"Isn't what?"

"It hasn't been accomplished at all," said Chico.

I looked at them, rather stunned. These two were always talking in riddles. "What exactly do you mean? Apparently, the spy is sitting in a cell at this very moment, awaiting his fate. Bentley told me so himself."

"Yes, I'm sure he did," said Harpo.

Chico stood up and paced the room. Then he leaned against the wall, took a cigarette packet from his pocket and lit one up. "Didn't we tell you that not everything is as it seems?" he said lightly.

"Yes, but…"

"The spy isn't a spy."

"Pardon?"

They were making no sense.

"Rather," amended Chico, "he is a spy, but he works for us."

"I'm sorry … he … does what? He works for you?" I could hardly believe my ears.

"Yes." Chico casually finished his cigarette before stamping it out on the floor. He returned to his seat. "He is one of ours."

"But … he was photographing secret documents, and he shot me, for God's sake!"

"Yes, I'm afraid we told him to."

I stood up then, pardonably annoyed. "*You* told him to *shoot* me? I could have been killed!" I was not at all amused to hear this admission.

"We told him to wing you, if he had to. He's an excellent shot."

"Well, I'll be…" It was my turn to pace the room. Just when I thought everything was plain as a pikestaff, these two jokers came along and turned it all upside down. "So, you're telling me you instructed one of your spies to come and spy on our squadron, and then shoot me in the arm?"

"Precisely!" said Harpo, smiling faintly.

"Whatever for? What possible reason could you have for doing so?"

"Because, old man," said Chico, "the real spy was going to ground. You were obviously getting too close. We had to do something to make them think they were in the clear."

"Hang on, wait ... what?" I sat down, trying to assimilate this information.

"The real spy is still out there, Flying Officer Mackennelly, and we need to catch him. So, we set up a decoy. We had to make it look convincing, naturally. Now Bentley and everyone is convinced that the spy has been caught, the real spy can continue his work." Harpo spoke slowly, as if explaining himself to a five-year-old.

"But how did ... I mean, that whole thing about me discovering him in the act, that was arranged too?"

"Of course," said Chico. "He simply waited for the opportunity to lure you in."

"Lure me in! For God's sake, I mean, whose side are you on? I still got shot!"

"Yes, that's an unfortunate risk we had to take."

"A risk *you* ... had ... to ... take?" I was almost rendered speechless by this callous admission. "Well, I'm so glad you are happy to take such risks on my behalf."

"Don't mention it, old boy," said Harpo, unmoved by my sarcasm.

"And you actually want them to keep on spying? The real spy?"

"Of course we want them to keep spying — how else can we catch them, or rather how else can *you* catch them?"

I digested this snippet that he handed out so casually. "Me?"

"Yes, you."

"But Bentley stood me down," I objected.

"He may have, but we are standing you up!"

"That's all very well, but I don't work for you, I work for Bentley." I was feeling rather recalcitrant now. This pair's actions had resulted in me being shot, and I wasn't enamoured of it in the least.

Harpo was unperturbed. "You work for King and Country, just as we do. You might work for the Royal Air Force, but you are also working for us, until we say otherwise."

He removed a piece of paper from his pocket and placed it in front of me. I looked at the standing orders signed by Fighter Command. There was no arguing with *that*.

"You will find the spy. Bentley is not to know. We know you've accomplices, and that's fine — just get the spy, that's all we are asking."

"And then it's all over? I can go back to just being a pilot?"

"Of course," said Chico in a way that didn't make me entirely believe him.

"Why *did* you choose me? Because I get the distinct impression that it wasn't Bentley's idea after all."

Chico laughed and said to Harpo, "He catches on quickly, doesn't he?"

I didn't rise to the bait but waited for him to explain, which he did.

"In spite of your dreadful womanising ways, and your entirely blemished record, you've nevertheless got the skills we were looking for."

I ignored this jibe and said, "Which are?"

"You are tenacious, you buck authority, you watch people's backs. You're a smart thinker in the air, with quick reactions. Oh yes, we've enquired, discreetly."

"Oh, I see." I was quite surprised by this somewhat complimentary assessment.

"In short," said Harpo, "you are a bit of a maverick yourself. We need someone who isn't hidebound, who will think outside the usual, shall we say, constraints."

"And that's you," Chico put in.

"Oh, right then." I decided to ask them something else before they left. It was something I had been pondering for a while. "And is Corporal Kensley … I mean … does she have as high clearance as she says she does?"

"She has access to information that would make your hair stand on end."

This didn't mollify me at all. "Is she working for you?"

"No, she isn't, more's the pity, but we know all about the people who can see the country's most important secrets."

"So, she's off limits?" I wanted to be sure and hoped the answer wasn't in the affirmative. I was particularly glad she wasn't actually a spy herself.

"Not at all. The only thing off limits is what she knows."

"Right."

Harpo cut in, "You need not worry about that particular ladybird. We have no concern about her knowing anything at all."

"I am much obliged to you." I couldn't help the acid retort. It didn't help; they simply ignored it.

"Find the spy, there's a good chap. He won't suspect a thing now."

"What will happen to your … man … in prison?"

"Oh, don't worry about him. We'll take him for questioning, as it were, and all of the associated documentation. Then he'll go on to other operational duties, where he's needed."

"Of course." I should have expected they would tidy up their own mess.

"Just a word of advice, old bean. Concentrate on the spy and don't concern yourself with things that don't concern you," said Chico, giving me a friendly smile. There was menace behind his words, however.

"I have no intention of doing so," I informed him.

"Good, that's the ticket."

The two of them stood up and I did likewise.

"Good luck, old chap," said Harpo, offering me his hand.

I shook it, and Chico's too. It was completely outlandish. Totally peculiar. I felt as if I was entering a completely different reality every time I met with them. I heartily wished them to the devil as I watched them leave. One thing I was right about. It had been far too easy catching the so-called spy. My instinct had been correct.

No sooner had they left than the door opened, and Angelica entered.

"Hello," she said with a smile.

"Hello."

"Those agents, what did they want?"

For some unaccountable reason, this annoyed me. How she knew they were here and had come to see me, was probably not that much of a puzzle. I was rattled by the meeting with them, and I took it out on her. "I'm sure you know already," I retorted. "You seem to be apprised of everything to do with this. Did you also know that the spy was a fake?"

"What? No, of course not…" She looked surprised by my tone, and I softened it at once.

"I'm sorry, I'm a little discomposed by events."

"Tell me?"

I furnished her with a summary of what I had been told, and what was now my mission.

"Oh, I see," she said at length. "I promise you, I didn't know anything about this at all."

"Right. I'm sorry for being a little on edge."

"That's what these people do," she said. "Try gaining top-secret clearance. They ask you everything, intimate … things."

I took her by the shoulders. "Will you still help me? To find the spy, I mean?"

"Of course. You know I will," she said at once. "Will you still … kiss me?"

"Of course. You know I will."

She smiled. I held her in a long, passionate embrace. Each time I kissed her, and it was becoming more often, desire burned within me. There was also something more, a fluttering in my stomach, and a feeling in my heart as if it might burst.

"I can't wait much longer," she whispered.

"For what?"

"To have you, Angus. I want you … so much… I've … got to… I've got to … go…"

She was blushing prettily as she turned and walked away. I knew what she was asking, but I did not know how to arrange it. I was also in two minds about it. Barbara was one thing, a married woman, but Angelica was different. She was young and single, and I couldn't help feeling she shouldn't be quite so forward. I wasn't sure how to deal with it and at the same time, I wanted her just as much.

It turned out that in the end, I didn't have to arrange anything. Angelica proved once again how enterprising and single-minded she was. Not long after we had spoken, she came to find me as I was waiting for Tomas to return from a sortie.

"I'm glad I've found you," she said, coming up to me as I leant against the hut.

"Did you lose me?"

She laughed. "Not yet … shall we walk?"

"All right."

She wanted us to be out of earshot, I could tell. When we were a fair distance from the hut and could not be overheard, she stopped and turned to face me. "I wanted to tell you that I've got some leave, forty-eight hours, starting tonight."

Being dense sometimes, I wondered why she'd come to tell me. Perhaps she didn't want me to worry about where she had gone. "Oh, are you going to go home?"

She looked at me strangely. "Good Lord, no!"

"What are you going to do then?"

She shook her head in resignation. "Really, for a Flying Officer you don't catch on very fast, do you?"

I was missing something obvious, and I was trying to figure out what when she laughed.

"Honestly! Men! I'm going to find somewhere nice to stay, and you are going to take me."

I stared at her, dumbfounded. "What? I mean, of course, I would … but I haven't got any leave."

Her eyes danced. "You're wrong there." She waved a forty-eight-hour pass with my name on it in front of me, signed by Bentley himself.

"However did you wangle that?"

"It pays to be the friend of his adjutant. Audrey's a darling. She arranged it. Besides, he was happy to, since you are still grounded. It was the perfect time."

I caught her hands in mine and held them. "Remind me to thank her."

"No need."

Now I was faced with a fait accompli, the stark reality of what she was asking was borne in on me. She saw it in my face and frowned.

"What's the matter?" she asked at once.

"I..."

"Are you shocked, is that it? Am I supposed to be a good girl?" she chided me gently, picking up on my thoughts as if I was an open book.

"I am a little taken aback, if I'm honest," I admitted.

"I told you, I wanted you," she said quietly.

"Yes, I know."

"Don't you want me?"

"I do but..."

"But your scruples won't allow it? Is that it?"

I sighed. This was incredibly difficult, and I was sure I wasn't the only one struck by the hypocrisy of my attitude.

"Listen to me, Angus. I may not get another chance; you might be killed tomorrow or the next day. That's the reality I'm facing, and to never have known you ... like that, it would break me." She dropped her eyes. When she looked up again, they were wet with tears. "Which is the bigger regret? Ask yourself that question, before you turn me down," she added, suddenly throbbing with emotion.

It was enough to break my already shaky resolve. She was right. Neither of us knew the future, and I might be shot down the very next day after my leave. I'd crossed so many lines; this was simply one more.

"OK," I said with a smile. "Sorry. I mean yes, let's do this."

She smiled at me tremulously. "Thank you."

Another objection raised its head. "But we can't just book into any old hotel as a single couple, can we?"

Now I was over my scruples, I was becoming more practical. I was pretty sure most country and small hotels were sticklers for these kinds of things. It was too far to go to London, I felt, if we wanted to make the most of our time together. Besides which, there was all the bombing. We'd spend half of it in a shelter, and that would defeat the object entirely.

"You are exasperating sometimes, Flying Officer Mackennelly." Angelica laughed. "Of course we can't, and that's why we'll say we are married."

Naturally, there was a simple answer.

"You've thought all this through, haven't you?" I said admiringly.

"In immaculate detail … yes."

"Then I suppose I will have to accept your invitation with good grace."

She put her lips up to mine and I kissed her. "You jolly well better, Flying Officer Mackennelly. I've been waiting for this for a long time," she whispered. "A very long time indeed."

This was food for thought as our lips met again. There were depths to this woman I didn't know and could not even guess at.

"Thank you," I whispered back, when our lips parted once more. "I'm looking forward to it immensely."

"Me too."

"You know," I told her between kisses, "for someone who was incredibly reluctant to kiss me, you certainly have changed your tune."

"I'm making up for lost time, that's all."

She smiled, and then in the distance I heard the familiar whine of the Merlin engines. The squadron was returning.

"Pick me up at five," she said. "Bring a bag. Fred has sorted out some transport."

"You're a treasure."

"I'm glad you are starting to realise it."

The sound of the planes got louder, and soon they would begin to land. She gave me one last peck on the lips and skipped away.

I turned around and watched them flying in. I couldn't help but feel choked up as I counted the planes. They were all there, thankfully. At least today they were home safe.

"Hey, Scottish," said Willie as the pilots began to head for their hut and he spotted me waiting.

"How are you, you reprobate?" I smiled, and he clapped me gently on the shoulder.

"That was a rum do, as Bentley would say."

"Oh?"

"For sure. Too many of them for us. Judd nearly bought it from a 109 that came out of the blue."

"What happened?"

"Jonty shot it down, so he's in Judd's good books for a change."

I laughed. "I suppose there's going to be a ball—"

"Don't even mention the word, for the love of God!" Willie interjected.

I chuckled and held my peace. Jonty arrived in short order.

"Hello, Skipper, old sport."

"Jonty, I hear you did a good deed."

"Oh, it was nothing," he said. "Just doing my job, as always."

"Can you fly again soon?" Willie asked me anxiously.

"No, not yet, and I'm going on leave for forty-eight hours."

"Really? Somewhere nice?"

"Yes, at least I hope so." I dropped my voice. "Angelica's arranging it."

"Oh, right. I see…" Willie grinned.

"Who's a sly dog?" said Jonty, who had overheard.

"That's enough, leave the man alone."

"Yes but…"

"Come on, Jonty, let's grab a cuppa before we go up again."

"Yes, and before all the biscuits get eaten! See you, Skipper, enjoy your, erm … leave…"

The two of them left, chuckling away. I stayed where I was, waiting for Tomas. He appeared shortly afterwards.

"Scottish, how are things?" he said, smiling broadly. "The spy business is finished, no?"

"Actually, no."

"What? Come on, Scottish. I mean, come on!"

"Come over here."

I jerked my head towards the edge of the field. We walked in silence, although I could feel Tomas was eager to know what was on my mind. When we were standing far enough away and out of earshot, I told him.

He let out a low whistle. "So, this wasn't the spy, eh? These MI6 Johnny boys, they are tricky bastards."

"They fooled me, and they've fooled Bentley. Hopefully, they've fooled the real spy too."

He digested this for a moment. "So, what do we do?"

"I'm not sure. We wait a little, perhaps, and think how best we can discover him."

He scratched his head and said, "We didn't manage before."

"No, we didn't, and perhaps we have to change our tactics."

"Like how?"

"I'm not sure, to be honest. I've got a forty-eight-hour pass. Let me think on it and we'll talk again."

"OK, fine, yes. You will think and I will think. Together we will find this bloody bastard spy, Scottish." He grabbed my hand and squeezed it.

"Yes, yes, we will. We have to."

"For sure. See you, Scottish. I must go, get ready for next sortie."

"Bye. Take care of yourself."

I watched him walk in easy strides to the hut. I hoped I would be cleared for action soon. I was chafing. On the other hand, there was something more immediate to look forward to. I went home to pack.

As I was putting a few things into a bag, Barbara burst into my room. She had the habit now of treating it as her own. She stopped dead as she saw what I was doing.

"Where … where are you going? You're not…"

"Leaving? No. I'm just going *on leave*, that's all," I said.

"On leave?" She echoed my words and then the realisation hit her — quite forcefully, judging by her expression. "Oh? With her, I suppose. You are, aren't you?"

I grew a little impatient. It was what happened when you felt guilty, I supposed. "And what of it?" I demanded tersely.

"Oh, nothing. Don't mind me," she replied bitterly. "It's no matter, after all. I can't exactly complain, can I, when I'm married? That's what you'd say, wouldn't you?"

I looked at her and saw that she was hurting. "It's true, though, isn't it?" I said more gently.

"Yes, damn you! Go on, go then! Enjoy her, every part of her. Just don't tell me about it."

"I wasn't planning to."

She softened and her eyes were wet. "I … I … sorry, sorry, I can't. I just … I'll see you when you get back."

She fled from the room with tears streaming down her face, leaving me feeling as guilty as hell. Though, I realised, not guilty enough to cancel the weekend. That told its own story, if only I would listen.

The Plantagenet King was a small country hotel far enough from the airbase that we wouldn't be recognised. It had an olde worlde feel about it with oak wainscoting, and Angelica had booked us a room with a nice fire and a four-poster bed.

We signed the register as Mr and Mrs Trelawney, a name I had plucked out of the air. The clerk at the front desk looked us over, and perhaps because we were in uniform thought no more of it.

"Isn't this exciting?" Angelica squealed with delight after we were shown to our room. "Our very first holiday together."

"Will there be more?" I smiled at her indulgently.

"You can jolly well bet on it, if I have anything to do with it."

We ate supper together in the hotel dining room and then with the fire banked up, we retired to bed. I wondered how the night would go, but I did not have to wonder for long. I sat on the bed, waiting while she spent what seemed an age in the bathroom. Finally, she appeared wearing a short red satin nightdress and nothing else. It left me rather breathless.

"That's nice," I said, understating how I felt about it in every way possible.

"Do you like it?" she asked me nervously.

"It's charming," I said.

"Just ... charming?" She raised a quizzical eyebrow, coming closer.

"Well, if you must know, it's incredibly erotic..."

"Much better... Would you like to take it off me?"

"Very much so."

"Go on then."

I kissed her and felt the electricity as my hands went to her naked skin. We disrobed each other and then made love slowly and delicately. It was almost like unwrapping one's favourite sweet and savouring it for as long as possible.

It was as far removed from Barbara as it could be. With her, it seemed a polished performance, almost frantic at times, and filled with lust. With Angelica, there was a devilish kind of innocence about it. As if the angel and devil had combined into one and taken me to bed.

Afterwards, we held each other and watched the flickering flames in the hearth.

"That wasn't your first time, was it?" I asked quietly. I knew it could not have been just from her responses and how she had taken the initiative at times.

"Did you think it would be?" Her tone was frank.

"I didn't know what to think." It was true. I had entered unknown territory with her in many ways.

"You thought I was some kind of chaste virgin? Well, I'm not!" She tilted her chin defiantly, daring me to naysay her. Then her eyes softened, and she continued quietly, "Well, to be fair, it was just the one time, and I was a little drunk."

She seemed to feel she should mitigate the disclosure, in case I thought badly of her. I didn't.

"I'm rather glad of it, if I'm honest," I said. I didn't want her to think me judgemental.

In truth, I was relieved it wasn't more times, in spite of the many women I had slept with. I supposed I was selfish. I wanted to be her only one. I couldn't divorce myself from these feelings, no matter how at odds they were with my own behaviour. I pushed the thoughts aside. As a pilot, I'd learned to live in the moment. I needed to heed my own advice.

I laughed, and she kissed me.

"It was very good, better than good, but we are going to need more practice." Her eyes twinkled.

"We are?"

"Yes, starting now."

"Are you always like this?" I teased her.

"Like what?"

"Demanding?"

"You haven't seen anything yet, Flying Officer Mackennelly."

"Then show me."

"With pleasure."

Forty-eight hours go by quite slowly if you let them. We spent quite a good part of the time in our room, exploring each other in every way we could. She had been determined to have me and now she had, as I pointed out during an interlude.

"So, you've got your wish. What happens now?" I asked her.

"What wish?"

"You wanted to have me."

"Yes, of course, did you doubt I would?"

"I don't doubt anything about you, not for one second."

"Good."

"Have I been profligate enough for you yet?"

She pretended to ponder the question, with a smile playing on her lips. "I'm not sure you have, not in every way possible."

I laughed. "Then I must try harder … but apart from that, what now?"

I wanted to know if having got what she wanted, she would want more. I certainly did, and I knew I would continue to do so.

"Isn't this enough?" she asked me.

"Is it for you?"

"Yes, but only for now and for the moment."

"Will you … want me again, once we go back?"

"Of course I will, don't you doubt it, Flying Officer Mackennelly. Besides, we've still got plenty of time before we *do* have to go back. I'm going to make the most of you." She snuggled into me and held me close. "You have no idea, have you?" she whispered.

"About what?"

"What it is to be loved, completely loved."

"I think I'm beginning to understand it, yes."

"Good."

Her eyes closed and she fell asleep. I lay there, looking at her sleeping so peacefully, her head cradled against my chest. I wondered what the future would hold for us. I wondered about Barbara and what should I do about my relationship with her. God knew what my mother would have thought. I stopped myself there and told myself to simply enjoy this time. After all, it might not come again. The future would have to take care of itself one way or another. I would soon be flying again, dicing with death. It was a sobering thought, and one that focused me on the present. I had to learn to appreciate moments like these.

Sadly, all good things must come to an end. Our little sojourn finished too soon for us both, and we drove much of the way back in silent contemplation. As we stopped outside Angelica's lodgings so I could drop her off, she suddenly turned to me.

"You don't have to love me if you can't," she said seriously.

"I never said I don't," I protested.

"But you haven't said you do."

"No."

She smiled and then after a moment, she said, "No matter, I love *you* and that's what's important, for now."

She leaned across and kissed me, softly, tenderly. I didn't want to let her go.

"You can say it when you're ready to say it, Angus. I can wait," she whispered.

Then she was gone, carrying her bag and stepping lightly through the gate. I felt a sharp pain in my chest as I watched her leave. I started to wonder how long it would be until I saw her smiling face again. My heart was certainly telling me something, just as Gordon had described it. My head stubbornly refused to accept the ready explanation for my feelings.

"You idiot," I said aloud, but it was to no avail. To admit to something like love would be to become vulnerable. To someone not schooled in love, vulnerability meant you could get hurt. I did not understand then that this was the dichotomy of love, the two sides to the coin: you could not have one without the other. Would my naivety be my downfall? I didn't know, but I stubbornly refused to yield to my own feelings.

When I returned to Amberly, I didn't see Barbara at all. She didn't come to my room nor summon me to hers. She wasn't in evidence at dinner either. This went on for two or three days. I took the opportunity to ask myself if I missed her. In a way, I did, but another part of me was grateful for the respite. I had half expected her to come running to me on my return, although it wasn't really what I wanted. However, the fact she did not perhaps spoke of some self-respect on her part. I did not experience the same pangs at Barbara's absence that I had had when I'd dropped off Angelica.

Naturally, after our time away, Angelica and I met and went out together. There was no real opportunity for further intimacy, although I knew we both strongly desired it.

Finally, when on the way to see Doctor Vivek for yet another check-up, I asked Gordon what had happened to Barbara.

He looked at me in surprise. "Didn't you know, sir? She's gone down south."

"Oh!" I digested this information. I wondered if my developing relationship with Angelica was the cause of it. Perhaps fate had taken a hand after all. "London?" I asked him out of interest.

"No, sir, to their country house in Guildford, sir."

"I see."

"London is too dangerous, sir, with the bombing an' all."

"I didn't even know they had a country house in Guildford," I mused.

"Her husband has estates in many parts of the country."

When I frowned at this, he said, "Burke's Peerage, sir, fascinating reading."

"Ah." I fell silent for a while until Gordon spoke again.

"If you are thinking it was to do with your, erm … recent furlough, I suspect it might be. Lady Amberly was somewhat unhappy at your departure, so I gather."

"And where exactly *do* you gather all this information from, Fred?"

He shot me a conspiratorial glance. "Ah, now that would be telling. But let's just say perhaps the lady's personal maid is a little free with her confidences. A point you should take on board, sir, with respect to your liaison with a certain corporal."

"Tell me about it." I was painfully aware of the fact Barbara's staff had no doubt reported on my movements. "But, seriously, Fred, have you been on intimate terms with Lady Amberly's staff?"

"As to that, sir, I couldn't possibly comment."

I roared with laughter at this. He was ever the politician. Gordon was quite a handsome chap, all in all, and I could see why the ladies might fall for him.

"When might she come back to Amberly Manor?" I enquired, so that I could be prepared for the eventuality.

"I wouldn't know, sir, nobody does know."

"Right."

Doctor Vivek finally passed me as fit for duty.

"Yes, I'm satisfied the wound has healed and you can get back up in the air. I can tell you are anxious to do so."

"Indeed I am," I said, smiling. "Thank you, Doctor."

"Oh, don't thank me, oh no. I am not at all a fan of sending men off to die in battle. It's a job we have to do, but don't think it stands easy with my conscience, because it most certainly does not." He wrote out a note, signed it and handed it over to me. "Try not to get yourself killed, that's all I ask," he said affably.

"I'll do my best."

I was grinning when I left the medical unit, and naturally Angelica was waiting outside. I picked her up and whirled her around before kissing her soundly.

"What's brought this on?"

"Splendid news, I can finally fly."

"Is it? Oh!"

Her face fell ludicrously, and I realised what might be good news to me, certainly wasn't to her.

"Don't fret. I bear a charmed life," I told her.

"Oh, don't quote *Macbeth* at me, Flying Officer Mackennelly. Now I have to worry about you every time you go up there, you … you…"

I caught her hands in mine. "It's my job, for King and Country, remember?"

"Yes, I know that, but I can't help it. I'm scared, Angus."

"Of what?"

"Don't be so obtuse. Of losing you, you silly gudgeon." She punched me gently on my bad arm.

I faked a wince, though it had not hurt. "Easy, tiger, that only just healed up."

"Well, I wish it had healed slower," she said with pursed lips.

"You don't mean it."

"Yes, I do. I love you and I couldn't bear it if I … if I lost you."

Tears sprang to her eyes. Realising she wasn't playing, I folded her into my arms.

"I knew this day would come," she said against my chest. "I just didn't want it to."

"I know. I promise to be careful."

"Oh no, you won't." She looked up at me severely. "I know you, once you get up there. I've heard all about it, and don't forget I can hear you all chattering away too."

"I will, just for you, I promise."

She sniffed. "If you die, I'm going to come and stand at your grave every day and curse the day you were born!"

"You perceive me completely unmanned, penitent and suitably chastened."

"Don't joke, Angus! It's not a joke!"

She was smiling, in spite of herself. I silenced any further protest by kissing her, an act with which she wholeheartedly engaged herself.

CHAPTER THIRTEEN

It was far simpler for the Marx Brothers to talk of catching the spy than it was to actually do it. It was perfectly fine to look at one's fellow airmen with a suspicious eye, but none of them seemed to particularly merit the scrutiny. I knew that the spy wasn't going to stick out like a sore thumb, but I did wish they could be easier to spot. Neither Tomas nor I could think of anything especially untoward about any of them.

Once Bentley agreed to allow me back into my aircraft, I was once more rostered for combat missions defending our shores from Jerry, whose incursions seemed to show no signs of abating. I was soon flying sorties once more, and contrary to what Angelica thought, I did have at least one eye on self-preservation. More for her sake than mine, but I was never careless. That wouldn't do: careless got you killed. The spy conundrum was on my mind, and also Lawrence, who seemed to attract ME109s like flies. I had certainly intervened more than once, on his account, did he but know it.

It was, in fact, Angelica who began to cast doubts upon one of the airmen under Bentley's command.

"What do you know about Charles Forster?" she asked me one day while we were out for fish and chips. It was a habit we had fallen into, and one I rather enjoyed. We'd buy it from the local chip shop and eat it sitting on a bench on the village green.

"Not a lot," I admitted. "Why?"

"Just because I don't think he's who he says he is."

"Really? How do you make that out?" I still had not twigged where this was leading.

"His file says he's from a high-born family, but I've looked that family up in the Peerage and they don't exist."

"Have you been looking in his file?" I said with interest.

"Yes, of course. How else am I going to help you catch the spy? It's not as if *you* can look in his file."

"Yes, of course, how very thoughtful of you."

"I will do whatever it takes to help you, Angus. I have the right clearance to look in anyone's file."

I looked up sharply. "Have you looked in mine?" I knew it would be full of notes about the various affairs I had had and why I had been booted from squadron to squadron.

"I can't say."

"Or won't?"

"That too." She poked her tongue out at me and I was left wondering if she was teasing me.

"Going back to the matter at hand," she said, "he was apparently schooled at Rugby before going up to Oxford. His degree was interrupted by the war, and he became a pilot."

"OK, but apart from his parentage, which you say you can't locate, what else makes you suspect him, as I assume you do? After all, his family might not be in records of the peerage."

She popped a chip into her mouth, and then popped one into mine. It was her habit to share food with me, and it seemed to delight her to feed me the odd morsel, particularly with her fingers. I must say I didn't object to it either.

"It's too pat, I suppose. It's just how a person's past would be if you imagined them for a fictional novel as a descendent of someone well-off, or if you wanted to show they were terribly English."

"But surely," I countered, "other officers have been to such schools, like Eton and so forth. I went to a good school in Scotland myself."

"But his record is so clean — not one blemish, not one foot out of place. Doesn't that strike you as odd?"

"As opposed to someone like me, you mean," I said pointedly.

"Oh, well, very few officers have a record quite like yours," she laughed then.

"So you have looked at it!" I said triumphantly.

"I could not possibly comment, my darling."

"Well, you're still here. It can't be *that* bad."

"It's bad, Angus, believe me, but I don't care."

I thought about what she had said, not about me, but about Charles. I couldn't do anything about my past but if she was disposed to accept it, I was a lucky man. Then as I crumpled up the paper from our dinner to throw it away, a notion occurred to me.

"You said his record is unblemished?"

"Yes."

"Then why did he get posted to the Mavericks?"

She looked at me as if a lightbulb had switched on in her head. "Good point! I never thought of that."

"Are all the pilots here … let's say … bad boys?"

"I can check, now you've mentioned it, because…"

"You have the clearance to do it?"

"Yes, I can always find an excuse. I will take a look and I'll tell you what I find."

This was a revelation and one that I shared with Tomas. He agreed it seemed odd and vowed to keep an eye on Charles from then on.

Not long after our conversation about Charles, on yet another sortie, we scrambled to intercept a parcel of Heinkels coming in on their usual route to London. As I gunned the throttle and took off into the blue sky, it certainly did feel great to be flying again. I couldn't help feeling that I was born to be a pilot, although I wasn't sure what I would do after the war. None of us knew how long the war would last, either. This sortie began in the usual fashion, flying straight for the enemy positions and then watching for fighters as we prepared to attack.

Below us were the Heinkels, and on my wings were Jonty and Willie. I felt confident with those two as my section; we had been through a lot together. Lieutenant Judd was about to order the attack when I spotted a group of 109s coming in from the west.

"Bandits, bandits at three o'clock," I said. "Break, break."

The squadron peeled off as usual and I said to my two, "We'll take the fighters, come on."

"Tally-ho!" said Jonty.

"Let's just try not to get killed," I told him as we headed for the incoming fighters.

"Aye, aye, Skipper."

We broke formation and climbed so that we could have the advantage over the 109s. On the flat, we certainly did in terms of turning speed. The enemy fighters sped on towards us, and when they were in distance they split left and right.

I took one as my mark and screamed down after it. He was good, weaving left and right while I gave chase. I could hear Jonty hallooing in his usual fashion as if he was out on the hunting field. Willie was far more considered and less impetuous.

"That's got you, you bounder!" said Jonty triumphantly. In my rear-view mirror, I saw a smoking plane diving to earth.

However, my focus was on the Messerschmitt in front of me, which was doing a grand job of avoiding me. I had tried a couple of bursts, which were wasted as he evaded them.

Then suddenly he turned and headed for the coast. As he crossed the cliffs, I elected to stop chasing him and turned back to the main pack. I flew in to try and take a potshot at some of the bombers, and used up my ammo before Judd ordered us home. We landed, and I had declined Jonty's suggestion to buzz the general's house. I had every reason now not to want to be forced out of the Mavericks squadron, and I wasn't going to step out of line. I realised, too, that I hadn't even thought about Lawrence and was relieved to see his plane landing.

As we walked back from our planes, Jonty remarked, "Not like you, Skipper, to refuse a dare."

"No."

"And you let that blighter hightail it to France without giving chase."

"Yes, I did," I said.

"He's got something keeping him here now, Jonty. Leave him be," said Willie, coming to my rescue.

"Something keeping him here..." Jonty frowned, and then his brow cleared as he realised. "Oh! Oh, I see. Yes, the ladybird, indeed, I see."

"She's not a ladybird, Jonty," I objected. "She's a beautiful, smart, funny, gorgeous woman among other things."

"Oh dear, oh dear." Jonty shook his head. "I can see you are quite smitten."

I shot him a look. Was it that obvious? And if it was, why was I continuing to deny it to myself?

"Leave him alone, old chap. Don't tease the poor bugger," said Willie.

"A love ballad, that's what's needed," said Jonty brightly.

"No, it bloody well is not. It's the very last thing he needs, or anyone needs, and particularly not his lady friend," Willie said forcefully.

"Oh, don't you think so?"

"No, I definitely don't."

"Pity," said Jonty in a voice that left us both expecting the forbidden ballad would transpire regardless of Willie's strictures.

"Talking of your ladyb… I mean, your lovely young miss," said Jonty. "There she is."

Angelica had taken to meeting our flight when we returned, and she was there to put her arms around me. The other two chuckled and left me to it.

"You're safe," she said, kissing me. "Thank God, thank God."

"If you keep on doing this, people will talk," I teased.

"Oh stuff, everyone on the base knows by now that I'm your girl."

"Oh?" I raised an eyebrow. "You're my girl now, are you?"

"Yes, I am, whether you like it or not!" She stuck out her chin defiantly, daring me to naysay it.

"I suppose I'll have to accept the honour," I replied.

"Oh, you!"

"Just don't punch my arm, please," I implored her.

"You certainly deserve it."

Later on, over a soup supper, which we took at the local pub, she brought up the subject of Charles Forster.

"I checked on all the pilots," she said. "I made up a reason that I was doing it for someone up at Fighter Command, and nobody questioned it."

"Good thinking," I said.

"He is the only one who doesn't have a reason for being here. All the others have at least something on their record that is a black mark or similar. Some have a lot of them." She looked at me meaningfully.

"If you intend to bring up my past at every opportunity…" I said, picking this up.

"Not every opportunity, just some of them." She smiled at me sweetly.

"I deserve it, I suppose."

"You deserve a lot of things, but mainly you deserve love, kisses … things like that."

"I'm sure I don't deserve a woman like you," I said seriously.

"Yes, you do. You need someone to reform your profligate ways."

I laughed. "I thought you wanted me to be profligate, isn't that what you said?"

"I do." She smiled. "But I'd much prefer it if you were only profligate with me."

This was the first time she had intimated she wanted me for herself alone. I found myself feeling, for a change, that she was right. Whether I was able to live up to it was still in doubt in my own mind, given my track record.

"Going back to Charles," I said, changing the subject, "how *did* he get into the squadron?"

"It seems he was recommended. By someone high up in Fighter Command."

"How interesting, and does this person exist?"

"Oh yes, they are highly respected, with a lot of clout."

I pondered this for a while. We ate the rest of our pea and ham soup in silence.

"This squadron would be the ideal target, wouldn't it? For someone to gain information from the inside. After all, it consists of reprobates, and as such wouldn't come under too much scrutiny."

"Yes," Angelica said. "Yes, you're right. It's an ideal cover, if you put it that way."

"Even so, we've no actual proof, as yet, that it's him." I wasn't about to jump in headfirst until I knew what I was jumping into. But things were starting to add up.

"I'll dig a little more, if I can. I have connections in Fighter Command."

"Connections?"

"Other comms people, who I trust. I'll see what I can find out."

As always, I found a way to talk to Tomas after a sortie. We moved out of earshot.

"So, this all makes sense, yes," he said when I told him what Angelica and I had discussed.

"Yes, it does."

"Well," he said, "I have been watching Foxy, and I thought about what I have seen, you know, in combat."

"And?"

"He never shoots one Jerry down."

"Really?"

"No, I never see him shoot one down."

"Has he no kills to his name?"

"No, he has not. Somehow, he is always unlucky, you know. Unlucky Charlie. That is what the other pilots are calling him."

I must admit I hadn't heard that nickname, but then I didn't pay too much attention to these things. "So, you think he's avoiding shooting down Jerry's planes?"

"Come on, Scottish, come on. What do you think? Nobody can be so unlucky never to shoot down one plane. I mean … come on."

"You may well be right. I should pay more attention to these things."

"We must watch him carefully. He will make a mistake, and then…"

"Yes, but we need some evidence to accuse him of spying, or Bentley will hang, draw and quarter us and then put our heads on pikes at the gate."

Tomas laughed. "Ah, Scottish, you are a funny man, yes. A funny man."

We left it at that, but it had set me thinking. How could we catch Charles out, if it was him? I didn't want to try following him like the others. Every one of those attempts had ended in disaster. There had to be another way, although I had no idea how we were going to solve the conundrum.

That evening when I arrived back at Amberly Manor, there was a sombre air about the place. The staff who I ran into all wore long faces and I wondered what on earth had happened to cause it. I didn't have to wait for long. Since I had taken to eating dinner with Angelica, I rarely ate it at Amberly, so if there was any news, I had not heard it. However, I was in my room when there was a knock at the door. It was Gordon.

"Can I come in, sir, for a moment?" he said, looking somewhat grave.

"Yes, of course. What is it?" I let him in. "Everyone seems deathly this evening. Has something occurred to warrant it?"

"Sir, His Lordship was killed in action. A telegram was received."

"Oh, oh God. And is Barbara —?" It was my first thought. I wondered how she was taking the news.

"She arrived earlier, yes."

"Did she … ask for me?"

"No, sir," he said. "But I thought you should know about the colonel."

"Yes, well, thanks."

He left and I wondered why I had not been the first person she had sought out. The hurt I had caused her must have cut deep, perhaps. Nevertheless, I felt I should at least go to her and offer my condolences. After all, it was the right thing to do. The decent thing to do, I told myself. I went in search of her and found her in the salon.

She was standing with her back to me by the window. She must have heard the door. "Is that you, Angus?" she asked without turning around.

"Yes."

So, I was expected, after all. She just would not stoop to asking me to come.

"John's dead." It was a flat statement, devoid of emotion.

"I know and I'm sorry." It seemed a trite and worn phrase to me, but what did one say when somebody died?

"Are you?"

There was a long pause while I wondered at what she had just said, as if I would somehow rejoice in her husband's death.

Suddenly she faced me. Her eyes were red, and tears streaked down her face. "Are you?" she said again. "Because I'm not."

"Oh, well, I nevertheless am very sorry for your loss." I wasn't sure what else to say. In her tone was something I had never heard before, bitterness, perhaps even hate.

"Don't be, don't be sorry for me, or for him. I don't want your pity either."

"OK."

I was nonplussed, not sure where this was going. She walked up to me swiftly and kissed me hard on the mouth, taking me by surprise. I responded, which was only natural, I supposed, given what had gone before, but everything in me rebelled against it at this particular time. Not only had her husband just died, but I was on the brink of forsaking her and any other for one woman.

She pulled away, and I saw in her face something that smacked of desperation, fear even.

"What, exactly, do you want then?" I asked her, perhaps a little harshly.

She breathed a little fast, ragged. "I want … the things I could not have from him, love, happiness, ecstasy. I want … you!"

This rather hit me a little forcefully. It just seemed inappropriate to be discussing such matters.

"Surely this isn't the time to…" I tailed off lamely.

She strode away, pacing the room with energy. It was almost as if her soul had somehow been released. "Why isn't it? Why? All my life I've done the right thing, played the part, and for what?"

"Did you hate him so much, then?" I ventured.

"Hate him? No! I didn't hate him. At times I loathed and despised him, but I also loved him. Oh, Angus, Angus."

She burst into floods of tears and flung herself onto my breast. This I could at least understand, an outpouring of grief. I held her gently, stroked her hair, and wondered where this was going to lead, in the end. For a while she remained there, and then taking my hand she led me to sit down on the sofa beside her. She wiped the tears from her cheeks and smiled at me weakly.

"Don't you see? I'm free, finally free, to be me, have what I want."

"And what is it that you want?" I asked, dreading the answer.

"Silly boy," she laughed, but gave me a nervous look. "I want you, of course. It's always been you, ever since we…"

I must have looked a little too surprised, for she stopped.

"Don't you want that?" she said.

"What exactly are you saying?" I asked her, still not entirely certain, even though I was getting the gist.

"Oh, Angus, how can you be so stupid? I'm a widow now, free to love again, marry who I want … marry you!"

I was trying very hard not to resemble a startled deer in the headlights of a car. Things had very suddenly shifted in her universe from us being lovers to potentially life partners. I was hoping to let her down gently but instead, she had precipitated everything by bringing up the idea of marriage. I could hardly believe my ears.

"Isn't it a little early to begin talking of such things?" I said mildly, trying not to make it sound like a reproof. "Your husband isn't even in his grave."

"Oh, you! Of course, publicly, but … privately…" She laughed it off as if it was of no consequence, but it was of huge consequence to me. Particularly since I had no intention of continuing our affair, let alone marrying her. However, when a person was grieving, you hardly wanted to add to their load.

"I still think…" I began.

She looked at me strangely. "You know how I feel about you. I've already told you. I love you. I'd die for you! Surely you know that?"

"That's just it." I picked up on that point. "I may also die any day and at any hour in combat with the Germans. You've just lost one man, for God's sake."

She was silent, and a tear rolled down one cheek. I wanted to comfort her. Seeing her distress was too much, and I didn't want to be the cause of it. Just as much, I did not want to be railroaded into a conversation about something I definitely didn't want to do. In the end, she was determined to pursue it regardless.

"You don't love me, do you, Angus? I asked you before and you couldn't answer. That's the truth, isn't it?" she said simply, a catch in her voice.

"We shouldn't be talking like this now." I tried again to deflect her.

"You didn't say you *did* love me either! So, tell me now, tell me the truth!"

There was nothing for it but to come clean. It was perhaps one thing my father had taught me well. Honesty was the best policy. A fat lot of attention I had paid to it on occasion, but now I couldn't avoid it.

"I have some feelings for you, Barbara, I can't deny it, but..."

"Feelings?" She shook her head. "Love is stronger than feelings. I should have guessed it. It's that woman, isn't it? You love her, don't you? Don't you!"

"Barbara ... I..."

I was trying to find a way out of this, particularly since I hadn't had time to come to terms with how I felt about Angelica. Barbara was forcing me into admissions I didn't want to make just then. I needed time to think. My hesitation seemed to fuel something in her. Her eyes flashed.

"Get out," she said suddenly, raising her voice, anger replacing grief.

"What?"

"I said ... get out, I don't want to see you. Just get out!"

"Barbara!" I was shocked by her tone. "Can't we at least be civil to each other, talk about this at another time?"

"I can't, not now, just go … please … please … darling…"

She looked at me imploringly. Since I wouldn't say the words she wanted to hear, it seemed she could not bear to be near me at that moment. There was nothing for it. I stood up and bowed stiffly before walking out. I heard her voice break on a sob, and I wanted to turn back but I didn't. The endearment at the end softened it, meaning she didn't hate me. Of course, she didn't, but she didn't precisely like me either. I could not reciprocate her feelings and that was not going to change. Nevertheless, I didn't want her to despise me. What man would? After all, we had been very intimate, and loving at times. She cared for me; she had been kind to me, gentle. I didn't want to end things with animosity. Yet, for the moment, that seemed to be the way of it. There was no more to be said. One thing was for certain: it was over between us, and fate had indeed brought things to a conclusion. At the very least I could be faithful to Angelica. I owed her that much. I was exceptionally lucky, and I knew it.

I stayed away from Amberly Manor as much as I could. Preparations were underway for the funeral and the colonel's body was being returned to England. He had been killed abroad, but I supposed because he was a lord and a colonel to boot, he was not to be buried where he fell. I would very likely be obliged to attend the service, whenever it might be, but until then I stayed out of Barbara's way as she did mine.

Besides which, the sorties continued to happen thick and fast. Jerry had not given up and was dropping as much ordinance as possible on London. If it was meant to intimidate the population, it was having the opposite effect. It simply made the Germans more hated and the British more determined to beat them. We flew into combat with a passion.

On one particular sortie, we had fared well, shooting down some bombers and ME109s. It had been exceptionally successful. We were returning to base, and not far from Banley.

"Don't look now, but there's a 109 following us," said Willie all of a sudden. We three had been trailing the rest of the squadron.

"What, just … following us?" I replied, puzzled.

"Yes."

I took a look in my rear-view mirror. I could see the enemy fighter a long way back, unmistakable by its yellow nose.

"What the hell is he doing?" I said as I took another look.

"I don't know."

"Well, why isn't he engaging?"

"No clue at all."

Jonty, ever eager for the fray, cut in. "Tally-ho, shall I go and shoot the bugger down?"

"Not just yet. Let's see what happens when we get to the airfield."

I wanted to find out what he was doing first. There would be plenty of time to engage him if he tried anything. The ME109 didn't close with us but maintained his distance.

"Keep an eye on him in case he does something funny," I said.

We all did, taking it in turns to check on him, but he never wavered from his course. Soon the airfield loomed, and it would be time to land.

"We're here. What shall we do now?" Jonty asked me.

"Jonty, you land first. We will circle back and get behind him."

"Righto. I'd rather shoot him, though."

"I'm sure you would, but just humour me and do what I asked."

"OK, Skipper."

He landed while we flew back in a circle to come behind the German plane. He still never wavered, though he must have seen us.

"He's lowering his undercarriage," said Willie after a moment.

"What?"

"He's going to land."

"What on earth…?"

"Yep, he's definitely going to land."

This being an unprecedented occurrence, I wasn't sure what to do. However, one thing I did know was that he would need to be taken into custody as soon as he stepped out from the aircraft. I spoke to the tower on the radio.

"Control, we've got an enemy plane landing on our airfield. Hold your fire but provide an escort, please, to pick him up."

"Roger, Red Leader. We've already been alerted and we've seen it; the escort is on its way," came the response.

"We'll follow him in and land behind him," I told them.

As we approached, I could see three vehicles heading out to the runway, one of which had a machine gun mounted on it. A number of ground troops were also in the vehicles, and the soldiers were bristling with armaments.

The 109 touched down and taxied to a stop. We landed and parked just behind him. I jumped down and so did Willie, drawing our sidearms as we did so.

The ground crew were already surrounding the plane, pointing their rifles at it.

"Come out with your hands up," shouted the sergeant in charge.

The cockpit slowly opened, and the German pilot emerged. He put up his hands and jumped down easily from the wing. The ground crew approached him and removed his pistol, patting him down for any other weapons. Once it was discovered he had none, they moved back while he watched them silently.

"What shall we do with him, sir?" asked the sergeant, coming up to me as the senior officer attending.

"I suppose he'll need to be taken into custody," I said. "But we ought to talk to him at least. Does anyone speak German?"

"I do," said a voice at my elbow. It was Charles Forster. He had appeared unannounced and as if from nowhere. It was all very strange.

"Fine, let's get him over to the hut and you can talk to him there."

I left the aircraft to be sorted out by Techie and his men, while we accompanied the German pilot to the hut. By then, Tomas had also joined me.

"Why don't you take him over there and find out what he's doing here? What he wants?" I said to Charles.

"For sure. I will speak to him and translate it for you."

He did so while the rest of us stayed within earshot. I motioned to the escort to keep back and give Charles some space.

Charles took a packet of cigarettes out of his pocket and offered one to the pilot. The pilot accepted it and allowed Charles to light it. There was something about the packet that triggered a memory — then I realised it was the same brand we'd found in the abandoned hut.

They began to converse in German. I noticed Tomas was listening intently.

"I asked him what his name is and what he's doing here," Charles told us. "He said, his name is Frederick Von Mayer. He's tired of the war, and of Hitler."

"Aren't we all?" said Jonty.

"Hush!" Willie admonished him.

"I asked him where he comes from, and he said Dusseldorf. He said he's a farmer and he doesn't want to fly planes. He was forced to fly them." Charles shrugged and continued to question the pilot.

"I said to him that he has come to the right place. He said he is glad to be here and doesn't want to fight for a madman." Charles turned to the pilot once more. After he spoke in German, the pilot looked at him, a little puzzled. "I told him that he's right: Hitler is a madman and needs to be stopped."

Then the pilot spoke again.

I saw the snarl in Charles's face, which disappeared as quickly as it had come. He then talked almost as if he was describing the weather.

"So, he said, he is glad to be among English people at last. We at least are sensible in preventing the Nazis from coming to our country. I'm just going to tell him congratulations once again for doing the right thing and surrendering to us. He will be taken to a prison camp and looked after properly. He should not worry about the rest of the war. We'll take care of it for him and his kind. Then I'll tell him goodbye."

He spoke in German again, then walked away from the pilot, who watched him with a strange expression, as if what had been said had staggered him slightly.

"So that's it?" I asked Charles.

"Oh, you know, there's nothing much else to say. He gave up, and who can blame him? We are beating Jerry at every turn. It's a shame there's not more of them turning themselves in and saving us the trouble of shooting them down, old boy. I doubt he knows anything of value."

"OK, thanks, Foxy," I said, but the casual way in which he said this didn't sit well with me.

Charles walked off into the hut.

"I guess you can take him away and lock him in a cell or something. Inform Squadron Leader Bentley and he can decide what happens to him," I told the sergeant.

"Sir," the man said, saluting. We watched as the German pilot was escorted to one of the trucks and put in the back under guard.

"That's that. I need a cuppa," said Jonty.

"Coming?" Willie asked me. "Show's over."

"Sure, Kiwi, I just want to ask Tomas something," I said.

"See you inside then."

I could tell Tomas was bursting to talk to me, and we walked to our usual spot to speak freely.

"What is it?" I asked him.

"Scottish, do you know what he *really* said to that pilot?"

"No, I don't speak German."

"I do. The first part of what he said was true. He asked the pilot where he came from, and the pilot did say his name is Frederick Von Mayer. He did tell Foxy he has had enough of the war and Hitler, and he came to surrender. He is also a farmer from Dusseldorf and doesn't want to fly planes. But what Foxy said to him was not what he told us."

"Oh?"

Tomas shook his head. "No, he said, 'You should be proud, fighting for the Führer,' and the pilot told him that Hitler is a madman."

"I see." I was thoughtful, hearing that Charles had lied to us. Tomas had more to say, however.

"Yes, but listen, Scottish. Foxy called him a coward and said in Germany he would be shot. The pilot asked him why did he care anyway, when he is fighting for the British?"

This was getting worse and worse.

"And what did Foxy say?" I was now terribly interested in hearing the rest of it.

"Scottish, listen! Foxy tells him, 'I care because I am loyal to the one true Aryan race. To the Führer. The stench of your traitorous actions make me sick. You are a disgrace. Here, have the packet. I hope it is your last. Enjoy your time in a British prison camp. If you value your life, tell them nothing. When we rule this country, if you betray us any further, I will personally come to find you and slit your throat like the pig you are.' That's what he said."

Tomas had the look of someone who'd just scored a Royal Flush at cards. I didn't blame him. We'd hit the jackpot.

"Well, I'll be damned."

"You will be damned, and so will Foxy, Scottish. He is a spy — I heard him, I heard him."

Rather impetuously, I made up my mind. All rational thought fled. We'd been hunting the spy for weeks and now we'd found him. Adrenaline was running through my veins in anticipation of calling him out. My blood was up; I was ready and spoiling for a fight. I was determined to confront Charles there and then.

"Come on," I said to Tomas. "Come on, let's get him."

We sauntered up to Charles, who was standing outside the pilots' hut, smoking a cigarette.

"Funny business, eh, Foxy, that pilot. What's the world coming to, with German pilots surrendering to the British?" I said.

"Absolutely. Well, I think I'll go and read the paper before we get called up again."

He seemed very anxious to go, as if he sensed something was up. A spy would be very attuned to what people were thinking or doing.

"Stay awhile, and talk."

"Why, what do you want?" He became belligerent at once. This seemed rather out of character for the urbane English gentleman he was supposed to be.

"Just a little chat, Foxy, that's all," I said quietly.

"All right, what about?"

"You've never managed to shoot down a German plane yet, have you?" I said to him casually.

He scoffed at the remark, as if it was of no consequence. "Yes, haven't you heard? I'm jinxed or something."

"Where did you learn such good German?"

"I … what? At Oxford, old bean. What is this, the Spanish Inquisition?"

I ignored him and carried on, ready to play the trump card. "It's quite lucky that Tomas here is fluent in German, or didn't you know?"

"Sorry, what?" Charles went white as a sheet.

I pressed home my advantage. "What was it you actually said to that pilot?" I said, as if I was making conversation, but in my voice was a hint of steel. He must have picked it up. He became nervous, looking for a way out.

"I told you already: he's sick of the war and wanted to surrender."

"So, you didn't tell him that you are loyal to the one true Aryan race. To the Führer. That the stench of his traitorous action makes you sick. You didn't tell him that you will slit his throat like a pig, then? Did you?"

Charles looked from me to Tomas, and back. There was panic in his eyes.

"You're a spy, Foxy, a damn traitor and a spy," I said suddenly.

One thing you learned in sport was never to take your eye off the ball. In the heat of the moment, I should have heeded that lesson. If I'd thought he would just give in, I was sorely mistaken.

Just then and without warning, he balled his fist and punched me full in the solar plexus. I doubled over, gasping for breath. From the corner of my eye, I saw him land another punch on Tomas, sending him flying. He set off at a run for the planes.

"Damn," I said, trying to get my breath back. "Tomas!"

Tomas was struggling to get up. "Come on, Scottish, we must stop him, we must stop him!"

He pulled out his sidearm as we started to run after him. Charles had reached his aircraft and was spinning it up. He started to taxi away towards the runway. Tomas levelled his pistol.

"Stop," I said, pushing his arm down. "Don't shoot the bloody plane."

"But he's getting away!"

"No, he's damn well not! Let's get him, come on!"

We both pelted for our own aircraft, jumped in and fired them up. We set off after Charles, whose plane was just taking off, and we followed him in short order. Almost immediately, I was challenged by the control tower.

"Red Leader, Red Leader, what are you doing? This is an unauthorised take-off," came the voice of control.

"Sorry, control, something's come up."

I was too intent on our mission to explain it all now. However, whoever was on duty wasn't having any of it.

"Red Leader, turn back, turn back now, and that's an order."

I replied tersely, the consequences be damned. Charles wasn't going to get away on my watch and that was all there was to it. "No can do, control, sorry and all that. Got a job to do, and I've got a traitor to catch."

"Red Leader, you are ordered to return to base immediately."

There was more of this, but I ignored it and kept flying.

"Come on, Scottish, we can't lose him," said Tomas. We urged our planes forward, as fast as we could get them to go.

"I don't intend to. It's very likely he's going to make for France. We have to get him before he gets there."

Then came a voice I recognised. "Angus, Angus, what are you doing?"

It was Angelica on the radio. She'd never talked to me on comms before, though I knew she listened in.

"Angelica, it's Charles — we found him out and he's making a run for it."

"Take care of yourself, Angus. I'll stay with you," she said.

Somehow, the very fact I knew she was listening to our conversations gave me heart. I renewed my determination to somehow capture Charles or if not, then prevent him returning to the Germans.

Charles's aircraft was away in the distance, and I wondered how we would ever catch him up. After all, we couldn't go any faster than he did. All we could do was doggedly stick on his tail in the hope that we could somehow cut him off. As we started to approach the coast, I felt that the task was impossible. We had only slightly closed the distance, and he was too far away for us to open fire.

"How can we get him, Scottish?" said Tomas.

"I don't know. Perhaps we can't."

I was becoming resigned to the fact he would escape. No sooner had the words left my mouth than Charles's plane turned without warning.

"What's he doing?" said Tomas, as the Spitfire loomed larger.

"I don't know. Perhaps he's going to surrender after all?"

It seemed unlikely, to be honest. Then, just as he got within range, I realised the danger. He wasn't giving up at all, quite the opposite.

"He's going to attack! Break, Tomas, break!" I shouted, banking immediately left, as Tomas banked right.

We did so just in time. A hail of bullets ripped past us through the spot where we had been flying a few seconds before.

Then Charles's voice came over the radio. "Damn you, Scottish, you bastard. I've always hated you anyway. I'm going to kill two British pilots before I head for the Fatherland! *Deutschland Uber Alles!*"

The urbane British accent was gone, and I heard what must have been his native German brogue underneath.

He turned and gave chase to Tomas, who spotted this manoeuvre and began to take evasive action. Tomas was weaving, banking, left and then right, with Charles right behind him.

"No kills, eh? Well, I'm going to get two kills today," Charles said.

I turned and banked too, heading on an intercept to try and head Charles off. He saw me and broke off his attack, then fired. I narrowly avoided getting hit once again, while Tomas recovered and fired at Charles.

Charles, for all his lack of kills, was a skilled pilot. He evaded the bullets and banked again to get behind Tomas. How he thought he could win against two of us I didn't know, but he wasn't doing a bad job of it so far.

"Tomorrow I will return in a Messerschmitt to get all of your friends, and this time I will have many kills," Charles gloated.

The whole thing was becoming preposterous, like a bad film with a manic, cackling villain trying to kill the good guys.

Tomas tried to pull up and into a loop, but Charles fired again and this time he shredded part of Tomas's tail. Tomas's craft bucked and rolled, as he tried to get it under control.

"Scottish, I've been hit, he got me."

"Easy, Tomas, easy," I said, throttling up and screaming in on the attack. It was time to end this ridiculous farce. I hadn't spent hundreds of hours in combat for nothing.

Charles had obviously been too preoccupied with chasing Tomas to see me closing in. He clocked me too late. I fired, once, twice. It was deadly. The bullets shattered his cockpit and then one must have hit the main fuel tank. The front of his plane exploded and dived down towards the ground, gathering speed as it did so. It smashed into the earth with another explosion, sending shards of his aircraft flying in all directions. I circled around, but Charles would definitely not have survived it.

"You got him, Scottish, you got that bastard spy!" Tomas was jubilant.

It didn't feel particularly glorious to me. It was rather ugly, in fact — I'd just killed a British pilot, albeit that he was a Nazi spy. It was hard to make the switch when up to now I'd thought of him as one of ours.

"Yes, yes, I did, Tomas. But now, can you make it home?"

Now Charles had been dealt with, that was my next worry. How would Tomas get back to the airfield?

"I will try. It's not easy, but I will try."

I escorted Tomas as he nursed his kite all the way to Banley. With one half of his tail missing, it was difficult, but he managed it, nevertheless. A credit to his flying skills indeed.

"Are you ready to face the music?" I asked him as we prepared to land.

"For sure, what can they do? We got the spy!"

I didn't share his optimism. At the end of the runway, there was a reception committee waiting, including Bentley himself.

We landed, parked our aircraft and left Techie tutting over the shredded tail of Tomas's kite. I wasn't in any hurry to see Bentley, but the inevitable could not be put off forever.

We walked over to where he was standing with Audrey beside him and a couple of other officers. Tomas and I saluted while Bentley regarded us with barely concealed rage.

"What I want to know is," he began, "what the hell were you two playing at?"

I opened my mouth to start to explain, but he was in no mood to listen.

"Don't even try to flannel me, Angus, no indeed. You went up on an unauthorised mission and disobeyed direct repeated orders to return to base. Now, what's it all about, and where is Pilot Officer Forster?"

I hesitated. He most certainly wasn't going to like what I had to say.

"Well?" he demanded in irascible tones when I didn't answer right away.

"We shot him down, sir," I told him.

He looked at me as if he could not believe what he was hearing. "Sorry? You did what?"

"Shot … him … down … sir," I repeated and saw his face suffuse with colour.

"You did WHAT? God almighty, what is happening in this squadron? You mean to tell me that you went up there and shot down one of my damn pilots? What on earth possessed the two of you? Have you gone mad? In all my years, I've never heard… Good God!" He looked as if he was about to succumb to apoplexy. "Explain yourselves, and it had better be good."

"Sir, Charles Forster is a German spy and we confronted him with this fact. He took off in his aircraft and we pursued him to the coast. He turned on us and attacked us. We defended ourselves and in the course of action we shot him down, fatally, sir." Now I had managed to get it all out, I felt better. More confident.

"A spy? Poppycock!" roared Bentley. "You damn fool pilots went up there and pulled some stupid stunt, and now you are trying to tell me he was a spy? What nonsense! The spy was caught days ago. Now, try again."

His response sorely tested my patience. I was about to bite back when Tomas entered the fray.

"Sir, it is true. Charles is a spy. He told the German pilot, I heard him. He is a spy, sir. I mean come on, sir, come on. What Scottish said is true. He attacked us … he…"

"I do not want to hear another word. I have had it up to here with your ridiculous pranks, and now they've ended in the death of a good pilot. The two of you will stand down, and you will be heading for a court martial. No mistake about that!"

"Sir…" I tried again. It seemed so unfair.

"No, Angus, my mind is made up. Whatever you've got to say can be said at a court martial. Just consider yourselves lucky I won't be throwing you in a cell until then."

I looked him square in the eye, because he was so completely wrong. I was considering unleashing my own temper and furnishing him with a pithy rendition of what I thought of his opinion and what he could do with his court martial.

Before I could speak, Angelica appeared as if by magic at my elbow. "Squadron Leader Bentley, sir?" she said.

He swivelled his gaze to her, and she saluted.

"And who might you be?"

"Corporal Kensley, sir, from comms."

"Right, and whatever it is you've come to say, can't it wait? I have things to deal with here, like preparing orders for a court martial."

"No, sir, with all due respect it cannot." Her manner was so calm and efficient, I was full of admiration. I noticed how Bentley's temper also started to cool.

"Well?" He waited a tad impatiently, but at least he was willing to listen.

"What Flying Officer Mackennelly said is true, sir. Pilot Officer Forster was a German spy."

He bristled ever so slightly at this and kept himself in check with an effort. "And you know this how?"

"Sir, I work for comms, but I also have high security clearance. Pilot Officer Forster had a clean record, so to speak. He could have gone to any squadron, but instead he came here on the recommendation of an Air Marshall in Fighter Command, and he acted upon a recommendation given to him."

"Who was the recommendation made by?" said Bentley, clearly now interested.

"The Duke of Windsor, sir."

He coughed and stared at her. The Duke of Windsor's loyalty to England, though not openly questioned, remained under a cloud of suspicion. "I see."

"Not only that, sir. I was listening to the conversation on the comms, and I heard Pilot Officer Forster say he was going to kill Flying Officer Mackennelly and Flying Officer Jezek. They were simply defending themselves. He vowed to return in a Messerschmitt and kill more of your pilots, sir."

Bentley now looked horrified and annoyed at the same time. "Did he indeed?"

Angelica wasn't finished. "I believe, sir, if you were to question the captured German pilot, he might corroborate what Flying Officer Jezek told you Charles said to him in German."

"Yes, right, a good thought, very good." Bentley now regarded her in an avuncular sort of way. "What did you say your name was?"

"Corporal Kensley, sir, from comms."

"I see, well, Corporal Kensley, good work, excellent work. I should imagine I might recommend something for you, a promotion perhaps." He smiled at her somewhat benignly.

"Thank you, sir."

"Yes. Don't mention it." He turned back to me and Tomas. "Now, as for you two. Consider yourselves damn lucky you've got a clever young lady like this on our comms team. Had you simply explained it as she has, then we might have avoided some … erm … unnecessary unpleasantness."

Though the retort was sitting on my tongue, I did not utter it. I wasn't going to point out to him that I had tried to explain it and he wouldn't listen.

"Anyway, consider yourselves back on active duty, and well done. Well done. I want a full report on this as soon as possible, mind. I shall be contacting MI6, of course, and we'll see what we can do about finding Forster's plane. We'll see if we can't make sure you are suitably rewarded for your actions. Two spies in such a short space of time, extraordinary."

I refrained from informing him the first spy was simply a decoy and instead saluted and said, "Thank you, sir."

"Thank you, sir, yes," said Tomas, doing likewise.

"Very well, you are dismissed."

Bentley saluted and strode back to the main building with his entourage in tow. When he had disappeared from view, I picked up Angelica and whirled her around.

"You are an angel, a guardian angel."

She laughed with delight. I put her down, then kissed her soundly.

"Come on, Scottish, I mean, come on," said Tomas, laughing.

I let her go and when Tomas had finished thanking her, he left us to it.

"I really thought I was for it there," I said to her. "Then you arrived just like the cavalry in the nick of time."

"I was alerted by…"

"Audrey?" I finished it for her.

"Yes."

"Well, bless her, and thank goodness for you ladies' intelligence network."

She laughed and kissed me again. All was right with the world. Well, almost. I still had to resolve the small matter of my feelings for Angelica and soon.

CHAPTER FOURTEEN

The Marx Brothers arrived in short order, Bentley having called them. I found myself once more seated across from them in the now all too familiar room.

"So," said Harpo, "you found the spy."

"Yes. I have provided a full report."

I had done so almost immediately, and Angelica had helped me to type it up. It was sent to MI6 post-haste, and the next day they had appeared like the bad pennies they were.

"We've read it," said Chico, dismissively.

"And?" I didn't really understand why they were here, since there was nothing more I could tell them. I couldn't help wishing myself elsewhere.

"A bit impetuous, weren't you, Flying Officer Mackennelly?" said Harpo.

"What do you mean?"

"If you had discovered he was the spy, why didn't you simply alert us so that we could have captured him alive?"

"Instead," continued Chico, "you elected to try to expose him there and then, resulting in a chase where he nearly got away."

I was silent for a moment. Unfortunately, what they said made sense. However, what was done was done. "Heat of the moment, I suppose. We were angered by his brazen conversation with the German pilot."

"Yes, angered, that's it, you see. You'll never make a spy with a temperament like that."

"I don't want to be a spy," I said evenly.

"Just as well. We can't recommend you in any case."

The two of them laughed, as if this was some kind of inside joke.

"Is this what you've brought me here for? To make light of it? Is all this funny to you?" There was no help for it; the two of them riled me up almost every time we met.

"No, not at all," said Harpo. "You did well. We can't expect more from a pilot jockey, after all. You surprised us, actually."

"Meaning what?"

"We didn't actually think you'd find the spy," said Chico.

"Then why the hell did you ask me?" I demanded furiously.

"Everything in life is a bet, a gamble, if you like. We had no option," Harpo replied.

"So, I was Hobson's choice, is that it?"

"Yes, indeed, but there we are. You pulled it off with the help of your lady friend."

I waited for them to say more and when they didn't, I said, "Are we finished?"

"Not quite," said Chico. "Funnily enough, we've searched his lodgings and found the radio. We've also found a codebook, and other things. We'll be arresting several accomplices, so all in all it's actually been rather profitable, this whole caper."

"Oh, well then."

I shrugged, still not sure why they had come to see me. Then they dropped their little bombshell.

"It's all going to be hushed up, of course."

"What?"

"Yes," said Harpo. "For various reasons, Pilot Officer Forster will be reported as accidentally downed by friendly fire. Nobody will be any the wiser, and none of this will ever have happened."

"Just a minute, why ever not? Why can't the truth be told?" I protested.

"Let's just say," said Chico, "that it would cause much embarrassment in high circles if it was. The press is not to know, and you are never to say anything about the real circumstances."

I was pardonably infuriated all over again. "So that's how it's going to be, is it?"

He was unperturbed. "That is very much how it's going to be, old sport, yes. Don't worry, you and your pilot friend will get a deserved decoration. The corporal will be made a sergeant. All's well that ends well."

They stood up to go.

"So that's it?"

"In a nutshell," said Harpo.

"You won't be seeing us again, and I'm sure you'll be pleased about *that*," Chico smiled.

I didn't answer. They had very likely divined my feelings, in any case.

"Well played. Your country is proud of you," said Harpo in slightly mocking tones. "Toodle pip."

I shook hands with each of them, and then they were gone. I couldn't say I wasn't glad to see the back of these two.

Predictably, Angelica arrived in the room shortly after.

"Do you know everything that goes on around here?" I enquired, greeting her with a kiss.

"Practically, yes."

"So you know it's all to be hush-hush, now."

"Yes, they told me. I believe they've also spoken to Tomas."

"Tidying up loose ends?" I said with a wry smile.

"Something like it."

"And you're to be made a sergeant."

"Yes." She smiled prettily. "Do you think I'll look nice with three stripes on my arm?"

"Very fetching, I'm sure, and you deserve it. You did most of the work."

She demurred at once, not willing to let me put myself down. "Oh hush, you shot him down, and I don't care what they say. I'm not sorry you did!"

"Me neither, if I'm honest."

"Shall we celebrate?" she smiled.

"With fish and chips?"

"Sounds splendid."

After a pleasant dinner with Angelica, Gordon picked me up and drove me back to Amberly Manor.

"They buried His Lordship today," he informed me on the drive back.

"Oh." I had rather expected to have to go to the funeral but evidently, I had not been invited.

"The CO represented the squadron, sir. I believe it wasn't felt politic for you to be there."

"No, no indeed."

We fell silent while I wondered how Barbara had fared. Even though she seemingly despised her husband, the loss of him must have been hard to bear in many ways. However, as she said, it made her a very rich widow indeed. A catch for the right man. Just not me.

I was sitting in a chair in my room, thinking, when the door opened softly. It was Barbara.

"May I come in?" she asked tentatively.

"Can I stop you?" I said sardonically, and then seeing her expression I thought better of it.

"I'll go, if you want."

"No, stay."

She sat on the bed in silence, as if she was finding the courage to speak.

"How did it go today?" I asked at length.

"All right." She smiled faintly. "I wished you had been there, beside me. I know that's not possible, but one can dream."

"I suppose one can."

"There will be other men," she mused. "Just not like you."

"I hope you find the right man, after a suitable period of mourning, perhaps."

Her voice took on a teasing tone. "For example, there is Lawrence Calver."

"Lawrence!" I sat bolt upright at this. She knew exactly how to goad me.

"Well, he's a little handsome, I suppose."

"I'm sure, but … Lawrence Calver … Barbara … really?"

She laughed lightly. "Well, if you'd rather I didn't…"

"What I think is of no consequence, or should be … of no consequence," I said, trying to sound noble, but then jealousy got the better of me. "As long as it's not Lawrence."

She laughed then, almost like the old Barbara. "I would never go with Lawrence," she said. "For a start, he's queer."

"What?"

"Didn't you know?"

Suddenly it all made sense. His seeming hatred of Jonty. His antipathy to homosexuals in general. The preponderance of naked men in those magazines.

"Well, I'll be…"

"Oh, I could tell you things, if we can still be friends."

"Of course," I said, though I felt this might be unwise. Yet, I couldn't refuse her, not after what had gone before.

She smiled at this. I suppose if she couldn't have me, then she could at least have the connection.

"Then as a friend, may I offer you some advice?" Her tone suddenly became serious.

"If you wish to." I wondered what she could possibly want to say.

"I... Angus... I..." She stopped and seemed to be controlling herself with an effort.

"What is it, Barbara?" I asked her gently.

She got up from the bed and came to kneel beside me. Then she grabbed at my hand, held it in hers. I allowed it — after all, we had been lovers, and I owed it to her not to be unkind.

"Angus, it's ... it's very hard for me to say this to you ... because I love you... I love you so much it hurts just to think of it ... but..."

I waited. Tears ran down her face. I stilled the impulse to take her in my arms, to comfort her.

"I'm sorry, so sorry for the things I said to you that day, when John died. It was selfish of me, I know, but I ... I couldn't help it. I wanted you so much. Wanted what I couldn't have..."

Her voice broke then, and she took a few moments to bite back the tears. I waited, since there was obviously something of more importance to her. She composed herself again.

"Listen to me, Angus. Angelica is a lovely woman, a beautiful, sweet woman. I know. I spent that time in her company when I ... when I came looking for you. None of this is her fault, this ... what we ... what we had, it's not her fault."

"I know that, and she knew all along about you," I said softly.

"Angus, she loves you, I can see it. Nobody deserves love more than you do, believe me. If only … if only… Have you told her you love her?"

It came out in a rush. "No, I…"

"Well, you must, Angus, you simply must. Don't waste this opportunity for something so precious. For God's sake. For *my* sake. Please tell her you love her … if you do."

I looked at her then, surprised by her tone and what she said. "I do love her, at least I think I do."

"*Tell* her! Don't lose this moment … my … my darling. Take it from me, you'll regret it otherwise for the rest of your life."

"OK. I…"

"Promise me, promise me you'll do it."

"I promise I will tell her."

She held my hand up to her lips and kissed the back of it for a few moments. Then, seemingly unable to resist, she kissed me too. "Thank you." She turned and walked away, pausing at the door. "Angus."

I nodded. Quickly, she opened the door and left. I heard her sob as she closed it behind her. I moved swiftly to open it again, but she was gone.

What she had done took a lot of courage. I admired her all the more for it. She was right about Angelica, but I didn't know how to put it into words. I had never uttered those words before. It didn't occur to me to take the simplest course of action.

It was still on my mind the next day when Gordon drove me to Banley.

"Penny for your thoughts, sir?" he said.

"They're not worth a penny, Fred, or even half a penny."

He didn't try to engage me again. I felt a little numb, as if I'd lost something. Perhaps I felt something for Barbara after all, but it was nothing compared to what was in my heart for Angelica. Yet the words stuck in my throat. What would it take for me to simply say, "I love you?"

At the airfield, the others could tell by my silence that something was up, and they left me alone. Angelica had not come to see me, which was unusual, but perhaps also fortuitous as it gave me time to think. When was the right time to make a declaration?

The phone rang and we were scrambled for action.

As I left the hut to run for my plane, I saw Angelica running towards me.

"Angus, Angus!" she shouted.

I ran to her at once, held her tight. She was crying.

"Angus, come back to me, promise you'll come back to me."

"Of course I will. Whatever is the matter?"

"I had a dream, a bad dream."

I kissed her softly. "I'm coming back, I promise you. Wait for me, right here. I've got to go."

"Take care, I love you," she called after me as I pelted off.

She watched us take off and I saw her still standing on the airfield until we were out of sight.

"You all right, Skipper?" Jonty ventured once we were airborne.

"Never better, old boy," I said with more confidence than I felt. I tried to get my mind on the job. It wouldn't do to be distracted, not in combat.

We arrived at the coast quite quickly and went on the attack. A bevvy of Heinkels was coming in, with Stukas in their midst.

"Break, break, engage," came the familiar voice of Lieutenant Judd.

We peeled off and went in for the kill. I flew down from the front of the main force and fired, hitting one of the Stukas, which started smoking. I banked again for another run and then there they were, the fighter escort and closing fast upon us.

"Bandits at twelve o'clock. Red Section on me, break, break," I said, turning to meet them.

The battle was fast and furious. Twisting, turning, first I was being chased and then I became the hunter. On and on it went, in a seemingly endless set of loops and counter loops.

"Tally-ho, there goes another one," shouted Jonty in his usual enthusiastic style.

"Watch your back, Scottish, watch your back," yelled Willie suddenly.

In my mirror was a 109. I banked hard left, knowing I could out-turn him, and I did. I was faster and then all of my focus was on him. I had him in my sights in no time and fired. His engine began to smoke.

"Skipper, watch out!" Jonty's voice came in my ear.

Everything suddenly went into slow motion after a moment's inattention. I'd known it would catch me out one day. Today was that day. To the right of me, I had been caught by a 109. He had me in his sights, and there was nothing I could do. I started to bank left and thought of Angelica as the bullets ripped through my canopy and cockpit. I felt every one of them, with all the fibres of my being. I heard the sound they made ripping through the fuselage.

This is what death is like, I thought to myself. *This is what happens when it takes you.* In those split seconds I felt every moment I'd lived passing in front of me, and then it was over.

By some miracle, not a single bullet had hit me, and Willie was shouting in triumph.

"Take that, you bastard!"

I glanced to see the 109 explode in a fireball. Air was rushing all around me, and my canopy was gone. I secured my oxygen mask tighter.

"Skipper, are you OK? Skipper?" Jonty was shouting.

I couldn't speak; I was filled with emotion. I hadn't died — how was that?

"Disengage Red Leader, go home, return to base, that's an order," said Judd.

I gave Jonty the thumbs-up and turned away from the battle. Jonty and Willie settled on my wings. We flew back in silence, with the wind rushing past me. The noise from the engine was deafening now there was no canopy to muffle it even a little. As Banley hoved into view, I knew for certain what I had to do. Barbara's words came back to me, and I realised I had almost died without telling Angelica how I felt. Somehow, I felt released from whatever had been binding me, stopping me from expressing my emotions.

We landed and I could see a lone figure standing and waiting. Waiting only for me. My heart was filled at the sight of her. I taxied the kite to a stop and jumped down from the wing.

"Skipper, what about a..." Jonty began.

"Leave him be," said Willie. "He's got more important things to do."

"What? Oh, oh, yes."

I ran like the wind, closing the distance with Angelica. She saw me and broke into a run. And then we were embracing, kissing. I felt my emotions almost overflowing, like a dam that had suddenly burst its banks.

"Angus, Angus, you were nearly killed, Angus…" she began.

I put a finger to her lips. "Hush, my darling," I said. "Hush."

"Angus? What is it?" Her eyes searched mine, questioning.

There was no holding back, not anymore.

"Angelica," I said, "I want to tell you that I love you. I love you with all my heart and soul. I love you more than I can ever say. I love you so much."

Her arms went around my neck. Her smile was happier than I had ever seen it. "Oh! Oh my! Oh, Angus, *my* Angus. I love you too. I love you so much."

There were no more words. We kissed and I finally understood what it meant to love. I ran my fingers through her hair and then I tilted my head back.

"I love you, Corporal Angelica Kensley, and I want the world to know it!" I roared, laughing with joy.

She stood there, smiling still. I pulled her close. As the rest of the squadron flew in, I knew we would be all right. I had survived when I should be dead. I finally felt something I had not felt before. Hope. The fragile dawn of hope.

A NOTE TO THE READER

Dear Reader,

I very much appreciate you choosing to read my first book in the Spitfire Mavericks Series. I have been fascinated by the events of WW2 for most of my life, and I was born not many years after the war ended. Spitfires particularly intrigued me, and I remember making an Airfix model of one all those years ago, which I duly painted in camouflage colours. I also had a Lancaster Bomber and a model of the HMS Hood, among others. Alas, I no longer have any of these today; they have been lost in the mists of time and various house moves.

But the Spitfire, as with so many other people, always held a special place for me. I've seen a few flying over the years, and that tell-tale whine of the Merlin engine is something that is so incredibly evocative and stirring. Years later I've managed to achieve a lifelong ambition, which is to write a fictional series about a Spitfire pilot in the war.

I invented the Mavericks Squadron because though it never existed, I felt that somehow it should have. We've always been fascinated, I think, by those who bucked the system or somehow were considered outcasts. What happened to them? Well, I like to think they could have ended up like Angus, flying for the Mavericks. Heroes who served their country in spite of everything.

I always do my best to stay true to the times and events, but of course, fiction is fiction and at the same time one has to tell a good story. Again, I like to think that the events I fictionalised could easily have transpired, and who is to know everyone's story, in any case? Nevertheless, even though I already had quite some knowledge about the war, I still research thoroughly what I need to, remaining faithful to the capabilities of the aircraft, and all the other aspects, as far as possible.

I have to confess, though, to having a ready sense of humour. I find it impossible to write a dry thriller without some witty banter. Also, I like well-rounded stories, and thus the element of romance inevitably creeps in too. All of these aspects, I feel, are important to the way I write. I very much enjoyed penning the sparky exchanges between Angus and Angelica, and of course the added complication of his entanglement with Barbara. The human element is so important in a story — the interactions, the camaraderie and more. War adds new dimensions and exigencies that change attitudes, ways of thinking, and cultural mores. I am always drawn to writing that conveys such experiences and emotions as much as the very important action.

So, with all those things in mind, it's quite a lot to cram into a novel, but I feel that I have succeeded. I hope you will agree, and you enjoyed reading it as much as I enjoyed writing it. If you did, then I would be very grateful if you could spare the time to write a review on **Amazon** and **Goodreads**. As an author, these reviews are hugely important, and always appreciated.

You can connect with me in other ways too, via my **website**, **Facebook**, **Twitter**, **Instagram**, and a special **Spitfire Mavericks Page**.

I very much hope you were entertained enough to read the next book in the Mavericks series.

Warmest regards

D.R. Bailey

SAPERE
BOOKS

Printed in Great Britain
by Amazon

25131629R00165